U_p in the H_{ills}

$U p$ IN THE $Hills$

LORD DUNSANY

Afterword by Michael Grenke

PAUL DRY BOOKS

Philadelphia 2008

First Paul Dry Books Edition, 2008

Paul Dry Books, Inc.
Philadelphia, Pennsylvania
www.pauldrybooks.com

1 3 5 7 9 8 6 4 2
Printed in the United States of America

Library of Congress Cataloging-in-Publication Data

Dunsany, Edward John Moreton Drax Plunkett, Baron, 1878–1957.
  Up in the hills / Lord Dunsany; afterword by Michael Grenke.
— 1st Paul Dry Books ed.
       p.   cm.
  Originally published: London: W. Heineman, 1935.
  ISBN 978-1-58988-049-8 (alk. paper)
  1. Fantasy fiction, English. 2. Ireland—Fiction. I. Grenke, Michael W.
II. Title.
  PR6007.U6U62 2008
  823'.912—dc22
                                            2008030468

Contents

Up in the Hills

CHAPTER I

The Wolf at the Door

Over wide marshes in Ireland the sun had gone to his setting, either behind a long ridge of green earth, or into a mist that the cold was drawing up from the ground: above the mist, which was white and very low, the whole sky was shining, like a sapphire too pale for any jeweler to show, but clear, cold, and beautiful. From a patch of land not far from the edge of the marshes, but completely surrounded by water, a column of smoke was going straight and slow, a bulk of grayness into the lucid air. Streaks of scarlet and orange began to appear in the sky, as the rays of the sun tilted upward from down below the horizon, and then the glow of the fire on the marsh-surrounded encampment began to assert its beauty, first with a color that rapidly grew in splendor, when other colors were gone, and then with light itself. And it was this firelight glowing at night; more than their houses, more than their big spears, more than the palisade of slanting stakes which protected them; that persuaded the dwellers in the island encampment that they were certainly superior to all other forms of life and probably the equals of the stars. For, argued they, can the wolf or even the elk give light? Five beings alone can do it, the sun, the moon, the stars, the comet and man. Is he not therefore amongst these five, and far the superior of the wolf? Grunts of earnest assent from all men round the fire settled the question whenever it was asked; and yet it was still in the balance. Numbers, organization and cunning were about equal: it was a near thing yet. If numbers were equal the equality was illusory, for the wolves with their greater mobility might destroy an encampment of man, fighting twenty to one, and then go on to the next with the same odds in their favor. The cunning of man was mostly used in defense, the slanting palisades for instance, tall poles a bit thicker than broomsticks, planted deep in the earth all round the encampment and slanting outwards; a wolf could jump to the top of them and get hold with his fore-legs, but the slant gave his hind-legs no purchase and he could be easily killed on the poles with the thrust of a spear in his neck. And then there was the water all round, which would rob the wolves of their speed if they ever tried to cross it, though they knew that swimming they would be powerless against men standing in the marshes, and surprise by night was impossible because of the noise of the water: a causeway of stones a few inches below the surface let the island-dwellers in and out of their houses, the little cluster of huts with the roofs of reed, but the causeway was too twisty for any wolf to follow, or any man that was not of that tribe. The trouble was when the ice came.

It looked like freezing tonight, no mere white frost adorning the rushes with rime, but the frost that hardens the marshes; and a wolf on silent feet at the edge of the wood that darkened the higher ground was peering towards the encampment, green eyes gazing at night like two faint stars in the wood.

This is one of the beginnings of my story.

A century passed and the wolf came close again, or a wolf so like to the other that no difference could be seen, if any existed. It was his belief that everything came his way in the end. Man was still on the defensive; his children did not dare to stray, but the wolves did not dare to splash through the water to jump at the palisades; and nothing was decided yet. It seemed only a matter of waiting; the wolves were always ready, and some day sloth would come to the little encampment, and neglect of the palisades, and after that the wolves would cross on the first good ice. And so the centuries passed; and in the end it went the other way, man's way, away from the wolf.

Danes came and Normans came, and many another folk, and blended to make what we call the Irish race, in which perhaps survives some trace of those earlier men that dwelt in the marshy islands; or perhaps so many conquests were too heavy for them, and they survive only in legends of little people hiding themselves away, and coming out to dance on raths only by moonlight, or running small and swift away over the marshes. The wolves lasted longer than these, but the lights increased in the nights that had once been so still and unthreatened, and the menace of man became a thing to be felt.

Picture History turning her face away from the marshy encampment, a forgetful muse ignoring the wattled floors, ignoring the palisade and the roofs of reed, the crude brown pottery and the olden spears; picture Nature leading back to the little island her myriads of tiny children that man had driven away; weeds, flowers, blades of grass; and they hold it this time and thrive, and not a hundred years have gone over the marshes before they have covered stamped earth and reed and wattle, and every trace of the intruders is gone.

And so, in the lapse of I know not how many centuries, I come to another of the beginnings of my story.

In a district of Africa that had won its freedom from Liberia, and had lately declared its independence, the new parliament was in session. The Place of Assembly was built on the lines of our Houses of Parliament, so far as this could be done with reeds and thatch. Stout reeds of enormous height were used for its walls, their interstices filled with a wealth of long brown leaves, and over all there loomed the palatial thatch. It was their first session since Liberation Day; and the assemblage, in evening dress, had risen to await the President. He came, and standing alone on the dais before a table, on which he laid documents down, he delivered them his address. "Honorary Members," he said, "our State has already concluded a treaty with another Nation. Europeans come to this State and dig among our old ruins to find antiques. But do our folks," he said, with his powerful voice rising, "go and dig for antiques in Europe? Plenty much we don't!"

And then he lifted a document from the table and unrolled it and read it out; it was a treaty with the Irish Free State, allowing a party from the State of Liberissima to dig up a lake-dwelling at the edge of an Irish bog, in exchange for a favorable tariff on Irish coal imported to Liberissima. Lake-dwelling is the name that archaeology usually gives to a village of primitive man protected by water; it was in fact the very village that the wolf had watched for so long, and that fell in the end to the Danes.

CHAPTER II

~~~~~~

*The Coming of the
Archaeologists*

*T*he town of Cranogue was a street, perhaps two hundred yards long, of white-washed walls with deep thatch frowning down on them. There may have been stones or timber here and there in the walls, yet whenever one of the houses became deserted it returned so swiftly to earth, that I think there cannot have been much else in its building: the thatch would sag in the middle into a black cleft, through which the rain came in and rotted the ends of the beam, and when that slipped slanting down the occupant would depart; all that year the house would be an untidy ruin, next year a heap of rubbish, the year after a green mound, and after that the field would come back, level and calm, to its own. The town stood on good solid land, a field or so away from the edge of the marshes that still lay where they were when they protected the little encampment from the envy of neighboring wolves. The thick white-wash along its walls seemed filling the air with sunlight, as though the light lingered and danced on them, when the party from Liberissima appeared in four outside cars. They drove down the whole length of the street, to the hotel that had been built to cater for hunting men, but that since the Treaty was empty. Many eyes saw them coming, but there was something so strange in their appearance that the boys who saw them first dropped down behind whatever hedge or wall they had peered from, or ran indoors to their mothers, so that the party of strangers seemed at first to be coming to a village as silent as the one they meant to explore. They were dressed in frock-coats and tall hats, meaning to give importance to their new State, but importance in dress is a narrow and slippery ridge, and it is easy to fall over on to the other side. And there was a peculiar difficulty about the appearance they wished to present, a difficulty that had haunted Mr. Washington, Mr. Johnson, Mr. Japhet and every other elder of the church in that party since first there had insisted on accompanying them a certain Umbolulu, an African whose dress above the waist was nothing more than a necklace of copious bones, and who was never without his drum. It had been impossible to leave him behind, because of the important part he had played when they broke away from Liberia; some revolutionaries soon kill such men, others attempt to civilize them, while others put up with them as these were doing. The first and the third course are the only possible ones.

So down the road drove the party in the four Irish cars, with not another soul in sight, until they came to the open doors of the village, where the women stood in their doorways regarding them keenly, but without any expression that could betray to the strangers what view they took of their arrival; and in and out among the cars danced Umbolulu, while Cranogue throbbed with his drum.

Among the first of the grown-up people to see Mr. Washington's party enter the village was old Mickey Ryan, who had been butler at the Big House for thirty years, until the old Lord died. He was the first in the village to see these people, partly because his cottage was the last or last but one at the end by which they approached, and partly because he liked to sit in his door all day to see if anything should come by, and to estimate it and then to put it away in his mind among all the other events that he had seen pass, life being no longer to him so much a thing to live as to observe, as it marched through his memories past that strange day when the old Lord had made him his butler, and brightly with sunlight on it through the present, and away into the future towards salvation, provided a few sins had been forgotten by now, as he had been given reason to believe they would be. They were black, he noted. That meant that they came from a long way away, further than France even, for he had known a Frenchman once, and they were not black in France. And they were going to the hotel: he knew this because the cars were driving on the side of the road upon which the hotel was. A party of them like that would be coming for some particular purpose, and the second car hadn't passed him before he got near enough to what that purpose would be: archaeology. Not that he used to himself any such queer word as that, but "everything," he had often said, "is very ancient round about here;" and he thought to himself now, "they'll be coming to take a look at some of the old things." Old things there were in plenty, old stones that the devil had thrown, standing up now in fields for the cattle to rub on; old ruins and old woods. And, talking of the devil, he was in those parts once when the blessed archangel spotted him, and makes a dive at him, sheer out of Heaven; but you don't catch the devil as easy as all that, the cunning lad; he saw Michael coming, and he dives too, right into a field, and comes out on the other side of a hill, knowing the undermost parts of the earth by grubbing about, in the way that the blessed angels would never think of doing; and you can see where he dived in and where he come up, to this day; there's a river running that way, right under the hill.

And another that saw the party arriving was Mickey Connor, or Young Mickey, old Ryan's grandson, who had been working in one of the fields at the back of the houses until he heard the drum, and ran to his mother's cottage, in through the back door, to peer out over the front window-sill and see what was coming. For a bare moment perhaps the black faces bore out what the drum promised with its wild beating, but a single peep from the window-sill showed the strangers to be too few for anything so exciting as invasion, and the boy of eighteen had to take farewell of that thought.

Then there was old Fanny Maguire, the wise woman of the village, or one of them; she heard the drum and looked out over her half-door, and blessed them in her heart; a change, she thought, something new, something strange and dark like her moods. Curses were more in her line than blessings, and yet she welcomed their coming; better have some one to curse than have all her powers rusting away in idleness.

And, just as old Mickey had supposed, the cars drew up at the hotel. And Mr. Washington, Mr. Johnson, Mr. Japhet, and half a dozen others, walked in with considerable gravity, while in a semi-circle about the door Umbolulu ran up and down sideways, and smote his drum as he ran.

Pat Sharkey, the owner of the hotel, was in the doorway waiting to receive the party, for their coming had been announced to him, and the rooms reserved, by the Liberissiman Minister in Dublin. And a fleeting thought came to him that it was like the old times come back, when his hotel used to be full for the whole of the hunting season.

"We am come," said Mr. Washington, "on behalf of de Republic of Liberissima to investigate de very interesting lake-dwelling dat's near here."

"So I heard say," replied Sharkey.

"And would you direct us to its situation?" said Mr. Washington.

"I heard tell it was down by the bog," answered mine host.

"Can we see dat from here?" asked Mr. Washington looking out of the window of the front room into which they had now been shown, where officers on leave and others there for the hunting used to sit and smoke after dinner.

"Sure, it's only a couple of perches beyont that hedge," said Sharkey, pointing out over three large fields. And the hedge to which he pointed was as far as one could see from the village; after that the land tilted downwards and came to the bog.

"We shall require a shed for to store our discoveries. We shall find pottery, spear-heads, bones, and de heads of elks."

"Do ye tell me?" said Sharkey.

"All two or three thousand years old," went on Mr. Washington.

"B' the holy," said Sharkey.

"We hab discovered ax-heads, and other relics of man, before now, dat was over ten thousand years old," boasted Mr. Washington.

"The dirty heathen," muttered Sharkey turning away, for something in the Liberissiman's estimate of ten thousand years conflicted with his religious beliefs. Pat Sharkey instantly transformed his turning away from his guest into an obsequious withdrawal, and his mutterings into a request that they would be all pleased to follow him in order that he might show them to their rooms.

Meanwhile the people of Cranogue, who had watched with immobile features the procession of four cars, did not long withstand the throbbing of the drum; and, reluctant though they were to show curiosity, or any other emotion to a stranger, they were soon gathered outside the hotel, from old Mickey Ryan to the youngest child that could walk, in a large semi-circle, while along a smaller arc Umbolulu leaped on and on, and flogged the resounding parchment of his African drum as he leapt.

CHAPTER III

The Soul in the Rib

Early next morning the party of archaeologists set out eagerly over the fields, guided to the edge of the marshes by Sharkey himself, while to and fro behind them Umbolulu ran with his drum, and the villagers of Cranogue came out of their houses and gathered to see them off. To those between the ages of seven and seventy there seemed nothing odder in Umbolulu's drumming than in the idea of coming to Ireland to dig up bones in a bog, but to the children and the old men and women a menace seemed to float up from the African drum and to hang in the air above the roofs of the village, though what the menace might threaten not any one of them knew. They heard the drum-beats throbbing all the way to the marshes. The marsh lay very much where it had lain during the writing of all the volumes of history that the world has amassed, and during one whole page of geology; though it was a bit shrunken now by the deepening of the bed of a little stream that ran through it and by the digging of two or three ditches. This shrinkage would have been considerable, but that the ditches soon filled up, and the river gradually smoothed its hard man-made bed, padding it first with mud and then with weeds; and a generation would often go by before any one dug it out again. As soon as the party saw the shape of the marshes and the position of the sun, they identified the site of the lake-dwelling by a map they had had from a traveler, the kind of man we should call an adventurer, who had shown it to the President in confirmation of some sort of scientific status that he was trying to make out for himself for the furtherance of whatever game had brought him to Liberissima; and the President had been delighted with it, and this expedition to the Irish Free State was the outcome. Pat Sharkey returned to his hotel, and the archaeologists, who had brought their spades, began digging at once; and very soon they came upon bones of cattle, and then to the tips of the poles of the palisade. These poles were sodden with water that had soaked them for thousands of years, and brown on the outside, but were not otherwise altered from the poles that had protected the huts on the island against the waiting wolves. They began to dig up horns three or four inches long, and noted the preference of those ancient lake-dwellers for veal or very tender beef. They dug on all the morning, undisturbed by any one, though eyes watched them from several points; it was even noted that they did not take off their coats to dig, and it was at once discussed in the village. Any criticism on that account was hard, since there were many in and about Cranogue who were soon to urge that Umbolulu ought to put on a coat, and it was only to emphasize the difference between Mr. Washington and such as Umbolulu that these frock coats were kept on upon all occasions. Once a herd came by, walking over the fields past the marshes to look at cattle, a man who came from the other side of the marshland and had not lately been in Cranogue, and had not therefore heard of the Liberissiman archaeologists. He glanced at them as he came near, and wondered at black men digging in a bog, but without any change in his features, and without surprise; for somehow he looked for wonders: all the stories he heard or told were of wonderful things; fairies, witches, banshees and little people; his world was full of wonders, sensible wonders; while from the noisy world beyond him, the world of towns, there sometimes came crazy wonders, such as a motor car hooting past the white-washed cottages of Cranogue. And so it was that when he saw the archaeologists digging, he wondered without surprise. When the herd had gone past with his dog the diggers were quite alone, except for the watchers, unseen by them, on the high ground near Cranogue; and gradually they uncovered the palisades and began to find traces of wattle, and soon they saw the old village, with its huts all huddled together within the protecting poles, as the scientific eye is able to see such things under the stimulus of a little material, such as their spades brought up. And by lunch-time they had found a piece of an earthenware pot. Everything that that traveler to Liberissima had said to the President was true, as is often the case with the white man traveling in Africa, where he feels that truth is expected of him and rises to the occasion; on the other hand it should definitely be set on record that he is *not* able to control eclipses of the moon. They returned for lunch to Sharkey's hotel, bringing with them their piece of earthenware. "Isn't it nothing only a bit of an old pot" said Sharkey, out of their hearing, to others to whom it had been exhibited. But some took the view that, whatever it was they had come for, and though what they had found was worthless, the party from Liberissima knew what they were doing. For a few days the decision of the united opinion of Cranogue as to what they were up to hung in the balance, this decision being further delayed by a suspicion that must always attach to any one digging in Ireland at the edge of a bog. There are certain suspicions indigenous to certain spots and districts; a man for instance seen loitering about a bank in London soon incurs the suspicion of being in search of gold. It is irrelevant that the gold may not be there, either because the bank does not keep much wealth at all at that branch, or because its safes are mostly full of unnegotiable paper: these are matters of high finance. What is relevant is that gold is supposed, and very likely rightly supposed, to be stored in banks, and this supposition would lure a thief, and the same supposition would cause him to be suspected. In just the same way any one digging all day in a lonely corner of an Irish bog cannot expect to escape the suspicion that he is after a crock of gold. The little people, the leprechauns and the fairies may have buried no gold in earthenware pots in any bog at all, but that is not so easily proved by a man found busily digging in such places; and of all the indefinite suspicions that attach to strangers, this was probably the most definite that followed the Liberissimans. It was for this reason that they were watched at first by many eyes at their digging, while the countryside seemed to the archaeologists to be all empty of men. Again in the afternoon they went back, Umbolulu and all, to their digging: it was spring, for they had chosen a time when there could be no ice in the marshes to interfere with their spades, and the evening was long enough for them to come, here and there, in sight of the wattled floors by the end of their first day's work. While they sat late in the hotel writing their notes, several of the inhabitants of Cranogue were peering into the hole they had dug; and this inspection, combined with the report of those that had peered at them beyond hedges, and checked by the observations of the servants at the hotel, established, when there had been time for proper discussion that they were not after a crock of gold. This took some days, on three of which they were working, and the fourth was a Sunday. They began to feel the suspicion that was all round them, and somehow thought that this would be abated when they went to church on Sunday, as they all did, except Umbolulu, nearly doubling the number of the congregation. But this had no effect on the public opinion of Cranogue. It was to the Protestant church that they went.

In the mind of Mickey Connor there was no suspicion of the Liberissimans, but rather a hope that, strange as they were, they might bring something stranger, a longing that from the throbbing of Umbolulu's drum-beats any event might come, mysterious or thrilling as what the drum seemed to promise. Once he had taken a great walk over the hills, impelled by some wandering impulse, and a long way away towards evening had come to a farm, in country he did not know, and there had met a girl going home through an orchard to the house that was quite near, its windows flashing with sunset: the apple was blossoming; it was a year ago; and he remembered the apple-blossom and her and the low light on the windows, all in one memory. Her name was Alannah; she was a year younger than he; they had talked for a while and parted; and ever since that day there was this strange longing on him that there might be changes, events and sudden happenings, things that would alter life in the street of Cranogue, so that instead of digging rows and rows of potatoes for his mother in the field at the back of the house, anything new would occur.

It is strange that the absence of Umbolulu from church gave more joy to the wife of the Rector of Cranogue than the presence of nine new parishioners, all of them elders of the Church in their own country; but so it was. After the first excitement of the march of the nine Africans up the aisle, two and two behind Mr. Washington, had subsided into intense interest, it was noted that Umbolulu was not among them. Now proselytizing was regarded by both sides in Cranogue as something so damnable that I can only use one word for it; and that word is *unsporting*. It was almost as though, before a game of cricket, you should attempt to lure one of the other side's bowlers to play for you against his own team: that was how they all felt about it. So Mrs. Patrick, the Rector's wife, did all her proselytizing in Central Africa. And it took a good deal of money to send a missionary to Africa, and a long time to collect it, so that by the time she had collected money for a year from the few Protestants in her neighborhood she could not feel that her labors had resulted in saving the soul of more than one African. But here was an African all ready to hand, a heathen out of the depths of the dark continent, and without any expense to the little fund she had gathered. From that day she started preparing his path to heaven: it was the first proselytizing she had ever done in Cranogue.

❧

On Monday morning Mrs. Patrick called at Sharkey's hotel and talked with Umbolulu. Hers was a noble work and it prospered in such a way as to promise triumphant success; yet it is a pity that, encouraged by Umbolulu's rapid progress, she boasted, for the Roman Catholics got to hear of her boast, and watched the conversion of Umbolulu so closely that only by following the standard set for themselves by the saints could he have hoped to escape from all criticism. During those first hours of Umbolulu's tuition the archaeologists went to the bog without him. The people came nearer now and watched the digging openly, though while they had still suspected the strangers of digging for gold, they had hid themselves as though made ashamed by their own suspicions. The Liberissimans, feeling at once the change in the villagers' attitude t'wards them, held up their little discoveries as fast as they dug them out for the onlookers to inspect; the bones of cattle, more earthenware, the poles of the palisade, fragments of wattle that had made the floors, sections of thatch that crumbled as it was lifted, but revealed bulrushes to the careful eye, small ornaments made from bone; the muddy makings of a little history that had never been put upon paper by any pen. They felt that things were going well with them, not only from the scientific point of view, but in regard also to a thing that, unguessed by Cranogue, these grave Africans set some store by, the friendliness of their neighbors; and that day for the first time the broad stripes of the Liberissiman flag, green, red, yellow and blue, floated from the highest window of the hotel. It was at lunch-time that Mr. Washington and Mr. Japhet exuberantly lowered the flag over Mr. Japhet's window-sill, and all that afternoon they worked again in the bog, and a little cluster of people watched them digging up bones. As one of the spadefuls came up, a young man left them and walked over the hill to the village.

That evening as they worked on while the sun was red and low, and Umbolulu sitting beside them was quietly drumming, an old woman appeared coming over the rising ground and walked towards them with a long, ragged stick. She came up to them at their work without any word, though she jerked her head at their greeting, and when she was standing beside them she stood in silence, leaning upon her stick. It was a long while before she spoke, or made any movement, except for the rapid movement of her eyes, peering from heap to heap of the archaeologists' little treasures. She scrutinized them all and then she spoke.

"There was a soul in that rib," she said, pointing. Nothing more did she say, but stood there looking fiercely into the African faces. And sure enough it looked like a human rib. Then she strode away back to Cranogue, with two long strides and then a stride of her stick, two strides and the stick again, and so soon disappeared in the dimness of evening.

That there had been a soul in the bend of a human rib was a religious fact that the Africans accepted, and they thought little more of the matter. But next day no villagers gathered to watch their work; and, when evening came over their lonely digging, another old woman came down the sloping ground from the other end of Cranogue, and stood beside them awhile and shook her head, and then went away muttering. When they went back in the dim light to the hotel Mickey Connor met them and turned away, as though he had been frightened of them. Next day they worked again alone at their digging, till another old woman came over the hill on the far side from Cranogue, and looked at them and walked away nodding her head, but saying nothing at all. The avoidance of them that evening when they returned from work, that had so surprised them when they had met Mickey Connor, was unmistakable now; every one that they met in the street hastened the other way. And somehow the elation that they had been feeling about their finds that day, little rarities that would be treasured by scientists, had the effect of increasing the depression that they felt from this reception; and the gay stripes of the republican flag seemed now to hang limply, disconsolate and forlorn from that upper window. And night came on with an uneasiness all along the street, of which the Liberissimans knew nothing. Later Mrs. Patrick came to the hotel to teach his catechism to Umbolulu, with the help of one of his countrymen, for Umbolulu knew no more than five or six words of English; yet, magnificent as his progress was, justifying her boast as fully as a boast can ever be justified, she was not yet able to part him from his drum, upon which he would beat in times of doubt or difficulty as well as in times of triumph, seeming to get a certain light in his mind from the rhythm of its strange throbbing, though darkness is what Mrs. Patrick feared that it brought, a pagan darkness from the black heart of Africa. He went out now into the fields between Cranogue and the bog and sat down and drummed for five hours: sometimes his voice rose tentatively to the tune of a hymn that Mrs. Patrick had taught him, and sometimes he sang the war-inspiring melody of an old African song.

CHAPTER IV

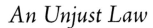

An Unjust Law

From now on the Africans worked unvisited, the brief friendliness they had found in Cranogue having utterly left them; they saw fewer people in the fields, and fewer seemed to pass them even in the street; while, if they bought anything in either of the two little shops, it was put down in silence upon the counter, and their money received with the curtest word of acknowledgment. Again they saw Mickey Connor one evening, and this time there seemed terror in his face as he hastened away from them.

"What was Mickey Connor afraid of?" they asked Sharkey.

"Ah, sure, it would have only been the way that he looked," said Sharkey.

But Mr. Washington and Mr. Johnson stuck to it.

"Ah, sure, Young Mickey's an odd lad," was the answer this time. And from none from whom they inquired could they get more than this.

"What hab we done to frighten folk?" asked Mr. Washington of Mr. Johnson. And a sad look of complete perplexity was all Mr. Johnson's answer.

"Mebbe they's frightened ob our black faces," suggested Mr. Japhet. But there was no sense in that, for they had had people smiling all round them only a day or two earlier; and Mr. Japhet's remark received little attention.

"It's de black heart, not de black face, what frightens people," said Mr. Washington. "And we ain't got no black hearts."

More than one of them glanced then in the direction of Umbolulu, as though a moment's doubt of him troubled them, but they were too good republicans to utter a word against one who had worked so recently only too well for the Cause. The whole party sat disconsolate, all feeling the ebb of the tide of sympathy that had swept far out away from them, leaving fear upon chance-seen faces, like dark and jagged rocks that the sea lays suddenly bare. But it was not the Africans that Cranogue was afraid of.

One day Mrs. Patrick called, on her work of redemption, and from her they heard, what nobody else would tell them, what it was that was frightening the village. The wise women were cursing. Three of them had seen the human rib that the Liberissimans had dug up, and the word had gone round the wise women that they were disturbing the bones of the dead. And so they were all cursing, and such curses might fall anywhere, and it was best, the people thought, to keep away from these strangers.

"But, Mam," said Mr. Washington, "we don't want to do no harm to dead folk. We only want to find out how dese people lived, in de interests of science. We don't want to hurt 'em."

"I know you don't," she said sympathetically, and it was the first sympathy they had heard in a voice for some days; "but that's what they think. The wise women are cursing; and all the people of Cranogue are frightened."

"What are dese wise women, Mam?" asked Mr. Washington.

"Well, the people think they are witches," replied Mrs. Patrick.

And a look of fear came over the faces of the archaeologists, not that they were afraid of witches, but these good Christian men were none of them so far away from another religion, and some remembered their mothers worshiping strange women, and others knew that their grandfathers had danced before witches by moonlight; so that witchcraft was as near to them as the cliff to the mountaineer, and they knew the way that a backslider would go if there should be one among their party.

"We don't believe in no witches, Mam," said Mr. Washington.

"Oh, no, no," came from the rest of them.

"I know you don't," said Mrs. Patrick again. "But that's what the people think."

And she said it with the finality of some one warning a traveler of some huge natural obstacle that there was no way round. And soon after that she left them, for there was nothing that she could do, and, though she was sorry for them, she could not feel for them the interest that she felt for Umbolulu, who needed her more sorely than he could know, while the souls of these others were so obviously saved already. To Umbolulu she said nothing of witches: it was not for her to point out any broad paths that might lead away from the strait one, and she got on with the catechism. When she left she left full of rejoicing at Umbolulu's progress, and yet she felt regrets for that little party of Africans that had become the object of curses that were terrifying the village all round them. As she walked away from that house, and noticed that the Liberissiman flag had now been hidden away, she saw more than one cross over the road to avoid her, and knew from this how pervasive must be the curses the wise women had aimed at the Africans.

Religion, Science, Politics: if I mention these three great powers, can I mention in the same breath so humble a guide as Tact? The Liberissimans were absorbed with religion, because Christianity was fairly new to them; Science called to them from the bog, where they had made real discoveries; and Politics urged them to remain at their work, for the treaty between Liberissima and the Irish Free State was the only treaty their country had ever made. Yet if the voice of Tact could have been heard above these mighty voices, Tact would have told them that it was time to go. What were the curses of a few old women? But their own mothers could have told them, from many a tale they remembered of old days in Africa. And any one in Cranogue could have told them. Anyhow it was plain to see that the whole village was terrified. They made a great mistake in remaining. Oh, what harm the world has suffered from mere errors in tact.

"Disturbing the bones of the dead is it?" said one that night at the cross roads. "There'll be a curse on that."

And that was the opinion of the whole of the little group that was gathered there a little way from the town, to discuss the whole thing quietly. But there was a curse already upon it; old

Fanny Maguire had laid it, heavy and deep on the marshes; so that it must be lying there now, like some deadly mist of the tropics, and rising, maybe, at evening against the walls of Cranogue. Few would walk down there now, even by day; but by night, when the power of rational things is abated, and the power of runes and curses come into their own, there was not a man of the young men gathered there at the cross roads that would go down to the hole in the marshes where the heathen (as they called them) were digging, and the curse of Fanny Maguire lay silent and terrible, protecting the bones of the dead.

"Will her curse follow them Liberissy men into Cranogue?" asked Young Mickey.

And others shook their heads. That was the question. And there was no way of answering it.

"And it isn't only she that's at it," said Jim Brannehan after a while, another of the young men, "for there's old Julia Hegarty, from over beyont."

"And Nanny Moran," said another.

The whole place was full of curses.

"Begob, it was better," said Jim Brannehan, "that they respected the bones of the dead."

And so said all of them; but it was too late now.

"Let us turn the whole lot of them out of it," said Jimmy Mullins, the blacksmith's son.

"I would not," said Jim Brannehan, "and I'll tell you for why. They'd go to Dublin and complain to their Minister, and then they'd invade Ireland. Aren't we only after driving out the English? We don't want to have to drive out the whole of Africa."

"Begob, we could do it," said Mullins.

And most of the little group were with Jimmy Mullins.

"And what would Sharkey say?" asked Jim Brannehan, a question that took all the fight out of them; and it was agreed that they'd have to leave the heathen alone.

A curse doesn't seem so much by day, still less if you are only reading about it; but discussed there in the night with low voices, while a wind moved wizened old thorns that nodded and nodded, as though they themselves might have been witches once, and the bark of a fox sounded over a mile in the stillness, and might have been the cry of something else; in such an hour and in such surroundings a curse not only seemed a thing of terror, but actually began to work, as they all could feel.

As Young Mickey went home that night he was forming a resolution that is not always taken by the young, and that had strange consequences for him: he was wondering whether to consult his elders. He passed Sharkey's hotel, where the flag of Liberissima had once more been hung out, in no glad confidence this time, but in an almost despairing effort to flaunt the courage of the little party of Africans in the face of so much unfriendliness; yet it hung there very limp and very gray in the night, and flapped in a gust that rose just as Young Mickey passed, and looked like something awful clambering up the hotel. It was then that he suddenly took the resolution to go to his old grandfather and ask him what should be done.

It was not so much respect for his grandfather's years, though this should have influenced him, that made Young Mickey resolve to go to the old man for advice; but he knew that old Mickey Ryan knew more of the big world than any one else in Cranogue, through listening to all the talk that there was at dinner in the Big House, during the years that he was butler to the Old Lord: gentlemen used to come there that had traveled as far West as India, and there would be great talk when he used to give them their port. And in politics too, which means so much in Ireland, he had played his part in his time, when many of the men that were ministers now, and members of the Dail, were only in their cradles. And it was that that had led so strangely to his becoming the Old Lord's butler; and if no man was ever appointed butler in such a way before, yet this is just how it happened, as all Cranogue knows. It was long ago in the eighties, when every one was very much interested in Mr. Gladstone's first Home Rule bill, and Mickey Ryan had received orders to shoot the Old Lord while he was at his dinner; and it was a summer's evening and the dining-room window was open, and Mickey had shoved his rifle in over the window-sill, kneeling on a flower-bed of geraniums, and took aim at the Old Lord, and the Old Lord saw him and said to him, "That's not the way to hold a rifle." And then he called out to him again and said, "And you're aiming it all wrong," which it is likely enough he was, in the trepidation of being discovered. And then the Old Lord said, "You want to take a finer sight, and get a better grip of your rifle, and hold it steadier. Now pull the trigger, and see what you can do." And poor Mickey got all rattled with so many instructions, yet he did what he was told, and pulled the trigger just as the Old Lord said. And he missed, and hit the wall. And then the Old Lord had looked at him. And after a while he said to him "There's one thing certain in an uncertain world."

"And what is that, my lord?" asked Mickey.

"That you'll never be any good with a rifle," said the Old Lord.

"Sure, that's God truth," said Mickey.

"Then hadn't you better give up politics?" said the Old Lord.

"And what would I do for a living then?" said Mickey. "Sure, your lordship wouldn't employ me as your gamekeeper."

"And indeed I would not," said the Old Lord, "when you can't shoot better than that. I'd have my woods overrun with every kind of vermin."

"You would," said Mickey humbly, for he knew it was true.

"But I'll take you on as my butler," said the Old Lord.

And years afterwards, telling the tale, "that's the way they used to arrange things in the old days," Mickey would say; "when a man would know a man by the look of him, and trust him all the days of his life. And he had a bald-headed fool of a butler that never did a hands-turn of work, except to brush a thin wisp that he had over the middle of his head, and that thought himself wiser than Solomon on his throne. He was well rid of that lad. Ah, God give rest to the Old Lord. The light of Heaven to him."

So Young Mickey went to Old Mickey to ask him what he should do. He went next morning and found his grandfather sitting with his old pipe in his hand, looking out into the street through his open door so as not to miss a sight of anything that might be going on. And the old man saw by his face that Young Mickey was troubled, and wagged his head gravely, giving to the scion of that much younger generation the impression that he knew already all about Young Mickey's trouble. And this added weight to his advice when it came.

"Good morning, Grandfather," said Young Mickey.

"Good morning, Mickey," said Old Mickey. "These are terrible times."

"Begob, they are that," said Young Mickey, "and cursing everywhere. They're disturbing the bones of the dead."

"The black heathen," said Old Mickey.

"Would curses aimed at them hit a young fellow like me?" said the grandson.

"Bedad," said the old man, "I made a great study of curses, but you couldn't tell that. Sure no man could say where they'd light."

"Couldn't you ask Fanny Maguire to stop it?" said Young Mickey.

"Sure, don't they deserve it, them Liberal Issy men, disturbing the bones of the dead?"

"Sure, they do, but it's on us they may light. Sure no one's safe with all that cursing going on in Cranogue. Couldn't you ask her to stop it?"

"I could not," said the old man. "And I'll tell you for why. I had trouble with her once over a hen."

"Did you that?" said Young Mickey.

"I did," said the old one; "and she was very bitter."

"She's a terrible old soul indeed," said Young Mickey.

"Now I'll tell you what to do," said his grandfather. "There's more in curses than any of us can know. But there's one thing sure about them, and that is that the further you are off from them, the less they can hurt you. I'm so old now that the doctor tells me I can't catch measles, and maybe it's the same with curses, though we can't be sure; but for you, Mickey, it's best to be out of this."

"It is so," said Mickey.

"And I'm telling you," said the old Mickey, "the widow Maguire is a terrible wicked woman. Many's the time I watched her at her cursing, and there's times I've admired the wickedness of her. Mind you I've nothing against her, nor against any wise woman, but she's terrible wicked."

"She is that," said Young Mickey.

"And when she has that mood on her, you couldn't say what she would do. Nor there's no knowing what she has done in the past. I quarreled with her over a hen, and God spared me. But Mike Kinahan had words with her once, and away with him out of Cranogue soon after, or out of the world for all any of us can say, for none ever saw him again. Unless . . ." and the old man stopped, with his eyes full of thought.

"Unless?" repeated Young Mickey.

"Boy," said the old man after a while, "do you mind that goat that came to Cranogue about the time Kinahan left it? An old goat with big large sorrowful eyes, and I saw a tear once in one of them."

"I mind the old goat," said Young Mickey almost in a whisper.

The old man nodded his head slowly a few times. "We shall never be sure what happened," he said, "to Mike Kinahan, till we know where that goat came from."

"Grandfather," said the boy, "I'll be going out of it."

"Aye," said the old man, "do. And maybe if you come back in a few weeks' time them heathens may all be gone, and the old woman will have done with her cursing."

"You wouldn't care to come too, Grandfather?" said Young Mickey.

But the old man looked at the cold outside his door and away from the bright fire blazing on his big hearth a little behind him. "The doctor said I was too old to catch measles now," he repeated.

"Begob," said Young Mickey, "I think I'll start tonight."

"That's best," said his grandfather. "And what will you do, away from Cranogue?"

"Sure, I'd like to be a general," said Young Mickey.

"It's a grand profession," said Old Mickey.

"It's what I'd like," said his grandson; "and to go up into the hills."

"Begob, ye might," said the old man. "Ireland's free. There were unjust laws in the country when I was young. And the unjustest law the English ever made was one that said that none might levy war without the King's consent. That was the wording of it, 'to levy war.' It was an old law hundreds of years old, but they kept to it just the same, and they let no one go and have a fight in the hills, though he might be spoiling for a fight. But if they wanted a fight for themselves, didn't they go and have one all over the world. Begob they did. Sure that was one law for the rich and another for the poor."

"It wasn't fair," said Young Mickey.

"Well, no matter," said the old Mickey, "they're gone now, and their old laws with them. And you're better out of this away from old Fanny Maguire."

"I'll go up into the hills," said the boy.

"And take some of the young lads with you to make an army," said the old man, and began to nod his head and look at his pipe; and the boy saw he was tired with all the advice he had given him, so he thanked him and said good-by and went back to his mother.

"Mother," he said as he came into the house, "Fanny Maguire turned Mike Kinahan into a goat."

"I never told you that, Mickey," his mother said. "I kept it from you, if ever it happened at all, and how can we know that it ever did? We've no way of knowing them things. And best not to be thinking of it, whichever way it was, whether it happened or not."

"Begob, I wouldn't trust it not to happen again, with the mood old Fanny Maguire's in," said the boy; "and I'm off to the hills."

"Indeed and you might be better up there for a bit," said his mother, "till Fanny Maguire's done cursing. And what'll you do while you're up in the hills?"

"Maybe we'll have a bit of a war," said Mickey.

CHAPTER V

The Army Marches

Young Mickey hurried from his mother's house to Mullins' forge, on the other side of the street; and when he got there he leaned against one of the door-posts and watched the blacksmith and Jimmy, shoeing a horse. This was one of the occupations of Cranogue, and another young fellow, Pat Geraghty, by the other door-post was already engaged on it, gazing into the dark forge, where the glow rose red from every snort of the bellows and the yellow sparks soared up from the ringing blows. Yet it was not to see a horse being shod that Mickey had come today, but to talk to Jimmy Mullins. After a while he caught Jimmy's eye, and Jimmy went on with his work, and soon after slipped out of the forge.

"Jimmy," said Mickey, "it's time we were out of this."

"It is, sure," said Jimmy. And he looked uneasily, both ways up the street.

"She turned Mike Kinahan into a goat," said Mickey.

"There's no limit to the malice of an old woman," said Jimmy.

"Will ye come up into the hills?" asked Mickey.

"I will that," replied Jimmy.

"Good for you," said Mickey.

"When will we go?" asked Jimmy.

"Tonight," Mickey answered him. "As soon as it gets too dark for them to see us carrying our rifles."

Jimmy and Mickey had both got rifles, the Army rifle, .303, once the property of the War Office. I do not say how Jimmy and

Mickey got them, because that is no part of this story, but if a reader should think that they got them in any illegal way, I would point out that there are no such ways; since their way of getting them, however they got them, was legalized by Act of Parliament in 1921. Did I not say what year it was in which these events were occurring? It was 1922, and a fine spring morning.

From Jimmy Mullins Young Mickey went on to find Jim Brannehan, and luckily found him on his way to the forge, to which he had been coming for company, which he needed in the anxiety that old Fanny Maguire had cast over the whole of Cranogue.

"Jim," said Young Mickey, "let's get out of this."

"Begob, that's best for us," said Jim Brannehan.

"Come up to the hills," said Mickey. "Jimmy Mullins is coming. Maybe we'll have a bit of a war up there. So bring your rifle."

Jim Brannehan thought for half a minute; but, whatever he thought, fear won. At any moment old Fanny Maguire might come out of her house and go down the street cursing. It was best to be out of Cranogue. "I'll come, Mickey," he said.

"Good for you," said Mickey.

"Will I bring Pat Kelly?" asked Jim, for he knew that Pat had a rifle.

"Do," said Mickey.

The three had all been boys at school together, and Jimmy Mullins had been attending school about the same time.

From house to house Young Mickey hurried on, getting together his army, and found the young men ready enough to come away from the village with him, for the curses of Fanny Maguire had not merely frightened one or two, but had hit the public opinion of Cranogue: I can only compare the spiritual effect of her, and the two other wise women, on the minds of all their neighbors, with the material effect of one of those mists that sometimes rose up at evening out of the bog; it was pervasive, chilling everything. And as night would come down, and blend with the mist, making the chill and the darkness deeper, so all manner of fears out of the dark of the future began to mix with the fear that these people had of the witches. It was time, the young lads agreed, to be gone out of it. And you, reader, should you incline to mock these fears, think first of whatever eerie surroundings you have ever moved in yourself, some house perhaps all wrapped in the dark of midnight, or some later eerier hour, yet rebelling against the hush as though of its own volition, with the sudden creak of a board, or the wandering fall of some fragment in hollow walls, or the whisper of curtains coquetting late with a draught, and through all this the hint of the sounds of feet; or recall some night far from houses in lonely places, with a voice in the wind that seems sometimes to wish you ill and sometimes to want to warn you, and a certain movement among the shapes of the trees as though they were watching you furtively. Whatever feelings the wind and the night may have evoked in you then, even though faintly, Fanny Maguire had called up over the whole of Cranogue, strong and lasting as her own indignation against the disturbing of the bones of the dead. And so Mickey got Patsy Mulligan, and Christie Ryan, no relation of old Mickey, and young Hegarty and Mick Geogehan and one or two more, who all had rifles; and he told them to dig up their rifles, and to meet him at the edge of the bog on the side of Cranogue as soon as it got dark. Then he went back to his mother's house and sat by the fire and said little, but gazed into the big fireplace, thinking. And, young though he was, his thoughts were of those fundamental things of which Victory makes the pedestals for her statues. First he thought of blankets, then of food, then of ammunition, then he thought of methods of carrying these things up to the hills, and then of transport. And he thought of little things, such as matches, and paper and paraffin to help in starting a fire with damp wood, and a piece of canvas that could be made to serve as a bucket and could be put to other uses when dry, and plenty of knives, and a spade, and if possible one or two axes.

"Will you be fighting against England, Mickey?" asked his mother.

"I will not," said Mickey. "Sure, isn't their army all routed? It'll be a private war."

"Don't be having too much war, Mickey," she said. "It's dangerous."

"Sure, it may not come to it at all, mother," he told her. But he had his plans for getting provisions from the far side of the hills, where Patsy Heffernan lived, and he had the sense to know that Patsy Heffernan would not easily let those provisions go, having fought in thirty battles against the English.

That day that faded away till the far hills darkened, till the ducks had gone over on their way to the bog, till all the lights were lit in the town of Cranogue, went too slowly for certain young men. They had forgotten the fears that troubled the rest of the village, no longer wondering what Fanny Maguire, Nanny Moran or Julia Hegarty would do to it one dark evening, for suddenly Cranogue seemed in a different world to them: its little shut doors, its little windows shining, its thatch and its white walls, seemed as far off now as infancy; while the night-wind, the earliest stars, and the hush, and the mist rising, seemed to be their world now. One by one they came down the slope and gathered beside the marshes, and waited for Mickey Connor. They began to talk in low voices, and already the talk of this band of armed men was different from talk that any of them had had with each other before. Soon they began to speak of Fanny Maguire. What could she do to them? they began to ask; and the tide of their talk was turning against the wise women; when some one looking across the glimmer of marsh, still lit by streaks of red in the fading sky and darkened by tufts of rushes, asked what the dead might do. The question was to the point. Small doubt that the dead had been wronged, having their ribs dug up by black heathen from Africa; and there they lay on the other side of the bog, and wisps of mist were coming from their direction, long and damp as winding sheets. If Fanny Maguire couldn't curse, who could? And wasn't a curse due? And if Fanny Maguire didn't curse for the dead, what would they do for themselves? And the wisps of mist crept on and on t'wards Cranogue. And then Young Mickey appeared, suddenly out of the darkness. "Hullo, Mickey," they shouted, and "Evening, Mickey."

"Fall in," he answered.

Talk stopped, and he looked at them, and read their names, and gave a pull to a blanket here and there to make it hang more easily, for each of them had a rolled blanket over his left shoulder. "Into file, right turn," he said, and marched them off; in file because that way they looked more like an army, making a longer column than fours. And, as they marched, the new world that they entered began to show them its mysteries. It was not that they had never been out at night before, but never before had the night seemed theirs as now. Going out to bring in a horse on a cold night, they were still the inhabitants of the world of walls and lamps, to which they were bound to return: the night showed them its wonders then, but only as to strangers; as a jeweler might show them his wares from a lighted window; but now they were theirs to handle. They were themselves of the night, and up in the woods by day they would keep some of its mystery. The village, they felt, though they did not frame the feeling in any words, was an island rising up above the tides of mystery, holding them back: they were out upon those tides now.

"You're not going the right way," called out Christie Ryan to Mickey.

But Mickey never answered him.

Young Mickey saw that they were all much too heavily laden for a march, especially up hill, and he was leading them to a farm that he knew of under the hills and a bit away to his left. He did not speak till he halted them all under a hedge, that bounded one side of the farm; and, taking Jimmy Mullins with him and telling the rest to wait, he went on quietly to the farm buildings.

"There's an ass in there, Jimmy," he said in a low voice. "And we'll want him."

One window shone in the night. All round was hush, only broken, when at all, by a sound in the byre, as a cow in her sleep moved some of her weight from one leg on to another and struck a board as she did so. As Mickey and Jimmy crept through the stillness and darkness that lay wide round the buildings they thought of all the things that roamed the dusk, either real or imagined, that had ever frightened them or given a somber splendor to starlight, and each felt that he himself had at last his share in these things, a kind of fellowship with the terrors of night, that threatened comfortable houses such as these. They were soon in the blackness of the byre among the breathing animals, and Mickey struck a match and found the donkey, and untied him and led

32

him out, when a dog barked. The dog was tied up, but Mickey knew that from the time he began to bark they had only about a minute to get away unobserved with the donkey, so they hurried and the donkey noticed the hurry at once, all the more because it was so new to that quiet farmstead, and protested against it, and it was all that the two could do to get him away. The dog barked on, and then slow bolts began to stir in a door, but they got the donkey on to the grass, and by the time a flood of light showed the open door of the farm-house they had just got out of hearing. And so they brought him quietly to where the other lads were waiting, and Mickey told them to take off their blankets and strap them on to the donkey, and the spade went on and two axes, and packets of various provisions, and the donkey became the transport of their little army; and, rested and very much lighter, they marched away to the hills. This was the first military requisition that they had made, and it seemed to give them the status of an army; it was also the first of those acts that were soon to confer on them what is the ultimate raison d'être of every army, an enemy.

CHAPTER VI

Night in the Hills

Young Mickey and his army, marching light, with all their outfit on the donkey, came to the great demesne of Knocknavogue, lying dark with woods in the night round the house at which old Mickey had been butler for thirty years in the Old Lord's time. They pushed down a bit of the wall where it had already crumbled low, till they could get their donkey to climb in over what remained and the heap of big fallen stones. The demesne lay wide before them and Mickey remembered the lines of Padraic Colum:

> An old man said "I saw
>> The chief of the things that are gone
> A stag with his head held high
>> And a doe and a fawn."

For he had himself seen just the same thing in this very place, before the troubles came and they were all killed. A few large horns shed by the stags in spring, could be still seen lying about. They passed by the house standing gray, like a huge ghost in the night, and all along one side of it the graves of flower-beds. There was the geranium bed by the dining-room window, though without geraniums now, on which Mickey Ryan had kneeled when he came to shoot at the Old Lord. Young Mickey, as he went by, had a feeling that something had deserted Ireland, though he did not know what it was.

They came to big woods, and marched down a long ride. Knocknavogue lay in the plains, but when they came out of the blackness of the wood, and saw at the end of the ride such luminosity as there is in the night sky, the slope of the hills was before them. They had marched hushed through the wood, but now in the starlight their spirits rose, and talk began among them. As they climbed the hill and the world seemed all below them and all asleep, their spirits rose higher still and their talk increased, even though the slope steepened and they needed all their breath for meeting the hill. Sometimes a dog barked, far off, and they welcomed the sound of the wild and wakeful voice, feeling wild and wakeful themselves in a world tamed by sleep and snug houses; the contrast between what walks the night and what shelters by firesides being greater now than they were ever to feel it again; for the night had yet to show them rain, wind, hard ground and cold, and many other discomforts, but now was only showing them freedom, and revealing to them too, as though the majestic night had honored them with her confidence, the mystery that cloaked the stars and the hills. They were going by no track, across the little fields that were bounded by walls of rounded stone, which were easily toppled down to get their transport through. And then they came to the wood. The whole of the tops of the hills were black with wood. Young Mickey halted his army just inside the trees; below them they saw the plain stretch far into darkness, above them the deep woods rose, and soared into night. They gathered round their donkey and sat down.

"Transport lines over there," said Mickey pointing, and the donkey was tied to a tree by Jimmy Mullins a little way off from where the rest were spreading their blankets and softening the hardness of the ground with bunches of bracken. Later they found it better to wrap their blankets round them standing up, and then to lie down; but this was their first night in the hills. At first the wind running cold through the trees and fanning their faces was a joy to them, a kind of welcome from the woods and the night to those who hitherto had only known sleep in houses; but soon there came the chill against which the first inventor of houses had built his walls. Young Mickey noted that one blanket each was not nearly enough. And he watched the sky anxiously. If it rained on the first night, how many would remain with him? He began to feel the anxiety that statesmen know when first they fear the defection of an ally. A miniature anxiety, my reader may think. No, it troubled him with all the force with which anxiety can trouble youth, though he showed it no more than a statesman would show it, if ever he felt such anxiety. This army of his was everything to him: would it melt away? The clouds were not high, but a wind was keeping them up, and he was afraid of nothing but rain. He would need more blankets in future, but tonight a good fire would keep them warm enough. He made two of them get up. "Take the axes," he said, "and get us some timber, and we'll have a good fire."

"We can't light a fire," said one of them, Jimmy Mullins.

"Why not?" said Mickey.

"Sure, they'll be looking for that ass of theirs, of course," replied Jimmy, "and if we light a big fire up here they'll know where to find us."

It was a trifling conversation; yet, if it had ended there, the leadership would have probably passed to Jimmy Mullins.

"Go all of you," said Young Mickey, "and get all the bracken you can, and let each of you put it in ten heaps, ten or twelve yards apart, and let you keep a good tidy line; and put a few sticks on each heap, and we'll have eighty camp-fires. Begob they'll not come for our ass then."

And this they did, working for nearly an hour, and any who watched from the plain saw the lines of an army flickering along the edge of the wood. Even far away in Cranogue, like sparks they saw the fires. An army up in the hills! But they had their own troubles in Cranogue, where the heathen from Africa were disturbing the bones of the dead and the wise women were angry; and they did not inquire what army. Many of the fires died down, then went out altogether, but not until stay-at-homes were long a-bed; and no one came near them that night. And when the sun unseen by them was climbing the hill behind them, unseen by the blackbirds in the dark of the wood, though greeted by them tumultuously, and the gleam of dawn was lighting the slopes below, the sentry that Mickey had posted just at the edge of the trees saw no one on all the hill coming up to look for the donkey. During that night Young Mickey learned a good many things, things that man in his principal cities during the last few centuries has concentrated a good deal of attention upon forgetting, things such as cold and the hardness of the earth, and other natural enemies of sleep. He did not even know, until taught by the experiments to which discomfort drove him, that there is no ease in a bed of earth until a hole has been dug for the hip. And not to know this is an ignorance as eccentric, among those that sleep under the stars, as it would be not to know the need for a pillow and bolster, among those whose rest is in houses. But that night he learned it, and even came soon to cultivate little luxuries, like digging another hole for the shoulder. Yet the one essential need was more blankets, and that he planned to secure before another night. In the cold before dawn he had their principal fire replenished and gathered his army round it; it is usual for armies to expect an enemy half an hour before dawn, but here the half-hour before dawn *was* the enemy: if that cold got through their single blankets and through their flesh and blood into their spirits, he feared that his men would be routed. Then came out the kettle, and the saucepan, and a dozen eggs, and the teapot; and as the kettle began to steam, and they saw that their fire was doing its work, and as they got warm while they watched it, their leader felt the lifting of an anxiety that he had never shown, and knew that the discomforts of the first night in the hills had not defeated his men. They had been a bit silent at first, but when the tea was made and the eggs were boiled, they all began to talk, and Young Mickey felt flushed with his first victory; for the stars had retreated, and his army was still in the hills. Twelve eggs were all they had, and the difficulty of carrying even them had cost them some thought; they had a side of bacon, that one of them had brought, but no frying pan: their commissariat had in fact been left to chance fancies. They had one bottle of milk, a large bottle that once had held whisky; and plenty of tea and sugar. Water they had not yet found, the water that made their tea having been brought in two bottles; the mysterious river, down which Satan had once dived,

37

ran far below them, for though on most of its course it ran only about five or six feet under the surface, it went here through the deeps of the hills. And it stands to reason that five or six feet of turf would have been no protection against a sword such as the one that the blessed Archangel would be likely to have; had Satan stayed at that level, he might just as well have run through the grass like a rabbit. No, he put the big hills between him and Michael. "And a pity for some of you that he did," said the parish priest of Cranogue one day, in one of his sermons, looking round him at some of those to whom the remark especially applied. It was nearly a quarter of a mile to where the river came out on the Cranogue side, and only a little less to the point at which it entered the ground on the other. So Mickey sent one of them to find a stream, while he watched the rest of them finishing up their eggs, and made his plans. In Mickey's plans his commissariat had an unusual relation to strategy. In most armies the commissariat is supplied in accordance with the work that the army is expected to undertake in the field, which is to say its tactics or strategy. With Mickey it was the opposite; he was not as yet at war, and his warfare would depend on the enemies that he made, and he would only make enemies as he replenished his commissariat. And what a dull world it would be if left was always on one side and right on the other, top above and under beneath: in Ireland left is often right and *vice* is *versa*. Cranogue was barred to them for many reasons, the most sufficient of which being that they had come to the hills to get away from whatever curse was going to fall on Cranogue for violating the bones of the dead, either to be brought on it by the wise women or by the dead themselves. And that meant that the commissariat would have mostly to be supplied from the other side of the hills, where Patsy Heffernan's influence was like that of a little king; and it would lead to a war with Patsy Heffernan's men, though he would not fight as hard, Young Mickey hoped, as when he fought with the English.

"Jim," said Young Mickey to Jim Brannehan, "we'll want provisions. Let you guard the camp with Paddy and Christie, and I'll go and get them."

"We could snare rabbits," said Jim. "The wood's crawling with them."

"It doesn't look well for an army to be snaring," said Mickey. "We'll shoot them."

"Can we do that?" said Jim.

"We'll have to get a shot-gun," said Mickey. "And we want a lot more blankets. Tell young Hegarty when he comes back from looking for water to bring the ass through the woods, and wait in the woods by the side of the Lisnane road, for we'll want him on the way back. But let him keep to the woods and not be seen with the ass."

Then Mickey marched off with four others, through the wood and over the hill, all carrying their rifles. None of them had ever been up to the top of those hills before; their dark line seen from Cranogue had always represented romance to them, and the hills seemed to stand in the land in which any dream might come true. And something in the early morning seemed so to haunt the still-ness and loneliness of the wood, that disillusion, which so often reigns in the purplest hills when once the traveler comes to them, seemed not to have reached their mosses. Had there been any armies in those parts they would have heard of it in Cranogue, and Young Mickey would not have gone out in broad daylight with only four men; but the only rumor of an army anywhere near those hills was the rumor that was running now through the fields below, from the eighty fires of his camp that he had lit the night before. They came out of the hills on to the other side; came to a road and marched down it; and quite a different country lay before them, to the one on the West of the hills. There were small fields, and neat white houses of many farms, great hedges, and no bog. Young Mickey marched first to the furthest of the farms that he meant to visit; he went up a bohereen to the house and knocked at the door. The farmer came out, a large man nearing sixty, with orange-colored whiskers round his red face once, as you still could see, but they had been whitening fast during the last few years; he stood in the doorway in his breeches, gaiters and waistcoat and asked them what they wanted.

"We want provisions for the army that's up in the hills," said Mickey.

"What kind of provisions?" asked the farmer.

"We want sixteen blankets," said Mickey, looking at the list he had made.

"Begob, I have not that many," said the farmer.

"No," said Mickey, "I don't want to take that number from you. Could you let me have five?"

"I might get you five," the farmer replied.

"And could you let us have a frying-pan?"

"I could."

"And how many eggs could you give us?"

"I might let you have twenty."

"I shouldn't take all that from you," said Mickey. "Give me twelve."

"Begob, and gladly," said the farmer.

"And have you e'er an old shot-gun?"

"I have a very old one," replied the farmer, and he went in and brought out a muzzle-loader.

"The very thing," said Mickey.

And the farmer went back and got the other things he had promised, as well as a flask of black powder for the old muzzle-loader, and some percussion caps and a bag of shot.

"Is there anything more you'll want?"

"There is not," said Mickey, and he marched on to the next farm.

From none of these farms could the line of Mickey's camp-fires be seen, for they were on the other side of the hill, but rumor had got round the hills, and it was known that there was an army up there. A woman came to the door of the next house where Mickey asked for more provisions for his army up in the hills, and she apologized for her husband's absence and gave them some loaves and butter and more eggs and a handy basket to carry them in. And they took a few blankets from her, and asked her the way up to the house on the next farm, and she showed them the shortest route, and they marched away.

And at the next place they saw several men in the farmyard, so they went in there, and found the farmer among them. And there was a large number of cows, so Mickey took all the milk that he wanted from there, and asked for nine or ten blankets to make up the number he needed. As it was a good big farm and looked as if it could spare them, Mickey asked for twenty eggs.

"Could you spare that many for the army up in the hills?" he asked.

"I could surely," said the farmer.

So Mickey and his men went with the farmer to his hen-house, while one of the farm-lads went to the house for the blankets and milk.

"Would you like a ham?" asked the farmer.

"I would surely," said Mickey.

So that was sent for too. And when everything was collected, it looked more than they would be able to carry, and march as soldiers ought to march. So Mickey asked: "Could you let us have a man to carry all the provisions as far as our transport?"

"I could," said the farmer. "Where have you the transport?"

"It's on the Lisnane road," said Mickey, "only half a mile away."

"Hi, Johnny," called out the farmer to one of his men. "Carry all these blankets for the general a bit of the way along the road."

And when they had Johnny well loaded they marched off, and were soon at the spot where the wood came down to the road and Young Hegarty would be waiting with the donkey. There they halted.

"The transport will be here soon," said Mickey. "Put everything down beside the road, and you may go back to the farm."

For he wouldn't let the man see that their transport was only one donkey.

"I'd like to be a soldier myself," said the man to Mickey, instead of going away.

Mickey thought for a moment: nine men would make a better army than eight; on the other hand what mattered most for the present was the repute of the size of the army that lit all those fires in the hills. So he said: "We have too many already. It might be hard to feed more." And he sent Johnny away. Then they put all the blankets and the ham and the old gun on the donkey, and marched away with their transport through the woods.

They came back to their camp in triumph. But a shadow dimmed the brightness of their triumph, only that evening. For while they were watching the sun setting, further off, as it seemed to them looking at that wide plain, than they had ever seen it before, a boy of ten or eleven came climbing the hill to the wood.

"Halt. Who goes there?" called the sentry.

"Timmy Halligan," said the boy.

"Advance and give the countersign," said the sentry.

"Sure, I don't know it," said Timmy.

Nor did the sentry for that matter, for there was no countersign. But soldiers often have to make the best of things in the face of all kinds of deficiencies, and he knew he had done right to ask for the countersign. But what to do next? He looked at Mickey.

"Don't let him advance," Mickey called out to the sentry, and went out through the trees to the open hill, and to where the boy was standing.

"What do you want?" he said.

"I've a letter for the General," said the boy.

"Give it to me," said Mickey.

It was addressed to the G.O.C. The Army up in the Hills. Mickey opened the envelope and read: "You are to cease as from this date from requisitioning any provisions in my Brigade area. Patsy Heffernan, Major General."

It meant war.

CHAPTER VII

The Two Generals Meet

*P*atsy Heffernan's embargo upon provisions covered the whole of the east side of the hills and was some miles deep, so that with the wise women down on the plain before them, and the probably angry dead in the bog of Cranogue, and with Patsy Heffernan behind them, Young Mickey's men were between the devil and the deep sea. He called them together by the embers of the big fire and read Patsy Heffernan's letter to them, and then tore it in pieces.

"Isn't Ireland free?" he said. "And what right has any man to prevent us getting provisions to keep ourselves alive?"

"Haven't we plenty of provisions, now?" said Jimmy Mullins, for the name of Patsy Heffernan was not without its terror.

"Only what will last us three days," said Mickey.

"Maybe we mightn't want to stop in the hills longer than that," said Young Hegarty.

"Patsy Heffernan will have to do more than write a letter before he can drive this army out of the hills," said Mickey, and noted how the boast had no effect; and added: "And besides that, anybody deserting this will be shot."

That had its effect. "We'll not go till you tell us, General," said one. And they all agreed to that.

"We'll have all tomorrow to get provisions," Young Mickey continued. "Because Patsy Heffernan won't know at once that we're not going to do as he says. But after tomorrow maybe it will be difficult, and we'll be only able to do it at night; so we must get all we want for a long while."

"Maybe we'd better start now," said Jimmy Mullins.

"We had not," replied Mickey. "For then Patsy Heffernan would know by tonight that we're not going to do as he says, and he'd be ready for us tomorrow. We shall want to have the whole day for all we'll have to get."

He went then to look at the pile of sticks and bracken that Jim Brannehan had collected during the morning. "Have you enough for the eighty fires?" he asked Brannehan.

"Sure, I've enough for thirty or forty anyway," said Jim. "And that ought to keep us warm."

"Have you no sense?" said Mickey. "What would they think of an army that shrinks to half its size in the night? Sure, they'd come and eat us. Go all of you and get enough for a decent army."

So they all went further into the wood, taking the two axes with them, and Mickey was left alone to think things out for himself. Ammunition began to be of importance now, though foremost in his mind was the need for protection against the rain, the canvas covering of some hay-rick that they could fasten to branches of trees, for it was still the rain that seemed to him to be the most immediate threat to his army. Then they would need provisions that would keep a long time, for food would not be so easy to obtain, once Patsy Heffernan got his army out. And then he began to think of tactics, the main idea of which was that Patsy Heffernan's army would probably be much too large, and that he would probably be able to keep out of its way, and to find it when he wanted to hit it. He had a lot to think of as he sat there watching golden stripes in the West widening slowly through a sky of greenish blue. Drilling, of recent years, had taken the place of greyhounds among the young men, so that they all knew a little of that, but he feared that they knew very little of shooting. So, as soon as they came back with the sticks and bundles of bracken he sent them all off in different directions to get a rabbit with their rifles while there was still a little light; there were plenty of rabbits out in all the grassy spaces in the wood, but in the bad light only one was shot, and the one that shot him Mickey made his musketry-instructor. They roasted the rabbit there and then, and he was tough, all except the liver, which they cooked by laying it on hot stones at the edge of the fire, and which made a very small dish, but one that might well have been served at any banquet. While the rabbit was cooking they laid out their sticks and bundles of bracken, and, as the nine men ate their supper, folk in the plain below saw the menacing lines of an army, glowing with eighty camp-fires. "They're still there," said some. But no one asked who they were, such questions being regarded as not having to do with a man's own business; which it was better for every man to follow, leaving other men's businesses alone, especially the business of men that might be up in the hills.

After supper, with three blankets each and some bracken under them, and their feet to good fires, and another night without rain, Mickey had his army well in hand. He posted a sentry and forgot him; and the sentry marched smartly up and down for the first hour, and then sat by one of the fires, getting up now and then to replenish the nearest. Towards dawn, when he wanted some sleep, he prodded one of the others with his bayonet, and persuaded him to relieve him in exchange for a packet of cigarettes. The relief was smartly carried out, for they had both watched sentries being relieved, before Ireland was free.

Dawn came up and found the rest of them harder to wake this time, now that they were all warm, and the sun itself had to come over the tops of the trees to do it. Then they put all the ends of burnt sticks on to one fire, and got out the frying-pan and the kettle. Young Hegarty had found a tiny stream quite near, trickling down from rock to rock that was deep with moss, past masses of the bright-green leaves of the wood-sorrel that have always seemed to me, if I may utter so great a heresy, to be much more likely than clover to have been the original Irish shamrock. The frying-pan made all the difference, and the army had a fine breakfast.

It was Christie Ryan that shot the rabbit, and Young Mickey sent all the men off with him now to a glade in the wood for an hour's instruction in musketry. Then began the work of the day, which was to obtain provisions for as long as they should be at war with Patsy Heffernan, or as long as the wise women were cursing Cranogue. More provisions they might obtain from time to time, but not with the ease with which they could obtain them now, and Mickey wanted to make sure of them while he could. Not only so as to be able to carry all the provisions they needed, but also so as to make as big a show as possible, Mickey took his whole army; and, having hidden their provisions, they went up through the wood and down the far slope of the hill, with Jimmy Mullins leading the transport. The rumor of the eighty fires in the hills had by now spread like their cousin, the proverbial wildfire; and the farmers were expecting them, with various provisions ready; for it had always been their policy to be on good terms with whatever army might be up in the hills.

Mickey went to farms that he had not visited on the day before, and got from the top of a hay-rick the broad sheet of canvas that he needed to keep his army dry, and took in large supplies of bread, butter and bacon. He found the canvas heavier than he had expected, and that this with supplies of food for twenty days would be as much as their donkey could carry. At the end of that time, if victorious over Patsy Heffernan, he knew that the provisions of the whole countryside would be at his disposal; while, if it should go the other way, he would be moving too fast to carry more provisions than such as his men might pick up at the houses they passed. And he took sufficient tea and sugar for those twenty days, and left the future to provide the milk, beyond what he had got for that day and the next. And just as he was about to turn back for the hills, he saw quite near him the farm-house by the orchard, by which he had met Alannah a year ago. He had not meant to take any provisions from this house, but ever since reading Patsy Heffernan's letter, it had seemed to him that he might have few opportunities of seeing Alannah again. So he halted his men by the road, and went up alone to the farm. At first he did not see her, and he did not like to go to the door, lest they should think he had come for provisions, which he had determined not to requisition there. So he walked about the farm, and presently saw her a little way off from the house. She recognized him at once, and was glad to see him. "I hear you have a great army now," were her first words to him.

"I have," he said, for it was not for him to undo the work that rumor had done for him.

"Where have you them?" she asked.

"Up in the hills," he said. "And I have a few of them out there on the road, part of my transport."

"What are your politics?" she asked.

And suddenly he knew that, brief though their acquaintance had been, he was something more to her than any young man that chance might have brought by, for one does not thus openly and without preliminaries inquire of any man's politics in Ireland.

"Just against the government," answered Mickey.

"Which government?" asked Alannah, for the English had only been gone a year.

"Any government," said Mickey. "Sure, what's the use of them? No man can be free when there's a government over him."

"He can not," said Alannah. "But who are you fighting against?"

"Sure, no one yet," replied Mickey. "But I got a very wicked letter from Patsy Heffernan."

"Oh, don't go to war with Patsy," she said.

"Why not?" he asked.

"He's terrible wicked," she said.

"So am I," said Mickey, and saw a look in her eyes that he long remembered, a look of interest certainly, and what seemed something more, only that it seemed too good to hope that it was so.

At such a moment it was good to part, for he might not easily waken such interest again; and he went back to his men and marched away, and became for Alannah part of the splendor and mystery that clothed the big hills.

With his head full of the glimmer of the dawn of a new happiness, and his men triumphantly supplied with provisions, Mickey was marching away by the road that wound to the hills, full of cheerful greetings to the few that he met, for whatever came near seemed to reflect some of his own cheerfulness; when he met a scowling face. For a moment Mickey stared; and then, though he had never seen Patsy Heffernan, neither he nor any of them doubted that the man stood before him. His words, when he spoke, made this certain. "I didn't drive the English out in order to let you march about here."

"Sure, I'm doing no harm," said Mickey lamely, the poor excuse of a boy caught in somebody's orchard.

"And you're doing no good," said Patsy.

"I'm doing a lot of good," said Mickey, becoming bolder.

"You'll get out of this," said Patsy. "Unless . . ."

"Unless?" repeated Mickey.

"Unless you've a bigger army nor what the English had."

"I have," said Mickey, and marched away with his men.

It was the right thing to say, and would have deceived a British statesman. But would it take in Patsy Heffernan?

CHAPTER VIII

The Conversion of Umbolulu

As Young Mickey's army came out next morning from under their shelter of canvas slung from four trees, to sit round a fire to their breakfast, an event occurred in Cranogue that was a shock to many good Catholics. For Umbolulu, as he got up that morning in a shed at the back of the hotel, was putting on a coat. There is of course nothing whatever in the religion of a good Catholic to prevent a man wearing a coat: on the contrary. But as soon as Umbolulu appeared in the street, wearing a long black coat, and without his drum, they perceived that in a matter of proselytizing the black Protestants had got ahead of them. Those best qualified to judge had given their opinion that a case such as Umbolulu's could not be spiritually cured in under a month; yet here he was after a few days of Mrs. Patrick's teaching presenting an appearance that seemed hardly possible to those that had so recently seen him dance to his drum, while the great necklace of bones bobbed up and down on his skin. When Mrs. Patrick later in the morning came down the street of Cranogue to Sharkey's hotel there was just that touch of bitterness added, for all who saw her, that a conqueror sometimes gives by marching his army through the principal streets of a defeated capital. Yet they were very tolerant of each other in Cranogue, the good Catholics and the black Protestants, and no trace of bitterness was exhibited.

When Mrs. Patrick saw Umbolulu in his coat, she experienced one of the great spiritual exaltations of her life. It should be borne in mind that the saving of souls was to her what having four aces in his or her hand, and a good sprinkling of kings, is to a bridge-player; and that, though this was her hobby and though she had saved souls, she had never seen the saving before in her life, the fruit of her labors having all ripened in Africa. From what was she converting him? She never knew. He spoke far too few words of English to give her any idea of what we call his religious persuasion. She guessed it weeks later, but not now. Whatever it was it was something far from that solemn frock-coat, the week-day coat that had been lent him by Mr. Washington, who henceforth wore his Sunday clothes all the week round. A starched collar and a gleaming triangle of shirt replaced the necklace of bones, and Umbolulu for the first time wore boots. He had not got a tie, but before that day was out Mrs. Patrick equipped him with an old cricketing tie of her husband's, and with the bright colors of the M.C.C. flashing from the darkness of his frock-coat Umbolulu was now outwardly a Christian, while inwardly his conversion proceeded apace, if he was not already perfect. Sunday came round again; and this time a little group at the other end of the town watching the Liberissimans crossing the street to go to the Protestant church saw one more than there had been last Sunday; they watched with tolerance, and if the faintest jealousy was aroused by Mrs. Patrick's capture of the soul of Umbolulu, it was soothed by the words of one of them, as the little party of Africans entered the Protestant church, "Isn't it a good enough religion for the likes of them?"

The church-door closed on the Africans. And another of the cluster in the street said: "There's an army up in the hills again."

"Aye," said another, "it's been there for the best part of the week."

"It's likely that's where Mickey and Jim and the other young lads have gone," said some one.

"Whist!" said Old Mickey from his doorway, near which they were gathered. "You wouldn't know where they'd be gone."

And talk died down at his warning.

When conversation awoke again they spoke of a force that was closer to them than the army up in the hills. Some one had heard an owl shriek down by the bog: it may have been meant as a warning, or it may not even have been an owl at all. Another had seen a gray mist at evening over the water, reaching out in long arms, and all of them pointing at Cranogue. "There's no doubt the dead are terrible wicked," said one.

"Wouldn't you be wicked," said another, "and heathens from Africa digging your ribs up out of your grave?"

And the first speaker shuddered.

"Don't the dead want peace?" went on the second. "Not to be dug up by black heathen."

"What's Fanny Maguire saying now?" asked another.

"Begob," came the answer, "she's wickeder nor the dead."

"God knows what's coming to Cranogue," said an old woman. "God spare it. It's terrible."

These were two of the topics that might have been overheard where any talk occurred in those days in Cranogue, the army up in the hills and the dead down by the bog. Who led the army up in the hills none knew, and it was safer not to talk of it. Fanny Maguire led the dead; and this topic, the more alarming of the two, might be spoken of to the heart's content. All other topics were of the ancient affairs of Cranogue, which changed little with the passage of centuries.

I do not include among topics Mrs. Patrick's conversion of Umbolulu, for it was almost too distasteful to count as a topic, this grab by the Protestant church being regarded rather as any of my English readers would be likely to regard shop-lifting. And it is curious that, though while Umbolulu was half naked, and actually a black heathen, he had from the people of Cranogue a certain amused friendliness; yet now in his respectable coat, and making daily progress in Christianity, he shared in the disapproval with which Cranogue regarded his party. A reluctance to sell them food now extended to him, a reluctance that only awaited an organizer to call up hunger against them.

I have little more to tell you about Cranogue; things never moved very fast there in any age. Umbolulu continued his progress, never free from the lash of Mrs. Patrick's zeal. A fear hung over the town as the mist hung over the marshes. Old Mickey watched from his door and saw nothing new. Let us get back to the hills.

CHAPTER IX

Mickey Prepares for War

On the day that followed Mickey's meeting with Patsy Heffernan nothing occurred in the hills. Mickey's scouts looking out of the woods on the eastern slope saw perhaps half a dozen young men during the morning on bicycles, on a road on which for the same period one would usually see only one or two. But there were no other signs of activity. That night it rained, and Mickey was glad of his canvas, without which his army would have been wet, and he knew that a wet army would have been hard to hold. Next morning his sentries saw men approaching the hill from different directions, and fired at them, and were fired at in return. Mickey had eight sentries out, as well as himself; his entire force in fact. In most armies sentries protect the army against surprise; but the important surprise in these hills was the smallness of Mickey's force, and this surprise had to be protected by his army. So he had a screen of nine sentries along the edge of the wood. At night he called them all in, for Patsy Heffernan would not be able to find out too much in those big woods by night, and they all had a good supper; after which Mickey went over the hill and down the far side to get fresh milk for his army's tea. He went to O'Dwyer's farm, the orchard farm, where Alannah lived; for it was necessary to go to friendly places now, and to go and return by night. Not that he knew if O'Dwyer would be friendly or not: he had never seen him. And he feared that any young men that he might meet would all be Patsy Heffernan's men. He met none as he went in the dark from the hill to the farm.

When he came to the farm the house was all dark, except for the glow that came from the curtained window. How could he find Alannah? To knock on the door might be to bring to it one of Patsy Heffernan's men; and he had come without his rifle. So he went to the window and tapped it very lightly twice, with the end of one of his fingers; lightly enough for any one's second thoughts to put it down to a moth, or a small bird, or a leaf on the wind, or imagination; loudly enough, he hoped, for Alannah to guess. And after a long time he heard a lock being turned softly; and there was Alannah.

"Have you any fresh milk you could let me have, Alannah?"

"Not what would do for any army," she said.

"I only want it for tea for a few of my officers."

"And what about your men?" asked Alannah.

"Sure, they don't drink it," he said.

"Is that so?" said she. "What do they drink?"

"Sure, they only drink whiskey," said Mickey. "They're terrible fellows. They wouldn't look at milk."

"Have you enough whiskey for them?" she asked.

"I have," said Mickey. "Barrels of it. But it's raw fierce stuff that those fellows drink. I'd be glad of a sup of the milder kind for my officers."

"What kind?" asked Alannah.

"Ah, any kind," said Mickey. "It's liquid fire those lads drink. It would blister your finger. Any kind you have would seem milk to it."

"They must be terrible, surely, them lads," replied Alannah.

"Sure, they are," said Mickey. "And I'm sorry for Patsy Heffernan."

Then she went quietly back to the house, telling him to wait there; and presently she brought him two large bottles of milk and a small bottle of whiskey.

"It won't do for many officers," she said as she gave him the milk. "But it's all we can spare."

"Ah, it's plenty," he said. "It's only the lads commanding battalions that drink tea."

"Why don't the others?" she asked.

"It's against the regulations," he replied.

You know, reader, a general that belittles his own army, that does not make the very most of it, that does not make it loom as large as possible, especially on the eve of a fight, is not worthy of his command. The various ways of making the most of an army are not laid down, and must be left to the individual commander.

"That Kaiser was a terrible fellow," said Alannah suddenly.

"He was that," said Mickey.

"And the English beat him."

"So I heard," said Mickey.

"And Patsy Heffernan drove them out of Ireland."

"Sure, doesn't every one know that," said Mickey. "Why do you tell me?"

"Because I'm thinking it might be better for you not to go to war with Patsy Heffernan," she said.

"Begob," he answered, "it's too late for that. Wouldn't I starve if I did what Patsy tells me. He wants me to keep an army without provisions. How would I do that?"

"Couldn't you do without a war at all?" she said.

"I could not," he replied. "Isn't Ireland free? And who's to stop me?"

It was on the tip of her tongue to say "Patsy Heffernan," but she wouldn't do it, only wishing to warn him, not to dispirit him.

From one practical business Mickey turned to another: he had done what he could to establish for his army up in the hills a reputation for size; he turned now to the question of further provisions. To march his men round the farms any more in broad daylight would be impossible, and even by night would be difficult. Surreptitious raids would have to be made, and hiding-places prepared in advance, for occasions on which they might not be able to be in the open long enough to get from the wood to the farmlands and back.

"Have you a good big hay-stack?" he asked.

"We have," she said. "Over there."

"Could I cut a hole in it with a hay-knife," he asked; "the way that, if I came down from the hills with a small escort of seven or eight, we could hide from Patsy Heffernan?"

"You could surely," she said. "But Patsy'd have a terrible quick eye for hay-ricks and the like of them, having been on the run for a year himself."

"Have you a hay-knife?" he asked.

"We have, sure," she said.

"Then let you and me cut a tunnel in the hay," he said, "and we'll close it up with a good thick bit at the end, and he'll not find us then, if we ever have to use it."

She was doubtful, but led him to the hay-rick.

They walked through the orchard and through a small gate in a hedge, and there was the hay-rick with wide flat fields beyond it. They got the hay-knife from a side of the stack in which the blade was buried, pulling it out by the wooden handle, and Mickey began to work at the end of the stack that was furthest away from the farm. Working hard he cut a tunnel in from the side along the end of the hay-stack, carrying out square pieces of hay, till he thought there was room enough to squeeze in nine men; then he put two big squares of hay to hide the end of the tunnel, and left it tidy and smooth. All the rest of the hay that he had cut out Alannah helped him to carry to the stalls in which the fat cattle were. And now he felt that the difficulty of obtaining fresh provisions was halved, as the big woods and the hole in the hay-stack gave him a hiding-place at each end of the journey. Beside the stack lay a duck-pond, bright and cold in the night.

Once more Alannah urged Mickey not to go to war with Patsy Heffernan.

"Sure, he's gone to war with me," said Mickey, "and we've started already. Didn't you hear the firing today?"

"I thought it was rabbits," said Alannah.

"It was not. It was men," said Mickey.

"Did you get any?" asked Alannah.

"We did not," said Mickey, "but there's time enough for that."

"Wasn't Ireland a dull country when the English were here?" said Alannah.

"Sure, there was nothing to do at all," said Mickey.

CHAPTER X

A Terrible Great Battle

With an extra blanket for himself, and the milk and the whiskey, and a packet of cigarettes and a little more tea, Mickey climbed the hill and came late to his camp. Through the huge solemnity of the woods in the night, and the cool air running between the trunks like a fairy, he came to the glow of his fires and the long shadows, and suddenly knew that he was home. Tired as he was, this knowledge that his bed was only a few yards away, and that the great wood was his house, gave him the delightful ease, long remembered and never quite explained, such as a tramp might feel, at night in the streets of a city, if a great palace lifting before him were all of a sudden to welcome him.

Soon he slept; the blackbirds woke them all; and they had their breakfast of boiled eggs, bacon and tea. And now Mickey put out only one sentry, telling him to move about a good deal and to watch the country at the back of the hill. He wanted to have the rest of his army handy, being sure that Patsy Heffernan would attack him very soon. And Jimmy Mullins was sure of it too, when they talked it over. "He's an agent of a big English insurance company," said Jimmy, "and goes about the country a lot on a bicycle. That's how he got to know it so well. But he'll want to be getting on with his work, so he'll come for us as quick as he can get his army together."

"That's so," said Mickey.

"What'll you do?" asked Jimmy.

"Sure, there's two ways of beating an army, and only two, in the books," said Mickey; "and many's the time I've read of them."

"What's those ways?" asked Jimmy.

"Two good ways," said Mickey. "One is to break its center, and the other to roll up one of its flanks."

"And which is the best?" asked Jimmy.

They were talking by themselves a little way off from the fire, at which the rest were seated.

"Sure, there's no comparison," said Mickey. "If we broke their center we'd have to go slap at them, and when we got there they'd be all round us. It'd be very close fighting, and we'd lose lots of men. That'd do well enough for big armies that couldn't move about quickly, like what the King of Babylon used to have. But we'll get away and attack one of the flanks. We'll have no one behind us then, and only one man in front of us."

"Only one man?" said Jimmy, puzzled.

"Sure, that's all," said Mickey. "If Patsy has a hundred men, and all in a row coming up the hill, and we get round and fire from a flank, there's only one man can fire back at us, but they all get our bullets."

"Begob, it's a great idea," said Jimmy, not knowing that he bestowed praise somewhat late on these tactics, which were well worn before Julius Caesar.

And as they talked the sentry came in, to tell that there was dust rising off a road a long way out in the plain.

"It'll be Patsy Heffernan," said Mickey.

"Are they within shot?" asked Jimmy.

"Sure, Patsy would never do that," said Mickey.

"They are not," said the sentry.

"He'd never bring a column along a road within shot of the wood," said Mickey.

Then Mickey gave orders to wrap all their possessions, except their rifles and ammunition, in the big sheet of canvas, and to bury it together with their two spades under a few inches of earth and moss, while he went with the sentry to the edge of the wood to watch the dust coming nearer. Before going he saw his transport tied to a tree with as long a piece of cord as they were able to knot together, and a pail of water by the trunk of the tree; and ordered two of his men to collect and throw down beside it a bundle of extra grass. It was a dry day at the end of March, and they saw the dust before they made out the men marching. They watched them marching until ten o'clock, then saw them halt and eat some meal by the roadside; and at half-past ten they saw them leave the road in two parties and cross the fields in opposite directions; they were in fact making a line across the country along the foot of the hills. Mickey saw at once what they were doing, and noted that there must be nearly a hundred of them.

"He's brought his whole army," he said to the sentry. But he need not have been surprised, for Mickey had done all he could to make out his own army to be one that merited such a display of force.

He saw them spread to about five paces between man and man, and by half-past ten they were coming up the hill, moving rather north-westwards. Mickey ran back to his men. It was the left flank that he fancied most. If he attacked the right he would be all in Patsy Heffernan's country, whereas attacking Patsy's left he could at least have his back to the country he knew. But first of all he lined up his men along the edge of the wood, and opened fire on Patsy Heffernan's force. They halted then at nearly a thousand yards, and lay down, and Mickey's men could hear them firing, fire that at first seemed unconnected with them, a noise in a far country. And then the first bullet arrived, dropping short and ricocheting, and going over them with a clear cry; and very soon several more. The trees were beginning to drop twigs on them. Mickey's men fired back as fast as they could, till he blew a whistle and stopped them. Then he led them back through the wood and over the top of the hill, and along the western side of it he must have run with them for nearly a mile, coming over the hill again when he was about opposite the end of Patsy's left flank. Unseen by the enemy he got to a point that was about eight hundred yards from Patsy's left-hand man, while they were all still firing into the wood. There he opened fire over a stone wall, and so well he achieved surprise that it was some minutes before a single bullet from Patsy's men hit one of the stones of the wall and screamed away upwards. Then Patsy's flank began to assort itself, so that instead of the one man who was able to fire at Mickey, there was soon a line of ten or a dozen; and bullets began to come over with that sharp crack, the intensity of which is the most noticeable of all the noises of battle.

Though Patsy's firing line was now a little stronger than Mickey's, and was even slowly increasing, as Patsy's officers began to understand what was happening and brought up a few more men, yet the advantage was still with Mickey, for all his bullets that went past that dozen men went right down Patsy Heffernan's line, uttering the single harsh syllable of which all men know the meaning. A little longer of this, and Mickey felt that his right to obtain provisions from any of the farms he had visited would not longer be questioned. And Patsy Heffernan's thoughts were not much different.

Suddenly there came a change. Again a haze of dust went up from a road. There was a flash from a brass button, far off, catching the sunlight. There shone some of the color so lacking in modern battlefields. The long rattle of horses' hooves floated up from the plain. And Patsy Heffernan ceased firing. Then, leaving the road, a column, bright with twenty pink coats, spread out and came up the hill between the two armies. It was the M.V.H., the famous Mountain and Valley Hounds, coming to draw those very woods for a fox.

"What are they doing?" said the Master to his huntsman, for Mickey's men were still firing.

"They're only having a battle, sir," came the answer.

"Well, tell them to stop," said the Master. "We can't draw the covert with all that going on."

And Old Jack cantered off, and came to the stone wall.

"What are you lads doing?" he called.

"Sure, we're fighting Patsy Heffernan," came the answer from the one that was nearest to him.

"Well, you can't do that here," said the huntsman.

"I don't know about that," said the other, slipping in one more cartridge for Patsy Heffernan's men. "You must ask the General."

"Where is he?" asked Old Jack. And the firing died down.

"What is it?" shouted Mickey.

"You can't fight a battle here," said Old Jack.

"Why not?" said Mickey.

"Because we're going to draw the covert," replied Old Jack.

"Can't you wait?" asked the General.

"We can not," said Old Jack. "It's our last meet near here for this season."

"We're fighting a battle," said Mickey.

"I know that," said Old Jack. "But we have to draw this covert. Or there wouldn't be a hen left in the whole country."

"Are the foxes as bad as that?" asked Mickey.

"Sure they are," said Old Jack. "Sure you don't see the claims on the fowl-fund as we do."

"Are they all in this wood?" asked Mickey.

"Look at the size of it," said Old Jack.

"Sure there's room for them," agreed Mickey.

"I'm telling you," said the huntsman, "there wouldn't be a hen left in the whole country. And you'll have all the people against you."

"Ah well," said Mickey. "Cease fire."

And the hounds went on up the hill.

The change that came over the battle was not due so much to this pause as that most of Patsy Heffernan's army, and the whole of his right flank, went up the hill to see the hounds draw the covert. On such occasions there is usually an honorable understanding not to change the position of troops, but no such understanding could hold against the Mountain and Valley Foxhounds: as well expect people to draw down their blinds when the hunt rode through a village. And by the time that the hounds left covert the whole strategy of that battle was altered.

Old Jack gave a wave of his hand and the hounds ran jubilantly into the wood, and there came that tense minute when all is silent in covert. Then a hound gave tongue, and then all of them; but not that high clamorous note with which they greet the enemy that they share with man; it was a cry angry and deep that they were uttering, almost a roar. "A badger," said Old Jack, as he heard the deep note of that tumult. Further and further into the deeps of the wood those voices roared away, till the badger came to a fastness of rocks wherein his family had dwelt for ages; the hounds were all round him and he was slow, but their teeth could not get through his skin, and he eluded them at a great shaft in the rocks that was called the Devil's chimney, because it went right down to the river that runs where the devil had dived, when he went under the hills to escape from the sword of St. Michael.

One whip went into the wood, but all the rest of the hunt rode on the slope outside, keeping level as they could with the pack for as long as they heard them. For a long while there was silence in the wood, when suddenly there broke out that cry that to hunting people is what cockcrow is to the farmstead, almost what dawn is to the world, the cry of a pack that has found its fox. After that everything that they had gathered there for began for them; the wide plain smiling in sunlight had now a meaning for them; hedges, streams, stone walls, that they had idly noticed, but as strangers having no share in them, became now so much a part of their own lives that their lives even depended on the skill with which they and their horses dealt with these obstacles. And the exhilaration with which they saw the hounds pouring down the hill from the wood, with the wide plain before them and great fields splendid for galloping, spread to all onlookers and the whole of Patsy's army. They watched the hounds, those men of Patsy Heffernan, till they could see them no longer, they watched till the last red coat and brass button were far away over the plain, and it was long before they slowly turned their backs to get on with their battle with Mickey.

The whole strategy of the battle was altered. Patsy Heffernan's right wing, in their eagerness to see hounds leave covert, had strayed as far as the wood, and the rest of them straggled all the way up the slope; while Mickey's army had not moved at all, except to show their heads frequently, by Mickey's orders, over different parts of the wall, so as to deceive the enemy as to their numbers; but no one had seen them, being all turned the other way to see all they could of the fox-hunt. Men who tell of that day tell of a marvelous fox-hunt, that carried the "Mountain and Valley" far over that wide plain, till one of the last of the watchers standing high on the hill and gazing into the blue distance said at last to another, "I can't see tail or trace of them:" they tell of a kill far off, getting on towards evening: they tell nothing of any fight. It is as though History willfully forgot both Mickey and Patsy Heffernan, and turned her back on that battle.

Yet all the more for the neglect of History must I describe the main features of this battle for my reader. They were these: Patsy Heffernan's army straggling all the way from his original line to the wood was now roughly parallel with Mickey's, while some of them straying through the wood in the hopes of finding a dead badger cut Mickey off from his hidden camp in which were all his provisions. Mickey opened a frontal fire, but realized that no good could come of it; and far from outflanking the enemy any longer, his own left flank was threatened by the men in the wood. Not only that but, from enfilading fire which must come the moment the men came out of the wood, the wall was no protection. Mickey increased the rapidity of his fire, and then slipped away down hill, under cover of the wall, as fast as he could move his men, before the men could fire at him from the wood. He was only just in time, and they soon came after him, and passed the news of his movement all along their line. The whole of Patsy Heffernan's army was now in pursuit of him, coming down from the wood, while he going down to the farmlands was leading his men into the enemy's country. Bullets from outside the wood now began to come over them, without the fierce crack that they make at shorter ranges, but hissing like rather lazy snakes. There was no flank of Patsy's that he was able to get at, and he continued his retreat down the hill. Soon his stone wall came to an end and he had to cross open fields in full view of the whole of the hostile army, and the number of bullets increased. At the first hedge he halted his men and fired at the enemy, but found that this did not stop them, so he stopped to fire no more, as it only lost time. Soon after his delay at the hedge he came to more level ground, while the enemy were still on the slope, and with the hill and victory to help them they were decreasing the distance between them and Mickey. Mickey's army ran on, while a strong wind that was rising seemed almost to push them back. If he stopped to fight there would soon be casualties when Patsy's line came closer. Suppose he lost two men! What general would risk, except for the most promising objective, a quarter of his entire force? The question was now where to go. O'Dwyer's farm with its haystack was now in sight. Could that haystack be his Corunna? No; for he was in full sight from the hill and, though the orchard might hide them as they entered the haystack, it would be a sufficiently likely hiding-place to be thoroughly searched if they went anywhere near, especially by a general like Patsy Heffernan who had lived much in haystacks himself, when freeing Ireland from the invader.

An hour ago Mickey had been fighting with a distinct advantage against an enemy that regarded him as an equal, and the advantage had been due to his own generalship. Then an event had occurred on the battlefield that had nothing to do with the battle, and as a result his superior position was utterly lost, and he was in full retreat, with the insignificance of his army known to the enemy. I cannot find any such effect on a battle by a totally extraneous force, in all military history. The only parallels that seem to suggest themselves are the angels at Mons, and the Russians a little later that, landing in Scotland from Vladivostok, fell on the German flank in the same advance, but acting independently of the angels. Yet neither of these so ruined a general's plans as that appearance of the Mountain and Valley Hounds treated poor Mickey's.

His rapid retreat was in exactly the opposite direction to that in which he wanted to go: if he could get to the woods a force like his was safe, but the enemy were all the way between him and the woods. And there was no getting round; they would be overtaken while they tried to do that: there was nothing for it but to keep straight on. The haystack was now before him, like a friendly but untenable fortress, only a few hundred yards away. Beyond it lay open fields, where they could never get out of view and must either be shot down or captured. And the enemy were closer, as they could tell without judging distance, for the bullets were now once more making their ear-splitting crack. And, more depressing than any of these things, came a question gasped by Jimmy Mullins as he ran: "Where are we going, General?" It showed Mickey that confidence in himself no longer went without saying.

"To that haystack," he said.

"We can't hide behind a haystack, sure," said Jimmy.

"I cut a hole in it that will hold us all," replied Mickey.

And that was a point to the General, till Jimmy countered, as Mickey had feared he would, with the remark, "They will search the haystack."

It almost forced from Mickey the words, "They will not." And as he said them there came to him an idea.

"Why not?" asked Jimmy.

"You'll see," said Mickey.

He increased the pace of his army and gained a little on Patsy. The wind that was blowing against them seemed even stronger now, and it was nine very tired men that reached O'Dwyer's farm. There were no men there except O'Dwyer, for the farm lads had joined Patsy Heffernan; and O'Dwyer was in the house. "Get a bucket each from the cowsheds," he shouted to his men. Then he ran into the house and found Alannah. O'Dwyer was there too. "What is it?" he said.

"Sure, it's a bit of a battle," said Mickey. "It would be best to stay in the house."

But he asked Alannah to come with him to the haystack and to bring two large jugs with her. He put her on the far side of the stack in case Patsy should be sending any more bullets, the side on which he had made his tunnel; and as his men came up with pails he told them to run to the duck-pond and throw palls of water over both sides of the haystack and the back of it and the top, but not over the front of it.

"Is it insured?" he said to Alannah.

"Sure, it is," she said. "What are you going to do?"

"Is it insured in Ireland?" he asked.

"It is not," she said. "Patsy Heffernan insured it with the big company."

"Ah that's in England, then, and it won't matter," said Mickey.

"It will not," she said.

"We'll have to burn it," he told her. "And I wouldn't burn your father's haystack if it weren't insured."

"Why will you burn it?" she asked.

"Sure, it's the only cover we have for miles," he said, "and they'd see us all the way over these fields. We must hide here."

"But why burn it?" she said again.

"Sure, isn't it the first place they'd search if we didn't. The water should prevent it coming along the surface to us, and this wind is just right. Say we lit it and ran on. And keep it as wet as you can for us."

"I will that," said Alannah, "and my father will help."

Whether she told her father they were inside or not Mickey never knew. But a hose was brought from the house and Mickey later heard it being played in the right place, keeping the fire from coming round the sides to the back of the haystack. It was a good big stack and Mickey had no fear of the fire coming through the middle for a long time, especially with that strong wind against it. Patsy's army was now so near that they could have seen Mickey's men throwing water over one side of the haystack if he had kept them at it any longer, so he opened his door of hay and got them all into his tunnel; then he went round to the front and lit the haystack and squeezed into his tunnel, and Alannah tidied up the pieces of hay behind him.

In about a minute Patsy's men came through the orchard, and Alannah explained to Patsy himself that Mickey had lit her father's haystack and gone on with his men over the fields. For all that, Patsy searched the house and the cowsheds.

"For the love of Heaven be quick," said Alannah, "or you won't catch him."

In the dark of the haystack Mickey listened to the crackle and roar of the fire, deciding to stay as long as he could. But after a little while his door of hay opened. "Are you hot in there?" asked Alannah.

"We are not," said Mickey.

"Well, you can come out now," she said, "for they're gone."

"All of them?" asked Mickey.

"The whole army," she said.

Mickey came out with his men, and got them at once round to the far side of the haystack into the smoke; but he himself stood and looked at Patsy's army, hurrying away from him over the fields. Then he fell in his men to march them away.

"Would you like any more ammunition after your battle?" said Alannah. "For we have a few rounds."

And he took from her twenty cartridges, for his .303 rifles; and thanked her, and Alannah wished him luck and cheerily said good-by.

But O'Dwyer was laying down his hose, as he looked regretfully at his burning haystack.

"Sure, such things must happen in war," said Mickey, and marched back to the woods.

CHAPTER XI

An Illegal Organization

Back in the woods Mickey's men dug up everything they had buried, and were soon sitting down to their tea, with water boiled at a fire that Mickey had watched very carefully, for they could have no more camp-fires now. They had had their first battle, and Victory had beckoned to them; and though she had soon gone over to the enemy, they had eluded defeat as Victory had eluded them. The tea tasted good. They had their big sheet of canvas once more above them, slung from its four trees; and, sitting there on their blankets, they heard from Mickey how they should have two more days undisturbed there; for Patsy Heffernan would have to spend all the next day on his bicycle looking after his insurance business to make up for his day off; and the day after that was Sunday, and Patsy would be certain to attend Mass, which would make him so late starting a battle that they could be sure of being unmolested till Monday.

"It was a great battle," said Jimmy Mullins.

"It was," said Mickey.

"It's a pity we didn't win it," said Jimmy.

"Ah, sure, if one won every battle there'd be no fun in them," said Mickey.

"Sure, didn't Napoleon lose an odd battle?" said Jim Brannehan, to comfort Mickey. "And he conquered the whole world."

"He did, sure," said Paddy Mulligan.

"Begob, he did," said all of them but Pat Kelly.

"Didn't they come and attack our camp?" said Pat.

"They did sure," said one or two of them.

"And aren't we still here?" asked Pat.

"We are indeed," came the answer from more than one.

"Then by all the rules," said Pat, "we won it."

It was a new light to them, and slowly spread in the wood. Mickey said nothing: he was glad that his army should feel victorious, but if he had shared their delusion they would soon have come on disaster. He sat thoughtful, trying to make a plan; but no plan came to him.

"Can we have a fire, General?" said Jimmy Mullins.

"No," said Mickey.

"Couldn't we light a row of a hundred?" said Jim Brannehan.

"They've seen us," said Mickey.

The idea that Mickey had had when first they came to the hills appealed to Jim Brannehan now. But Mickey knew that it was stale and useless. He sat and listened to them talking nonsense about their victory; but the more their spirits rose the more his sank, for the contrast between their boasts and the actual situation emphasized the menace to a small and beaten force of a neighboring army more than ten times its size. What was he to do? The two days' rest that he was sure of tempted him to wait and see what would happen; that is to say to trust to luck, or Fortune, who serves men well, but never the men that trust her like that. He had the sense to reject so mad a lethargy. But still he had no plan. The babble of his men's talk was all around him, while he sat deep in thought far far away from them. To stay there was impossible and, if he went away, beyond pursuit of Patsy, where would he go and what new enemies would he find there? And all of a sudden a plan came to him. He had not a hundred enemies until Patsy mobilized them again: he had only one enemy. If his eight men seized Patsy Heffernan, that would be victory. He never said a word; and his men never knew how deep he had gone to despair, or how far he had climbed up from it. That night they slept without a fire, but he promised his men one for Saturday night, as he counted on ending the war by the capture of

Patsy Heffernan on Sunday afternoon. The actual fire could not be seen by Patsy, and the rumor of it would not reach him before Mass on Sunday. And during Saturday evening Mickey allowed his men to take out the muzzle-loader and shoot a few rabbits, but not before, for he did not want any information of their movements to reach Patsy too soon. The day passed like others they had spent in the woods, Nature seeming to greet and welcome with freedom and boundless greenery men who had spent their nights in houses and their days at regular tasks. Mickey's plans were simple: he knew Patsy Heffernan's house, he would make sure he was not mobilized, as they could easily see from the hills, and then he would march on the house with his whole army. That evening they ate bacon and rabbits round a good fire, their spirits high after their day's rest, and after their victory, which had grown in the last day and night, drawing such sustenance from their talk that it sprouted wings.

"What are we going to do, General?" asked one.

"We're going to arrest Patsy Heffernan," replied Mickey, "for belonging to an illegal organization."

And all his men were delighted.

During Sunday Mickey carefully watched the plain on the eastern side of the hills, and saw nothing stirring but a few men on bicycles, and knew that Patsy's army was not yet out. In the afternoon he fell his army in and marched down to the plain with all except his transport, taking such advantage of stone walls and hedges that he could not be seen till he was quite near Patsy's house. And no one he met on the way did he allow to go on in front of him. When he could get no further without being seen from the house he waited with Jimmy Mullins under a hedge, while he sent the rest to double round from both sides and surround the house, three behind it and two on each side. While that was being done Mickey and Jimmy got through the hedge on to a road and marched up to the front door, by which a large brass plate shone in the sun and was engraved with the words: "Agent of The Dawn Insurance Company. Offices in London and Liverpool. Capital a hundred million."

As the two approached the house, two nuns, one young and the other maturer, came out of the house.

"Do holy women insure their lives?" gasped Jimmy in surprise.

"Begob, they must," said Mickey.

They passed the two nuns and took off their hats, and received a gracious nod of the hooded heads. They came to the door and grounded their rifles, and Mickey rang the bell. Then the nuns came back to the house again. Mickey did not want them just then, and, though he saw them coming out of the corner of his eye, he turned his face to the door and remained oblivious of them as long as ordinary politeness made this barely possible. His men were now round the house, though out of sight of him and Jimmy. Still Patsy did not come to the door. And then one of the nuns spoke to him, in a voice so gentle that none of the men at the back or the sides of the house could have heard her. Mickey heard her clear low voice, and so did Jimmy; yet neither of them believed that the words they heard had really been said, until they saw what the two nuns held in their hands. And after a long silence Mickey and Jimmy put their hands up, which was what the nun had asked them to do; and each of the holy women caught one of the falling rifles with her left hand, while the right hand held an automatic close to the faces of Mickey and Jimmy. Then one of the nuns leant a rifle against the wall and gave two short rings at the bell, and Patsy Heffernan came to the door. He also had an automatic. "Come in, won't you?" he said.

They all entered in silence, and Mickey's army was still surrounding the house, and had not heard a word. They came into the parlor and Patsy sat down at a table in the middle of the room, with Mickey and Jimmy in front of him and the two nuns behind them.

"Can I insure your lives?" said Patsy. "The premium is ninety per cent, but if you made a sound that could be heard outside it would go to a hundred."

"We'll keep quiet," said Mickey.

"That's good," said Patsy.

"Do you get holy women to do work like that for you?" blurted out Jimmy.

"Begob, we're not so holy as all that," came a voice behind him, telling him what Mickey knew already. And the automatics remained level just at the back of their necks.

"B' the holy, but it's a great make-up," said Jimmy.

"It is that," said a nun.

"You've seven men round the house," said Patsy Heffernan, "and I'd be glad for you to send them away."

"I'll go out and tell them to go," said Mickey.

"You will not," said Patsy. "But you'll write what I tell you. Take a chair."

There was pen and ink on the table, with a pile of insurance forms, and Mickey sat down facing Patsy, and the pistol behind him now slanted downwards, and Patsy dictated: "I am insuring my life with Patsy Heffernan, and Jimmy the same. And let you all go away, the way the Dawn Insurance Company won't have to pay up on me and Jimmy." And Mickey wrote as he was told. Then Patsy called to a small maid, who looked after the house, and she came in, with her blue eyes gazing at Jimmy, who was standing with the pistol to his neck. "Nancy," he said, "give this note to one of the lads outside." And when she was gone with it they heard talk round the house, rising then dying away; and after a few minutes of silence they heard the tramp of men retiring.

"That's right," said Patsy. "And now, what for did you come here?"

And some flicker of bravado rising up in Mickey, after all the humiliations of the last five minutes, he blurted out, "To arrest you for belonging to an illegal organization."

To which Patsy Heffernan replied, "If there's any law in these parts, I make it."

Mickey was silent.

"Do you understand that?" said Patsy.

"I do," answered Mickey.

"Take those clothes off," said Patsy to the nuns.

And they began to undress.

"Not both at once," shouted Patsy.

And he covered Mickey with his pistol while the nun behind him got down to shirt and breeches, and appeared once more as one of Patsy Heffernan's men that had fought in the battle on Friday. That was the elder one; the one behind Jimmy was a lad of seventeen, and very good-looking: he also returned to shirt and breeches, while Patsy with his right elbow upon the table leaned forward and covered Jimmy.

"Take this one away," said Patsy, nodding his automatic at Jimmy, "and lock him up in the shed."

"I've not taken off these boots for three nights," said Mickey to the two ex-nuns, "and they're hurting me."

He caught their attention a moment before they moved off with Jimmy, and working hurriedly he had off his boots by the time they were out of the room. Patsy was sitting with his back to the fireplace with the door on his left at the end of the wall that the fireplace dominated, the great fireplace of an Irish cottage, which had been left when the rest of the room had been given a genteel veneer: between him and the door was a big arm-chair.

"Did you order them to take all my money off me?" said Mickey.

"What?" said Patsy. "No."

"I thought not," said Mickey. "Well, they've taken a hundred pounds."

"A hundred pounds!" exclaimed Patsy. "No!"

"I'll soon prove it to you," said Mickey, going to the door.

As far as the door he was covered by Patsy's pistol: beyond the door Patsy knew his two men were still in the passage. Mickey opened the door and Patsy rose to follow, but the door shut as he rose. Patsy hurried out and saw his two men at the end of the short passage, but no Mickey.

"Did you let him past you?" he shouted.

"We did not," said one.

"Sure, we never saw him," said another.

Then Patsy shouted language at them that should not have been used to any one that had so recently worn the dress of a nun, and they carefully searched the house, after calling up another man who was waiting a little way off, and telling him to see that nobody left the house. There was no exit from the passage except at the ends. Patsy had never before seen a man vanish, and was driven to conclude that this was what had happened now. And so one must conclude it had, if we accept Patsy Heffernan's evidence that he saw Mickey walk out of the door. All strange stories are based upon evidence, and the honester people are, the angrier they become if you doubt it; and the dishonester they are, the more they simulate anger. The bare truth of what occurred is that Patsy did not see Mickey walk out of the door: he saw him open the door and disappear behind it, as we always do when we see anybody go out of a door that opens towards us, and saw the door shut; so that he would have sworn, in any court of law that he recognized, that he had seen Mickey walk out of the door. I suppose that is the picture that his brain actually did see. Mickey as soon as he was hidden by the opened door dropped on his knee and slammed the door, and was now hidden from Patsy by the arm-chair. That much was very easy: there is often a screen by a door; it is where any one who has a screen puts it; and, when there isn't, there is often some other furniture; and the trick can be played in most rooms. The difficulty was when Patsy began to move, as he immediately did; and Mickey had to slip round the chair quickly and quietly. It was for that he had taken off his boots.

There were two small windows, both shut and latched, and to get through either of them would be difficult, noisy and slow, apart from the man that Mickey was sure would be watching outside. And he certainly could not go on dodging round the arm-chair. But Mickey had seen the great fireplace, and the wide chimney that soon narrowed, offering less escape than the windows, in fact none at all; but there was a ledge just where the chimney narrowed, in sight of any one sitting close over the fire in winter, but not otherwise visible from the room. Mickey climbed up and sat there: the fireplace was so wide that he might almost have lain down on the ledge, but the ledge was so narrow all the way along that he could not stay there without support. There was nothing to hold to, and the only way to keep himself in his uncomfortable position was to push hard with one hand against the opposite wall.

Patsy soon returned, and sat down at his table, and Mickey heard the other two men continuing to search every room in the house, except the one in which Patsy was working out the accounts of his business with the Dawn Insurance Company. Outside he heard another man going round and round the house, opening and shutting the doors of sheds and outhouses. He rightly assumed that they had taken Jimmy off and locked him up at once. Whenever he heard searchers coming along the passage they stopped at the door and turned back: he knew they would not come to search the room that their general had told them that Mickey had left, to disturb him at his accounts. As for Patsy himself, his whole intelligence was a barrier against a glance up the chimney, which was the only possible hiding place for Mickey in that room: to have searched the room for the man he had just seen walk out of it would have been to deny the accuracy of his own observation, and if many were prepared to do that there would be very few really strange stories. Fortunately there is no serious tendency in this direction.

Mickey heard the rustle of Patsy's insurance papers as he sat at his work. Would he light a fire in the evening, he wondered? It was at the end of March, and he thought not. Would he be able to stay where he was, if Patsy did light a fire? Even this thought did not too much disturb him, for his head at least was well wide of the grate. But he had no plan of escape.

For an hour Patsy sat and rustled and wrote; more men came up and searched round and round the house; the patch of daylight that Mickey could see shining down the chimney grew dimmer, and still he had no plan. One thing was certain, escape up the chimney was impossible: there was barely room that way for his head. In great discomfort he had to wait, and see what opportunity Patsy would give him.

He heard Patsy light a candle. Did that mean another hour of the discomfort that had now become torture? No. Patsy rose and walked to the door, taking the candle, as racing shadows showed. Mickey was down off his cramping ledge almost before the door shut. He took two painful steps and was looking down on the table.

Was it credible? No. The pain of that hour in the chimney must have brought on hallucination, or the darkness of it had deluded his eyes. Yet there on the table by the right of the blotting paper seemed to be Patsy Heffernan's pistol. Any other man might have done it; but not Patsy Heffernan. And then he heard the key turn in the lock. Yes, it was credible after all. So long as Patsy locked up the room, it was credible that he had left his gun there. And certainly there it was, the gun of Patsy Heffernan, the gun that had driven the English out of Ireland.

CHAPTER XII

A Door at Fifty Yards

Young Mickey was alone in the locked room with Patsy Heffernan's gun in his hand. To return to the chimney was impossible, for as soon as Patsy missed his pistol and searched for him in the room, which he would not do till he armed himself, he would suspect the chimney at once; and when he did that he would fire up it. Mickey went behind the arm-chair, no adequate hiding place in itself, but the pistol made a world of difference. What hid him from the door did not hide him from the table, so he hid from any one coming in by the door, and prepared to move round. There he waited a long time, long enough to do a good deal of thinking, long enough even to act on one of his thoughts. For he went to the table and moved slightly a heap of papers, the concerns of the Dawn Insurance Company, which might have almost concealed the automatic, had it been where Patsy had left it; and this would give him many extra seconds, for no one finds anything amongst untidiness quicker than that, and those extra seconds would be all to the good. He returned to the shade of his chair, and again the minutes dragged by. He began to hear sounds in the house from whatever part any one moved in it, but no feet in the passage. And then a certain sound of clinking and clicking told him that Patsy and some of the others were having their supper. The sound brought to his notice intensely his own hunger. And somehow his hunger added a weight to the minutes, making them pass more slowly and more oppressively. The light grew dimmer yet, and in the dusk all sounds seemed to grow clearer, but none came to the passage. In the long wait he thought once of the windows, but luckily discarded the idea; for, as he rightly decided, the noise would bring some one up, and half in and out of one of those awkward windows his shooting would be only noisy.

He waited, and another twenty minutes went by. And at long last he heard steps in the passage. He was down behind the armchair. He heard the key turn in the lock, and Patsy Heffernan entered and went to his chair and sat down, Mickey moving round the armchair as Patsy passed it. He heard Patsy turning papers, but saw nothing of what he did, for Patsy was between him and the table.

"Patsy," he said, "I'm in the insurance business myself now."

Patsy never turned round: he knew now where his pistol was, and knew that Mickey had him covered.

"That's all right, Mickey," he said. "What do you want?"

"Same as you, Patsy, when you insure them," said Mickey. "I want to see you live long."

"All right," said Patsy.

"That's right," said Mickey, "then let me out of this."

"I will, sure," said Patsy.

They moved to the door.

"I'll open the door for you," said Mickey.

"I can do it for myself," said Patsy.

"Sure, I'm only a general and you're a major-general. I ought to open it for you. And besides that . . ."

He did not need to complete the sentence: Patsy understood such things well enough, and understood that Mickey knew that if Patsy opened the door himself he would slam it after him, and Mickey would not get another chance to escape. So he got in front of Patsy and opened the door with his left hand, from which now dangled his boots, and gave a little bow as Patsy went through, and went after him down the passage to the door.

"How ever did you get into that room?" asked Patsy.

"Down the chimney," said Mickey.

Patsy nodded his head, for he had seen the soot all over Mickey's clothes.

"I didn't know it was wide enough," said Patsy.

"Ample," said Mickey.

"But how did you get past those two lads?"

"Sure, they weren't looking," said Mickey. "Didn't you only tell them to watch Jimmy?"

"You're very spry," said Patsy.

"Sure, I am," replied Mickey.

"You ought to go over to London and shoot one of them, in order to learn them sense," suggested Patsy.

"Ah, I never like towns," said Mickey.

They were now at the outer door, which Mickey opened, and the two went outside.

"That was a great battle we had," said Patsy.

"It was surely," said Mickey.

"What for did you burn old O'Dwyer's hay-rick?" asked Patsy.

"Ah, didn't it make it more like war?"

"Sure, that's so," said Patsy.

"I suppose you couldn't let me have Jimmy," said Mickey.

"I could not," replied Patsy. "You see, there's three other lads with him, and if any one tried to get Jimmy away from them they'd all shoot. And you know how it is when young lads start shooting."

"Ah, well," said Mickey, "then I'll be going. And maybe we'll come back one night for Jimmy."

"Any time you like," replied Patsy.

And Mickey began walking away in the politest way known to man, which is to say backwards.

"One moment," said Patsy. "I've a sentiment for that gun. It's the one I shot at the Lord Lieutenant with. I'll give you a rifle for it."

"My rifle, is it?" said Mickey. "I'll change if you give me Jimmy to carry the rifle."

"I could not," said Patsy.

"Ah, what use are Jimmy and his rifle?" asked Mickey.

"He'd be fighting against my army again."

"Ah, what harm could he do if he did?" said Mickey. "Sure, I swear to you by all the blessed Saints in Heaven that he couldn't hit this door at fifty yards with five shots."

"Could he not?" said Patsy.

"I swear he couldn't," said Mickey.

"Ah well," said Patsy, "maybe I'll let you have him."

And he turned to the door.

"Best to call to them to send him out," said Mickey.

"Why?" asked Patsy.

"I'm still insuring your life," said Mickey.

So Patsy called into the house, "Have you Jimmy Mullins in there?"

"We have, sure," came the answer.

"Then send him out by himself to me."

And Jimmy came.

"Put your hand inside that door to the left," said Patsy to Jimmy, "and you'll find a rifle standing up in the corner. Bring it here, would you?"

"There's two," said Jimmy, opening the door.

"One'll be enough," said Patsy.

So Jimmy brought out the rifle.

"Give me my old gun," said Patsy, holding out his hand.

"Patsy," said Mickey, "when I was a gossoon, I wanted to be Prime Minister some day, having a great taste for politics. And my mother said I wasn't clever enough."

"Did she so?" said Patsy.

"She did, sure," said Mickey. "And she was wrong. For you can fool a Prime Minister, Patsy."

"Ah, well," said Patsy, "leave it on the big stone over there."

"I will, sure," said Mickey. "Come now, Jimmy. You're a great lad, Patsy."

"Sure, aren't we all great lads?" said Patsy Heffernan.

"Begob, we are," said Mickey.

And so they parted.

When Mickey and Jimmy had gone fifty yards they came to the big stone, and Mickey laid down the pistol on it. And not till then did he put on his boots, which he had all the while been carrying in his left hand, from the room in which he had taken them off.

"The blessing of God on you, Mickey," said Jimmy. "How did you do it?"

"I said you were no good with a rifle," said Mickey.

"No good with a rifle, is it?" expostulated Jimmy.

"Ah, I only said you couldn't hit that door at fifty yards."

"Begob, how far are we now?"

"Fifty yards," said Mickey.

"Fifty yards, is it?"

"There or thereabouts."

"Begob," said Jimmy, "I'll show you what I can do to a door at fifty yards." And he knelt down and took aim slowly. The door was shut, and they could not see Patsy. Bang. And the bullet went through a window a little to the right of the door.

"B' the holy," said Jimmy, "I've broken his window."

"Ah, Patsy will understand," said Mickey. And they marched off to the hills.

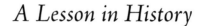

CHAPTER XIII

A Lesson in History

*T*here was a great reunion before Mickey and Jimmy came to the woods, for they met their army hidden by stone-walls and gorse-bushes, all watching Patsy Heffernan's house from a distance, where lights were gleaming now, in the late evening, from two of the windows.

"We were coming to get you tonight," said Jim Brannehan.

"You were not," said Mickey. "Patsy would have been expecting you. He'd have had fifty men round the house. You'd have had to have waited a week. And even then, Patsy's a smart lad."

"How did you get away?" asked nearly all of them.

"Sure, Patsy did what he'd never done before," said Mickey, "and never will do again. He left his gun out of his pocket. And I got it."

"Good for you," said one of them. "But he can't be well."

"He is not," said Mickey. "He's pining for the R.I.C. He never did anything like that when the constabulary were in the country."

"How did he get yez both?" he was asked next.

And Mickey told them how.

"Begob," said Christie Ryan, "I never saw two holier women, by the looks of them."

"B'Jabers," said Mickey, "when one of them kneels, it will be to look along Jimmy's rifle."

"Did they get that?" said Christie Ryan.

"They did, sure," said Mickey.

"Why didn't you take it off them?" asked some one.

"I didn't like to be asking for too much," said Mickey.

They went back in triumph to their camp, and lit a big fire, and the stars came out and watched them happy by the bright embers. Yes, I know what the stars were really watching, one of them was watching the warning fires that were lit before the armada, another the fire of London, and another the burning of Troy; but that is what it seemed to this little band of men, and I am rather recording their emotions and fancies than adding a volume to Science. And they were cheerful emotions and fancies that were felt round the fire that night: they had not exactly triumphed over Patsy Heffernan, but he had certainly not triumphed over them; and this gave them a certain feeling of equality with one whom, perhaps without very careful study of history, they regarded as one of the world's great leaders. Christie Ryan sang a song about a young lad that left his mother in the West of Ireland, and went to London for a holiday, and the English found him and hanged him. Christie had a fine voice, singing under the stars; and the night and the trees and the firelight seemed to add something to his song: they had had no singing in their camp before, and it helped to make this evening the happiest one they had had.

It was not till the following day that they began to feel a loss, that seemed to grow heavier and heavier as the days went by, the loss of Jimmy's rifle. Again I must beg to be permitted to check my reader should he think such a thing trivial. Imagine an army of eight or nine corps: suppose one of these corps to be completely disarmed: it is a serious matter. Jimmy and his rifle were an eighth part of Mickey's force, and the deficiency of his rifle was serious. Jimmy was given the muzzle-loader, but no student of military history will argue that an equipment of muzzle-loaders would atone to a corps for the loss of all its small arms and artillery; and only number six shot to fire out of the muzzle-loaders at that.

Except for this deficiency, that began to weigh on Mickey, he was more full of confidence than he had been since he took to the hills. Patsy it seemed to him had asserted himself by fighting a battle, and had nothing to gain by attacking him any more; they had parted good enough friends, and he had taken nothing that

Patsy wanted; on the contrary Patsy had got a rifle of his, which always means so much to a leader of irregular forces; and he knew that the broken window would be paid for by the Dawn Insurance Company. Provisions in the future, he felt, must be obtained by tact, without any show of defiance; and this could be easily done, as he had plenty of bacon already and could obtain rabbits in the hills; Patsy Heffernan in that case, he thought, would scarcely trouble to mobilize his men again to fight another battle against him. The one shadow that darkened the future was the loss of Jimmy's rifle.

They spent a happy time in the hills during the next two or three days, shooting rabbits and singing songs, and never disturbed by the army of Patsy Heffernan, who did not even send scouts to pry on them. And then one afternoon, while the birds were singing, and the twigs were murmuring to the softest breeze, and the chatter of squirrels were heard now and then in a pine, and the scurry and scratch of their feet, and Mickey was standing perfectly still in the wood to distinguish a blackbird's song from the song of a thrush, there came a new sound to his ears. Tap-tap-tap went its hurrying note above all the noises of spring. And Mickey knew that Patsy had got a machine-gun.

Had it not been for his sorrow for the loss of the rifle he might have put up with the sound, but as it was he could not help comparing his loss with Patsy's splendid abundance, and the lavish bursts of fire from where Patsy was practicing destroyed for Mickey the whole beauty of April. To all else who heard it, there was a new sound in the spring air, that an unsympathetic government had prohibited up to last year, except in the narrow limits of a few of their own rifle-ranges.

"Jimmy," he shouted.

And Jimmy Mullins came through the wood.

"Listen," said Mickey, as with another twenty rounds the machine-gun added its voice to those that were greeting April.

"A machine-gun, by the Holy," said Jimmy.

"And you've only a poor old muzzle-loader. B'Jabers if we had a machine-gun there'd be no army able to touch us in the world."

"There would not," said Jimmy.

"Where do you make out that it is?" said Mickey.

And Jimmy pointed. To Mickey also the sound seemed to come from the same direction. But they could see nothing, and did not know how far it was.

"Get all the lads," said Mickey. "And tell them to come quick."

Jimmy did as he was told. And soon all the army was there at the edge of the wood, looking out over Patsy Heffernan's country. And Mickey spread them out in a line six hundred yards long, and told each of them to point at the sound when they heard it again and to lay down their rifles aiming at it. There was one more burst of fire from the machine-gun, and they all pointed at it. By this means Mickey got a fair idea of how far it was; as, although the eight aims did not all accurately meet at the one spot, they all crossed the line that he and Jimmy had indicated, short of a certain landmark barely a mile away. It must be close to a small white cottage fourteen or fifteen hundred yards from them. Mickey gathered up his army, and walked with them back to the camp, depressed and thoughtful.

"We know where it is now," said Jimmy.

"Boys," said Mickey, "that only makes it worse."

A mother would not take her child to the Zoo and leave it negligently in a cage with tigers: Mickey knew that. And no Irishman would take his machine-gun out into the country without proper protection. What could he do? Into the void left by the loss of Jimmy's rifle, had come this new, glorious, triumphant, beautiful machine-gun. And the ache only increased.

Mickey was moody all day, and at night lay awake thinking. And, although thought is the fount of all human activity, my reader will perhaps not care to hear of Mickey's thoughts before they cast on the ground those shadows that are actions. The result of his night's brooding then was to send him down the hill by the earliest light, so that he arrived in Cranogue at eight o'clock, when he knew that Old Mickey, his grandfather, would be having his breakfast.

He walked into the house in the fresh morning, and there the old man was eating an egg.

"May I come in, Grandfather?" said Mickey.

"Come in, Mickey," said the old man.

"It's a fine morning," said Mickey.

"It is," said his grandfather. "Did you have a battle up in the hills?"

"We did," said Mickey.

"So I heard," said the old man.

"It was a great battle," said Mickey.

"Glory be to God," said Old Mickey.

"But we lost Jimmy Mullins' rifle."

"Bedad," said Old Mickey. "That was terrible."

"And Jimmy's without it."

"The poor lad," said Old Mickey.

"Patsy's got a machine-gun."

"You should get it from him," said his grandfather.

"Grandfather," said Mickey, "that's what I came from the hills to ask you about. How should I get a machine-gun from Patsy Heffernan?"

"Bedad," said his grandfather, "there's a lot to think about in that." And he was silent awhile.

"He was practicing with it yesterday beyont the hills," said Mickey.

"And so he would," said the old man, and was silent again.

And after a while Old Mickey said to his grandson: "Would you hand me my old pipe from the mantelpiece?"

And Mickey did so, and a tin that had once held tea, and in which black tobacco was lying.

"It helps me to think," said Old Mickey, filling the pipe. He smoked some puffs in silence. Then he took his pipe out of his mouth and spoke.

"That machine-gun's well hidden," he said.

"Is it so?" said Mickey.

"Aye," said the old man. "For Patsy has his insurance work to do, and he hasn't his army going around all day like yours. There's two ways to mind a machine-gun, and if he isn't guarding it he's hidden it. And a man like Patsy Heffernan would hide it well."

"How shall I find it?" said Mickey.

"That's the question," said Old Mickey, smoking again and puffing hard. "Begob, that's the question."

And for a long time the old man sat smoking in silence. When he spoke again it was only to say: "When I was young I had to be content with a very ordinary kind of rifle."

"Times have changed, Grandfather," said Young Mickey.

And the old man was silent again.

Then he said, "If you must have a machine-gun, there's only one way to get it. Patsy will guard it well enough when he takes it out, and until he gets it back. And you'll not find it by looking for it, when Patsy has hidden it. No, you'd never find it, the way that lad would hide it. He's a cunning lad. He's a cunning lad, indeed. Aye."

"How will I get it, Grandfather?" asked Young Mickey.

"Bedad," said the old man, "if he brings it out in a hurry, you might get it. It's the only way. Get him to bring it out in a hurry, before he has time to get more nor a handful of men to guard it. Aye, only a handful. You might get it that way."

"And how will I do that, Grandfather?"

"I'll tell you," said Old Mickey. "When he's going round the country visiting people on his bicycle, what time does he get back to dinner?"

"They say he has dinner at one, Grandfather," said Mickey.

"Would he get back about half-past twelve?" said his grand-father.

"Maybe," said Mickey.

"Then let you take out a pencil now and find a bit of paper," said Old Mickey, "and write down a proclamation as I tell it to you."

Young Mickey had a pencil and found a bit of paper that had wrapped up a piece of bacon.

"I'm ready, Grandfather," he said.

"Let you write this down," said Old Mickey. "But tell me first how far is Patsy Heffernan's house from the place where you heard him shooting with his new gun."

"Five minutes' walk," said Young Mickey.

"Then write this down," said Old Mickey. "There is to be no machine-gun practice in these parts before one o'clock. Signed Michael O'Rourke, major-general. On behalf of the Government."

Young Mickey wrote as he had been told.

"Now," said Old Mickey, "pin a few copies of that up on trees where he'll be seeing them on his way back to his dinner, and it may be that contrariety will make him go and get the wee gun to let rip a few shots out of it before one o'clock. And he'll be in a hurry that way and only get the lads that would live nearest to him, for to protect the wee gun. And that's one thing you'll do. And another thing is that you'll go to some of those lads living near Patsy Heffernan that morning while he's out on his rounds and get them to come away, the way they won't be there when Patsy wants them to be guarding his wee gun."

"How'll I do that, Grandfather?" asked Young Mickey.

"Sure wouldn't it be enough to ask them to lend a hand with a spade," said Old Mickey, "to do a bit of digging at the butt of a thorn tree, where you'd seen a rainbow touch the ground? You needn't only offer the lads a small handful of gold among the lot of them for their help with the spades. They'll know you're looking for a crock of gold. And, if they don't find it, begob it's you that'll be complaining, not them, for it's you that have located the crock."

"Begob, I'll try it," said Young Mickey.

"If he's set on letting the wee gun off before one o'clock, maybe he'll do it without having all the men he wants to guard it. You might get it that way, Mickey. It's all I can do for you."

"It's a great scheme surely," said Young Mickey.

"It's no scheme at all," said Old Mickey, "to take in a man of any sense."

"There's a lot of sense in Patsy Heffernan," said Young Mickey.

"I know that," said his grandfather. "But the wisest men in the world have been headstrong, and it's been the undoing of them. Look at Napoleon when he came leaping out of Elba to fight the battle of Waterloo; and what did he do when he got there only lost it? And the English took him to St. Helena and tortured him to death."

"They did that," said Young Mickey, who had learned his lessons at the same village school that had taught Old Mickey so many years earlier.

"He'd have been all right only he was headstrong," said Old Mickey. "And look at them Trojans too. The Greeks set up a big wooden horse for them to look at. They'd have been all right if they let it alone, but they dragged it into the town, and it was full of Greeks, and they lep out on the Trojans like a fox on a hen. They did that. And it's a lesson to all of us."

"Which side were the English on?" asked Young Mickey.

"They weren't fighting in that war," said Old Mickey. "But they'd put the Greeks up to it by bribery."

"It was a dirty trick," said Young Mickey.

"Bedad, it was," said his grandfather. "They were jealous of the trade of the Trojans, and they bribed the Greeks to smash it. It is what they do."

There was silence awhile, and Old Mickey smoked, gazing into the pale-blue haze that went reeking up from his pipe, and seeming to see the world in it and its strange ways, all leading to darkness; for he nodded his head at it and said: "Headstrong men, headstrong men, all rushing to find their dooms. And, bedad, if they didn't, wouldn't they rule the whole earth, and there'd be no freedom for any of us."

"Is Patsy Heffernan headstrong, do you think, Grandfather?" said Young Mickey gently, half fearing to disturb the old man looking into the smoke in order to regulate the world.

"He'll keep his wee gun if he isn't," said Old Mickey.

And then Young Mickey saw that he had got the advice he had come for, and that the old man had no more to give him. It told how to get the machine-gun from a headstrong man, and it indicated that men like that, men that had machine-guns of their own, were doomed to be headstrong. It only remained to do as the old man said, and to hope that the famous cunning of Patsy Heffernan would be marred by those hasty qualities that had ruined Napoleon and brought to ashes the tall towers of Troy.

CHAPTER XIV

The Plan

*F*rom his grandfather's Young Mickey went to his mother's house.

"Oh, Mickey," she said as she saw him, "were you having a battle up in the hills?"

"I was, sure, Mother," he said.

"Oh don't be having any more of them," she said.

But Mickey was a little disappointed. It reminded him of days when too many restrictions seemed to build a barrier between him and his mother.

"Ah, you wouldn't have grudged it to me," he said, "if you'd seen what a great battle it was."

"I'm not grudging it to you, Mickey," she said, "but you've had your battle now. Let that be enough to content you."

"We lost a beautiful great rifle in the battle, Mother," said Mickey, "and I couldn't be content till we get it back. It belonged to poor Jimmy Mullins, and he's without a rifle."

"How are you going to get it, Mickey?" she asked.

"I can't tell you that, Mother," he said, "for it has to do with the movement of troops. But we might get something better than Jimmy Mullins' rifle."

"Don't be trying to get too much, Mickey," she said.

And at that moment Mickey caught sight, through the window, of the black faces of three of the Liberissimans coming along the street. Suddenly he asked his mother: "How are things with the bones of the dead, Mother? And what is Fanny Maguire doing?"

"Worse and worse," said she. "The black heathen are desecrating them. And Fanny Maguire is wickeder nor ever, and Nanny Moran's no better."

"What'll happen, Mother?" he asked.

"God knows," she said. "What ought to happen, with all these desecratings? Something dreadful, I'm thinking. Let you get back to the hills."

"And what about you, Mother?"

"Sure, I never had any quarrel with Fanny Maguire," she said, "and maybe her curses will pass over me when they go to blast the Liberissy men. But let you get back to the hills."

Mickey lifted his eyes as he heard her, and the hills seemed to call to him very faintly, like music heard in sleep. They had a queer way of fading away, those hills, right into ghostliness. And they were like ghosts now, like ghosts far off and smiling. Only their outlines were there, drawn very faintly in pale silver and gold. Inside the outline was all filled in with haze, and there was haze beyond them too, so that only by some slight difference in the touch of the sunlight upon them could you tell which were earthly heights and which was sky. There had always been something in those hills that had called to him, and his mother saw that they were calling to him now and that he would go back as she had advised him, yet not because of her advice.

So she gave him a good bottle of milk for his army's tea, and bread and cheese and half a pound of butter, and he said goodby to her and opened the half-door. In the doorway she tried to hold him back, for she saw Umbolulu coming down the street, and wished to avoid a quarrel, thinking that the more the Africans were left utterly alone the sooner they would go from Cranogue, and the curses that were threatening it with them, and the just anger of the dead would abate. She feared a quarrel because Umbolulu had developed a tiresome habit lately, under black Protestant influence: he would see somebody passing him in the street or looking out of a door and, as soon as he noticed the look of honest scorn on the man's face, even though he never spoke, Umbolulu would say, "I pray for you, sah," or even sometimes he had been known to say, "I pray you not get damnation." When it was explained that his prayers were utterly worthless, Umbolulu could not understand, for he did not really know English at all. And this led to quarrels, and it was better to leave him alone to starve, as he would do if only the butcher and grocer stuck to ignoring him, instead of trying to argue. Mickey went out and passed Umbolulu, but luckily did not understand what he said, and started away on his long walk back to the hills. All the catkins of the willow were blooming near marshy lands, the gorse was shining all the way to the hills, becoming even more golden as the hills lifted, on many trees was a hint of bursting buds, air and earth were full of spring; but Mickey, so far as he knew, saw none of these things, being obsessed with his plans for laying a trap that would catch a headstrong man. Sometimes he paused a moment in his planning, to wonder if all men possessing the power of Patsy Heffernan were headstrong, so that the power must be thrown to others, like a gambler's money; or if there were men with the lavish qualities that made for such power and who yet had room in their characters for the qualities of the miser, so that they could keep it; and might Patsy be such a man? A while after mid-day he sat down and ate the bread and cheese that his mother had given him; his plan was now clear in his mind, and little remained for him upon which to ponder, but profitless doubts as to whether the plan would work. It was an idyllic scene in those days of triumphant spring, where he sat and ate his cheese, but these doubts on the brink of a venture that would make him master of the hills hid from his mind the beauty that was so abundant around him. He rose and went on, and soon the hills welcomed him. It seemed almost like coming home, to be once more among their gracious folds. All his life they had peered at him through the window of his mother's house, and had been for him a romantic land lifted above the fields that one had to dig and to tend; and, instead of being only a few hundred feet above those fields, had seemed to him to be almost half-way between solid earth and that blending of air and sunlight that haunted their slopes. All the great figures out of the legends, mixed with occasional facts, that he had been taught as history, had seemed to him to have walked in those hills.

"Halt. Who goes there?" rang out from the edge of the wood.

"General commanding the army up in the hills," repeated Mickey.

"Pass General commanding the army up in the hills," said the sentry. "And all's well."

"Jimmy," said Mickey, "I've the father and mother of a great plan."

"Good for you," said the sentry.

They walked back arm in arm to where the others sat round the fire, while Mickey explained his plans. The rest were watching a kettle boil, as Mickey and Jimmy came up.

"The General has a great idea," said Jimmy.

And then Mickey told his plan to them all, the plan of Old Mickey that was to catch a headstrong man. He showed the proclamation that he had written out while the old man dictated. "We must only give him half an hour," he said, "to rush out and get the gun; and he'll get the escort from the men that live nearest to him, and we'll have the most of them digging away for a crock of gold."

"Won't he get more then from further off?" said Jim Brannehan.

"He will not, for he'll be in a hurry," said Mickey, "and he'll take what he's got. And we'll be too many for them."

"Will we attack them while they're digging up the gun?" asked Christie Ryan.

"We will not," said Mickey, "for we'll never find it. My old grandfather said he'd have it well hid. And so he would. But we'll go to the place where he lets it off, and surprise them."

"Good for you," said the army, with an enthusiasm such as his cuirassiers showed for Napoleon before Waterloo, if I rightly interpret pictures that I have seen.

"Run, one of you," said Mickey, "and get me some ink and a couple of pens, and a dozen of good big sheets of paper, the way we can write out some proclamations."

And Pat Kelly got up and started off through the wood.

"Take your rifle," shouted Mickey after him, "in case they mightn't want to let you have it."

And Pat came back for his rifle.

And the rest he brought out through the wood on the eastern slope and they chose a likely thorn for a leprechaun to bury his crock of gold under; a gnarled and wizened tree that had gripped the earth with many a strong lean clutch, while the ages had bent its head away from the south-west. "It's a likely tree," said Mickey.

"Begob," said Paddy Mulligan, "if you saw a rainbow touch that tree there *would* be a crock of gold under it."

"We'll tell them we saw it," said Mickey. "Now let two of you go down and get as many as you can of all the lads that would be handiest to Patsy Heffernan, and get them to be up here with their spades round about half past twelve tomorrow."

And he sent two of them off without their rifles. He knew that all the men that they asked would come; and any man that wouldn't would be a man that would refuse to accept a ticket in a sweepstake, if it were offered to him for nothing. There was no sweepstake, in those days, of which any of these men could avail themselves; and the crock of gold had no rival.

They returned to their fire in the wood on the other side of the hill, and made tea and brought out bread and butter and, while they waited for the return of Pat Kelly, they heard quite close one of those triumphant voices that greet the spring, a haughty and somewhat harsh voice like the clarion of an Asiatic conqueror, a voice like another from Asia that has greeted our dawn for the last few centuries, the voice of a cock pheasant.

"Jimmy," said Mickey, "you have the shot-gun now. Let you go and get that bird. He'll be a great addition to us."

So Jimmy took off his boots and slipped away with the muzzle-loader and stalked the pheasant, guided by the sound of his crowing and the noise of the rapid wingbeats with which he always ended his challenge. And the bird was too much occupied with the spring, or with proclaiming the glories of Asia, for Jimmy crawled up close to him and shot him, and brought him back to G.H.Q., as they were now calling their camp.

"Isn't he a great bird?" they said, as they clustered round Jimmy.

And Mickey said: "Begob, we owe him to Patsy Heffernan, for no one was allowed to shoot a pheasant only a landlord, until last year. Many's the time I watched one with the sun on him in the spring, and daren't touch him because of the laws they had."

"Sure, that was terrible waste," said Jimmy Mullins.

"It was surely," said Mickey.

And while they plucked the pheasant Pat Kelly came back with the pens and ink and the big sheets of paper, and Mickey started writing out proclamations in the words that Old Mickey had told him. And so with the help of Young Hegarty, who had a certain gift with the pen, they wrote out the twelve proclamations, that all read: "There is to be no machine-gun practice in these parts, before one o'clock. Signed Michael O'Rourke, major-general.

"On behalf of the Government."

And when they had finished and they were all looking at the proclamations, Jimmy Mullins said, "It's a pity we couldn't put the royal arms on the proclamation so as to give it a finish."

But they could not, for none of them there could draw. So whatever they added to give the proclamation a finish would have to be verbal. And in the end they wrote at the bottom of each of the twelve sheets, in a straight line all by itself and a very large capital for every word:

And So Say All Of Us.

And then the two men came in that had gone to find the gold-diggers; they had found seven or eight of them, and they would all come up tomorrow at about half past twelve to dig by the thorn-tree, just at the time that Patsy Heffernan would want them. The proclamations would be pinned to trees near Patsy's house while he was out on his bicycle. Everything was ready for the coup that should bring out the headstrong in Patsy, and lure him to the downfall that had overtaken others whose possessions had been beyond reason.

CHAPTER XV

Night or Blucher

A lark from the fields below came up the hill, and went singing beyond the trees and woke the sentry. He filled the kettle and replenished the fire, and put the tea in the tea-pot; and when the water was boiling he woke the rest. Soon G.H.Q. was astir. The morning was early; and the men, peering out at it through the trees, saw its soft glimmer falling unfamiliarly upon common things, as though they had surprised Aurora up before man, and picking her way daintily over the fields. To Mickey it was no common morning, but the opening of a day that he hoped should give him, what a year ago could have been only a frustrated dream, a machine-gun. Then that whole range of hills would be his: he would be greater than Patsy Heffernan, he hoped, and at least the equal of England. They had breakfast on pheasant and bacon, and Mickey told off the men that were to put the proclamations on trees near Patsy Heffernan's house as soon as he should be out of the way, and chose Jimmy Mullins to superintend the digging for the leprechaun's crock of gold, as he had no rifle. And he explained how they should come on Patsy Heffernan when he got to the place at which he practiced with his machine-gun. He took them through the wood to the side of the hill that looked out over Heffernan's country, to examine the walls and hedges that ran near the place to which he wished to bring them. To the left of that line shone the thorn-tree, which had suddenly flashed into green on its southern side over-night. And they took this for a good omen. Gray and ancient as legend it seemed on the side to the north; on the south side bright as hope. How beautiful gold would look amongst that brilliant green, thought the young men that dug there later. And the thought seemed to make it more likely that the gold was really there. The red flower was out on the larch, but no other tree showed new green except that thorn. They returned to their fire in the wood. At eleven o'clock a watcher that Mickey had put out on the hill came in to say that Patsy had started out on his bicycle shortly after half past ten, and told the direction in which he had gone. Mickey sent off the men with the proclamations at once. He waited an hour, anxious, but full of hopes of success. That proclamation, he thought, was bound to sting Patsy. A proclamation in his own country, and interference by the government; both these things should make him do at once what the proclamation forbade. He did not plan to shadow him when he went to get the machine-gun, knowing that Patsy was not simple enough to be shadowed, and trusting his grandfather's dictum that the machine-gun would be well hidden. He meant to attack Patsy just as he got to his machine-gun range, as his grandfather had advised him, and of course before he got his machine-gun set up and loaded.

At twelve o'clock Mickey moved off. Patsy got back a bit sooner than he had expected him. They saw him arrive, from the hill, and go into his house. Then an electric buzzer sounded from the roof of Patsy's house, like what they have on factories, and there was almost immediate activity amongst the few who appeared on bicycles. Mickey was watching from a long way off. The bicycles disappeared, and for a long while he saw nothing. He moved nearer to the place that he knew to be Patsy's machine-gun range, for it was essential for him to get there before Patsy got his machine-gun ready for use. More time passed: it was just on one o'clock. And then Mickey saw a small party approaching the place, carrying a long bundle covered with tarpaulin. He counted them and they were only five; five to his eight. Add to that odds the surprise, and the chances seemed to promise to Mickey his machine-gun. He moved still nearer. The party of five were going along a road, and this enabled Mickey to get over open ground by rushes, whenever he saw that Patsy's men were about to be hidden by hedges, as they frequently were. A long gap in the hedge on the road would detain Mickey's force under a wall for a while; then he was on again. The machine-gun party certainly moved without scouts. When they reached their destination Mickey's men were little more than a hundred yards away. The machine-gun range was in a sandy hollow with gorse bushes at the edge, which enabled Mickey to get quite close to it. He dashed over the last hundred and fifty yards, to get there before the machine-gun should be loaded; and, lying behind the gorse bushes, he saw the bundle that they carried, now on the ground, pointing towards a target, but with the tarpaulin still over it. They were only forty yards away. The men were unarmed except for the bundle: they began to unwrap it and Mickey dashed forward with his men. Patsy Heffernan's men looked old, the bundle looked odd, and Patsy was not there; and then Mickey, about to shout "Hands up," dashed past them with one loud order to his men. "Come on," he said. "It's a trap." They were down in the hollow and up the other side. "Away from the hills," shouted Mickey.

He had seen, as he dashed past, that the machine-gun was a bundle of sticks and those men were not politicians. Patsy had fooled him; but, with his head in the trap, he had not yet sprung the spring of it. The moment he saw the sticks and the gaping men, he knew that it was a trap, and instantly knew which way the trap would face. It would be so arranged that he would be caught running home to the hills: so that to go straight on immediately, without even losing the impetus that he had from his rush down the slope, would be his only chance. The hundred yards or so that he gained while Patsy Heffernan was waiting for his dupe to walk right to the end of the trap were all to the good. Then bullets began to snap over, and Mickey heard Patsy firing from the hill. It was the buzzer that had done it, it had brought men from a wider area than what Mickey had calculated, and must have brought the men running down from the thorn-tree, to get their rifles and join Patsy. And now the fire was heavy. Mickey came to a wall that gave him cover, but he only utilized this to rest his men. Over the top of the wall he saw Patsy's men come forward, the moment his own army got out of sight: he saw that there were at least fifteen of them, and guessed that from then on the whole of Patsy's force would be gathering between him and the hills. He fired one volley, which he knew would be innocuous, with his men panting as they were, and then dashed on again. Now the bullets grew fewer, as Patsy raced after him. He had been completely surprised by Patsy; that was the main movement; that is what the battle may be said to have been about; but as soon as it started Mickey had surprised Patsy, by going straight away from the trap that was prepared for him between him and the woods. The perfect example of Patsy's strategy is to be found where men lay a net, clear of the ground, all along the edge of a wood in which rabbits have their burrows: the rabbits go out to feed at sunrise, then some one frightens the rabbits and the net is dropped as they all run home. But what if the rabbits ran straight away from their burrows? That was the maneuver that Mickey was practicing now; but, with a force certainly increasing between him and the hills, and a few more probably joining the pursuing force, what was he to do next? At the next halt to breathe, behind a wall, questioning faces began to turn his way. "It's night or Blucher," he said. "And as Blucher's dead, it will have to be night."

"We've a long way to go before night," said Jim Brannehan.

"So has Patsy," said Mickey. "Come on, lads."

And they continued one of the rapidest retreats that has ever been made by infantry. And as Mickey ran he wondered who had been headstrong. Certainly not Patsy. He began to see that, had he been content and aspired to no machine-gun, he might have lived happily in the wood. Greater than Mickey have had such reflections, and they have been recorded in diverse forms sufficiently often for it to be unnecessary for me to say more of them here: I merely call my reader's attention to the glittering prizes that, all through history, have ruined so many men. Perhaps Mickey had greater temptations than come to most, for not until a few years before its final retreat had the Government permitted any one to have machine-guns in Ireland, and all the earlier part of Mickey's life had been shadowed by this inhibition.

When, therefore, a machine-gun seemed near, he had grasped at it with some of that recklessness that his old grandfather knew of, but had so far failed to locate that he had attributed it to Patsy. Away on his left Mickey saw a group of men on bicycles. Bicycles! He must keep away from the roads. He edged away to his right, but before he was out of sight of the road he heard the sharp cracking and intense hurry of a stream of bullets. This was the real machine-gun. Once out of sight of the road they heard these bullets no more, but the irony of it was felt by all of them. "He loves having his joke," said Jim Brannehan.

It began to show that Mickey had five good runners, including himself, and three bad. The three were lagging behind. It was essential to his plan of joining forces with night before he should be defeated that he maintained the pace of men that could run well. He began to look for means of escape for the three men that were lagging, and could not find any escape for them. He was increasing the distance between him and Patsy slightly, even with these slow ones, but they were dragging more and more and he would soon lose what he had gained. They came to the road again right across their retreat, and had to cross it, and he got them all to the other side without meeting with the machine-gun; when, just as they were going to leave the road behind them, they saw a tricycle cart coming along it, a cart that a London firm was sending all through Ireland in order to sell chewing-gum: a man in a white coat and an odd cap was driving it. As STOP ME was written upon the cart, they stopped it, and took the man's queer coat and cap and gave it to the slowest, young Hegarty, and put him up on the seat and sent him off down the road. "Back to G.H.Q. how you can," said Mickey. And soon young Hegarty safely passed the machine-gun.

"'Ere. What's all this?" said the ex-driver of the little cart.

But Mickey hadn't breath, during that retreat, to explain Irish politics to a man who probably couldn't have understood them in any case. So all he said was, "Come with us." And to Jim Brannehan, "Bring him along." That Patsy Heffernan still saw eight men retreating before him was a by-product of Mickey's order to bring the chewing-gum man along, a chance gain, such as often accompanies a good plan; the reason of it being to prevent him from telling Patsy Heffernan's men where young Hegarty had gone to. Later they released him, still protesting, still wholly unable to understand the reason for the war in the hills, and making childish claims for his property, as though the Government of Great Britain cared what became of it.

Still in sight of the pursuing force and therefore still under fire, and with two men dragging wearily, they passed a cottage and came to a green dog-kennel, with a collie chained up outside, or a large dog that looked more like a collie than any other animal. He had four walls to his house, with a doorway by which to go in. Few people came that way, and dogs in such places are often resentful of strangers. But this dog was delighted. Perhaps the old man, his master, gave him little attention, so that his friendly nature was wasted. Whatever it was he ran the poor distance his chain allowed him, full of welcome to the eight men and pouring out canine greetings. A well-bred dog might have guarded the cottage and little garden better, but this mongrel was vulgarly friendly. "Quick," said Mickey to the weariest of his two stragglers. "In there."

That was Paddy Mulligan. And he went behind the dog as it greeted the rest, and crawled into the kennel with his rifle. The cottage hid the kennel from Patsy's men. Mickey stopped a moment while the rest ran on, to see that all would be well. The dog was puzzled; he turned round and saw the last of Paddy Mulligan retreating into his own kennel. He went up and sniffed at him to see if it was really a man, and found that it was as he had thought. He sat down then and considered. For a moment his considerations were interrupted by another matter, that does not concern this story, which he set right by scratching his left ear with a hind leg. Then he considered again, with his head on one side. And the whole thing became perfectly clear to him, a man had entered his own kennel and set up house there, his kennel that not even another dog ever entered. Still he was not angry, but he was hurt. Was he to remain outside forever, under the stars when they were cold, houseless like foxes? Very deliberately he determined to assert himself, though still without trace of anger.

He walked into the kennel himself. And, finding there was not quite room, he put his head out through the door. The moment Mickey saw that, he ran on after the rest.

When Patsy Heffernan's army poured past the cottage, the watch-dog came out to offer them the same courteous welcome that he had recently given their enemies.

And now Mickey was gaining no longer, his tired man holding back the speed of the whole retreat. Patsy Heffernan's men were obviously searching as they came, so that good hiding places were bad hiding places, being likeliest to be searched. No ditches seemed to give sufficient cover, yet a hiding place must be found immediately, if Mickey was not to lose at least a man and a rifle. A stone came in sight standing upright in a plowed field, with thorn bushes dotted round it, and pieces of rag on the thorns. The sight of the thorns undisturbed in a plowed field was sufficient alone, without the hundred fluttering rags, to show Mickey the stone was holy. "Go you," he shouted to the tired man, "and leave a hand on that stone. And don't take it off while there's one of those lads in sight; not if they offer you the kingdoms of the world. Give me your rifle."

And the man did as he was told. This was the Holy Stone of Maheragh, marking one of the greatest victories of the Church over a pagan and regrettable custom; for it used to be ignorantly believed that there was some protective virtue in the stone, and people used to come to it from miles round for its help and protection, until good men came and taught otherwise, and put the stone under the protection of the apostle James; and it is now St. James that protects people there, and not a mere stone.

The moment that Mickey was rid of the slow man he had a certain power of maneuver that he had not before. He began to slant away a bit to his right, with a view to returning at some time to the hills; but, whatever he did, he was most of the time in full view of Patsy Heffernan, for the slope of the ground was behind him from the hills, so that Patsy was always on slightly higher ground.

"Of all the silly gimes I ever 'erd of," said the chewing-gum man, making his first comment upon the battle.

"What about chewing-gum?" said Mickey, incensed by the criticism.

"Chewing-gum? There's money in that," said the man.

"But what's the good of it?" asked Mickey.

"I tell yer, it brings in money."

"But is it any use in itself?" persisted Mickey.

"Well, what's the use of this shooting you're doing?"

"That's war," said Mickey. "Have you never heard of war?"

"Been to one myself," said the man.

"Then why do you gainsay ours?" asked Mickey, very angry.

"'Cause it's no good," said his captive.

"What good was yours?" asked Mickey.

"Saved the world from a tyrant," answered the Englishman.

"I don't believe you ever go to war over there except with people you hate," said Mickey.

"Why should we?" asked the chewing-gum man.

"You should go to war for the glory and splendor of it," said Mickey.

"That what you're doing?" asked the Englishman.

"And why not?" replied Mickey. "Sure I don't hate Patsy Heffernan. He's a lovely lad. You don't understand war."

"And you don't know what war is," said the other.

"Ah get along, I've had enough of you," said Mickey, and he let the chewing-gum man go.

CHAPTER XVI

The Indolence of Historians

*E*vening was wearing away, and, as the pursuit still continued, Mickey perceived that he must have touched Patsy on the raw, by trying to get his machine-gun. And that much he might have known, without the sharp reminders that still cracked over his head whenever Patsy's army lay down for a moment's rest; for the machine-gun, besides being the emblem of liberty, denied to such as Patsy Heffernan for so long, was the very essence of his power, and was also quite new: to try to take a new machine-gun from such a man was as though one should try to purloin the scepter of an emperor, who but a few days before had been only a king. There was a certain bitterness in this pursuit, and the continued firing, that made Mickey wonder if, even when he returned to the hills, he would be able to live at G.H.Q. unmolested. Of his return he began to feel fairly sure, since a large body of men was unlikely to overtake five, from whom the slow ones were weeded out; and the shooting of men in such a race as that must continue to be negligible. Mickey was hungry, and it irritated his temper, so he stopped at the next stone wall and gave Patsy several volleys, though it only wasted time.

Another twenty minutes went by, and still Mickey had not shaken his pursuers off, and he decided the time was come to increase his pace. His method was a simple one; to get rid of the slowest man. Though all were tired there were no stragglers now, so Mickey waited until he saw ahead a good hiding place; and soon it appeared before him, a fox-covert of thick gorse. Then he warned his men that the last man would have to hide in it, and raced for the gorse. The last man to arrive at the near side of the gorse was Pat Kelly. "Come on now," said Mickey to him, "and get in from the far side."

"I'm not a fox," said Pat Kelly, looking at a million thorns, made worse by insidious brambles.

"And Patsy isn't a hound," said Mickey. "It would take a pack of hounds to get you out of that. Get in."

And Pat Kelly crawled in with his rifle, groaning as he crawled, and sometimes yapping out oaths. One of Patsy Heffernan's men could have crawled in where Pat Kelly did, but to have searched for him there would have been impossible. The rest continued the retreat and, from now on, gained on the larger army. They came to no more roads, and heard nothing more of the machine-gun. Presently they saw a river, slanting across their retreat so that they could either avoid it by edging more to their right, or cross it, except that there were no bridges.

"Take a look at that river," said Mickey to Jim Brannehan. "If it's shallow, we'll leave it alone and not be wetting ourselves. But if it's deep we'll cross it. Push in a stick."

Jim Brannehan did as he was told. "It's about five feet here, Mickey," he shouted. "But, oh Lord, it must be over our heads in the middle."

"Then we'll cross it," said Mickey; "and see what Patsy will say to that."

"It looks terrible deep, General," said Christie Ryan.

"No matter," said Mickey. "In with you."

He took Christie's rifle and cartridges from him, and in Christie went.

"And it's terrible cold," Christie added from the stream.

In the middle his head was under for a moment, and he swam a stroke and was standing again with his shoulders clear of the water. Before he got out Mickey took Christie's rifle in both hands, holding it across him horizontally, and threw it to Christie. Christie caught it in the water and climbed out. Then Mickey threw him his cartridges, quickly, one by one; but, finding that this took time, for there were thirty of them left, he wrapped his own in his handkerchief, which he held high over his head while he floundered over the deep part in the middle. And what odd words we find ourselves using sometimes: a flounder would have crossed that river with the most delicate grace, provided that the fresh water did not kill him; whereas Mickey, with his rifle held up in one hand and his bundle of cartridges in the other, crossed it uncouthly and ludicrously, so that some verb closer home than "to flounder" is required here to describe human clumsiness. Jim Brannehan came next in the same way. But, when it came to Mick Geogehan's turn, Mickey saw him gazing down thoughtfully into the water.

"General," he said, "it looks very cold."

"It's not," shouted Mickey, "it's hot."

"And it's deep," said Mick Geogehan. "Sure, you saw that yourself. And I can't swim."

But Patsy's men were getting within shot again, and Mickey grudged the time that it would take to persuade Geogehan. So he shouted back: "Can you run?"

"I can, sure," said Mick.

"Then look after yourself," said Mickey and ran on.

Mick Geogehan also ran on at once, in a divergent direction, and easily eluded the pursuing army. And Mickey, too, saw no more of them. They were eight hundred yards away when Mickey came to the river, four hundred by the time his force had crossed it, and when they reached it themselves Patsy knew that by the time he had got all his men over they would have lost sight of their enemy; so that the river was the decisive feature of that battle. Patsy lined up his army on the bank and fired for as long as he could see any men in front of him, then led his army home to a late tea. He might claim to have won the battle, but to compete with the mobility of a force so small as Mickey's had now become was beyond him. Mickey maneuvered his force gradually round to his right, recrossing the river this time by a bridge, and working his way back to his hills. It was a weary army that plodded home; and so bedraggled were they and so few, that at any farmhouses they came to Mickey explained that they were scouts of Patsy Heffernan's force; for he and his two men felt like wolves outnumbered and lean among shepherds, and feared that they might be set upon for their rifles as the wolves would be for their skins. And so by starlight they toiled up the hill to the woods, and found all the rest of the force already there, sitting round a discreetly small fire; and Mickey, interrupting their welcomes after a while, made them heap on more brushwood, and soon the clothes of the three that had crossed the river were drying about the blaze, while the men themselves, wrapped in blankets, lay close to the embers and rested.

This was the second battle of the war between Patsy and Mickey, battles that might have been told of at greater length and with far greater splendor, a work for the pens that make history. It is only the indolence or the ignorance of all the world's historians that has thrown this task upon me.

CHAPTER XVII

The Arts of War

As the three men wrapped in their blankets were asleep before their clothes were dry, the others gave them a blanket each, so that in addition to each man's own three blankets he had two more thrown over him. The rest had had their food, and, leaving the men that preferred sleep to food or clothing, they were soon asleep themselves, including the sentry.

Mickey was the first to wake at dawn, and dressed himself, and went and took the sentry's rifle, and stood with folded arms looking down at him; an impressive picture if the sentry had started awake, and seen his General standing there; but the sentry refused to stir, and would not wake till Mickey kicked him, after which Mickey's pose was all gone, and he resembled the print of a famous picture no longer. This annoyed Mickey, and after talking for a while of death to the sentry, he confiscated his egg.

Mickey had woken from his good night's rest with his plans clear in his mind, or at least the ground-work of them. The ground-work was that his force was definitely inferior to Patsy's, and all his plans would have to be made accordingly. After breakfast he therefore explained to his men that there were a great many thousand trees in the wood, and only nine of themselves; consequently, if Patsy came to attack them, which was likely enough, their defense would be concealment; in fact, in such a wood as that, they would practically vanish.

"What about our transport?" asked Jimmy Mullins.

"It will be captured," said Mickey.

That Patsy Heffernan would overlook Mickey's attempt upon his machine-gun, considering all that a machine-gun meant, seemed to be beyond the limits of Christian forbearance. And so he gave his men those instructions. He reconciled himself to the certain loss of his transport: armies had lost that before and yet been victorious. Another order that he gave was that all available sources of water in or near the wood should be found and noted as soon as possible. This he superintended himself; and, though they found no more open water, they found several holes where the underground river was only six feet from the surface, at the foot of the hill on Heffernan's side. And Mickey had got to know these holes very thoroughly, knowing that one water-supply would never be sufficient for men that might at any moment be driven from it, and that the danger to a party going in search of water would be divided by the number of pools from which they could choose. They lowered bottles by string into the underground river, and at first could not fill them with water; till Mickey told them to lower them by two strings, one at each end.

These were only immediate plans; but what afterwards? Success might have stimulated Mickey's imagination; but, as it was, he had no plans for the future whatever. I know of no other case in which a general in the field has actually sought the strategical advice of his grandfather, although a very similar case suggests itself, when the Crown Prince in front of Verdun received strategical advice from old General von Haselaer, who had been a kind of military tutor to his father. Young Mickey now put a similar trust in the wisdom that is undoubtedly to be found among octogenarians. He put Jimmy Mullins in command of the army, impressed on him what his tactics should be if attacked, and arranged a call, borrowed from the curlew, by which he should be able to find the army on his return, should it be in hiding; and set off at once from the hills. During the battle of yesterday, spring unnoticed by Mickey's soldiers had been sweeping over the plain; even while they were retreating thorn-trees had flashed into green in the sunlight of that day; and now the plain was dotted with thorn-trees that a clear view of the sun to the south and shelter from easterly winds had enabled to greet the spring with their banners of green sooner than most of their brethren. A little paler than these, or as though from a secret treasure they had added some mixture of gold, a chestnut or two had also broke into leaf. And banks of trees far off, clad with abundant buds, shone sometimes with a glance of the sun through cloudrifts of the variable Irish sky, while the foreground was under shadow, and appeared like enchanted mountains of faery gold. In such a golden land, thought Mickey, one might lead armies to victory: it was sometimes difficult here. As he passed by the edge of the woods of Knocknavogue, the laurels were all in bloom, scenting the morning. And daffodils flashed there by lawns no longer tended, their golden flowers giving a gracious air to the grass and woods about them, and seeming to beckon to memories to linger a little longer amongst what was else forlorn and lost and untidy.

All the morning he walked, not tired after his battle, but a little stiff, and reached Cranogue between twelve and one. He went straight to his von Haselaer, and found Old Mickey as usual in his doorway, watching the street.

"Good morning, Grandfather," he said.

"Good mornin', Mickey."

"Grandfather, I lost that battle," said Young Mickey.

"Did you so?" said Old Mickey.

"And I'm thinking Patsy's no headstrong lad; for he kept his machine-gun."

"Bedad," said the old man, "there's no saying where headstrongness lurks, only that it does be in the world in plenty, and that, where it does, there you find men losing the riches of the world."

"I'm thinking it's I that lost the machine-gun, Grandfather," said Mickey.

"Maybe," said the old man looking at him. "That could be. Aye, that could be. Your grandmother (the light of Heaven to her) could be wonderful headstrong. Aye, that may have been passed on. And, if there's anything headstrong in a man's blood, there's times it will help him, and give him the riches of the world, and times it will throw them all away to another."

"Grandfather, he has the machine-gun yet. And he's feeling very wicked."

"Is he so?" said the old man.

And then, just as the Crown Prince may have told von Haselaer of the powerful defenses of Verdun, he told the old man how Patsy had fooled him over the machine-gun and then chased him for miles.

"Aye," said the old man, "Patsy's a clever lad. A clever lad indeed. Patsy's the clever lad."

And he lit his pipe and smoked for a while in silence. Then he took out his pipe and said again: "Patsy's the clever lad."

"What will I do, Grandfather?" said Young Mickey.

"I'll tell you what you shall do," the old man said. "You shall do what Napoleon did when anything went wrong with his battles. What did he do when he lost a battle, and a lot more lads would be coming up from all the nations of the earth to fight another with him?"

"I don't know, Grandfather."

"Sure, you should know. It's lads like him and Hannibal and Julius Caesar showed you how to do it. They did indeed. Well, Napoleon would lose an odd battle and there'd be a lot of lads coming up to chase him, and what did he do?"

"What did he do, Grandfather?"

"Sure, he made peace."

"Did he do that?"

"Sure, he did indeed."

"Patsy's terrible wicked, Grandfather."

"Sure, there's men that's terrible wicked, and yet they make peace. Sure, if they didn't, wars would go on for ever."

"They would that," said Young Mickey.

"They would sure," said Old Mickey.

"There'd be the terms of peace, Grandfather."

"There would, sure."

"And he'd make me leave the hills."

"Even so," said the old man, "isn't it better to leave the hills than to be massacred, and to leave the whole world."

"It is," said Young Mickey, but rather doubtfully.

"Then what ails you?" asked Old Mickey.

"If I left the hills, where would I go?" said Young Mickey. "With the wise women cursing in Cranogue the way the air must be full of curses, and them black heathen disturbing the bones of the dead, till they're wickeder nor the wise women. Sure, I'd sooner be in the hills."

"Them black heathen will be out of this in a few weeks," said the old man. "And then you can come back."

"And what will I do in the meantime?" asked Young Mickey.

"Sure, what would Napoleon have done?" said Old Mickey.

"I don't know," said Young Mickey.

"I'll tell you," said Old Mickey. "Look you, he has his army in a place he can't hold, because there's too many lads coming up to chase him out of it. And some of them have beaten him once, and he knows they can do it again. And he doesn't want to go out of it for two or three weeks. If he stays where he is, they'll have him out of it next day, if you understand me. And if he makes peace they'll take the place off him. What does he do?"

"Sure, what does he do, Grandfather?"

"He makes poor parleys."

"Poor parleys?"

"He does that."

"And what's poor parleys, Grandfather?"

"Ah, how can I be talking to you when you don't know the simplest things of the conduct of war? Sure, war's a great art. Poor parleys are what you do when you want peace, but you don't want it in a hurry. Then you make poor parleys, which is talk and discussions and drawing up documents, and a great many other things; only it isn't shooting. And at the end of it all you have peace."

"And you can waste two or three weeks over it?" asked Young Mickey.

"Bedad, one lad wastes them," said Old Mickey. "And the other gains 'em."

"Sure, I'll do that," said Young Mickey.

"Sure, it's the thing to do," said Old Mickey.

"Will them heathen be here long?" asked young Mickey.

"Sure, they will not," said his grandfather. "Go and look at them. They're digging down by the bog now, disturbing the bones of the dead. They're all getting lean. Sure no one will sell food to them; and it's only scraps they can get. And, sure, who would sell good meat to heathen to make them strong, the way they could the more easily dig up Catholic bones. Sure, no one in his senses."

"They would not," said Young Mickey.

"Then they'll be soon gone," said Old Mickey, "and the wise women will be finished cursing, and the dead at peace again. And you can make your peace with Patsy Heffernan and come back. But, for now, let you make poor parleys."

"I will, then," said Young Mickey. "I'll go to him and say I want peace."

"You will not," said Old Mickey. "But you'll say to him 'I'll fight to the last man, for I'm fighting for freedom, and I've hundreds more men in the hills waiting to rise, and I can get guns from America, and if you want peace what are your terms?' Sure no man can say he doesn't want peace on any terms. And you'll get his terms that way. You will sure."

"Aye, Grandfather," said Young Mickey, "I'll do that."

"Then you'll soon get talking and disagreeing. And that's poor parleys."

"And they can take two or three weeks," said Young Mickey thoughtfully.

"They can, sure," said Old Mickey. "He says his terms are for you to be leaving the hills. And you say 'What hills?' And, sure, it isn't enough for him to say 'Those hills.' He must get a map and he must make out the boundaries, and the two of you must agree on them. Sure, did you ever hear of a war that ended when the last empty cartridge was thrown out of a rifle? Poor parleys begin then, and they rage for weeks; sometimes for years."

"Aye, I'll do that," said Young Mickey again.

"It's terrible the poor parleys they do have," said the old man, warming to his theme. "Worse nor the war."

And from this thought Old Mickey turned to watch the smoke from his pipe, and gazed into it so long that Young Mickey saw that he was either tired with all the advice he had given, or that he had forgotten him; and, without disturbing him by calling him back to the world that lay beyond the smoke of his pipe, he went out of the house.

A young man's love for his mother is a powerful influence, and Mickey went next to his mother's house. But I will be honest with my reader, and record that after Mickey's long walk from the hills, and the healthy life he was living there, the influence that drove him to his mother's house was his great need of a dinner. This he obtained, and in return he cheered his mother's heart by telling her that he was going to make peace with Patsy. "When will you do it, Mickey?" she asked. But that involved an explanation of the poor parleys, which were so new to Mickey himself that the importance of them greatly weighed on his mind, perhaps even slightly oppressing his sense of humor; for he felt that poor parleys were a matter for men, and would tell his mother no more than that peace would come as soon as the time was ripe for it.

CHAPTER XVIII

Promotion for Jimmy

As Mickey started on his long walk back to the hills he went down by the bog to see the Liberissimans. And there they were all at work, with Umbolulu doing most of the digging, in the black frock-coat from which now he was never parted, unless he took it off when he slept. It was a symbol to him of more than we shall understand, unless we imagine all that is most sacred to us represented by a single piece of cloth. Mickey walked by them scowling, and noted with some satisfaction that it was as Old Mickey had said and they seemed to be getting a little bit thin. "What for you not like Liberissimans, Sah?" said Mr. Washington wistfully.

"Digging up Catholic bones," angrily muttered Mickey. There was no time for Mr. Washington or any of them to answer, for at that moment Mickey caught sight of a wooden idol set up on a mound of earth, put there in a place of honor as the principal find of the day, a find of inestimable value to science; but to Mickey the squat and obese figure of wood, with a leer that seemed right and left to threaten salvation, was the idol of these men's heathen religion that they had specially brought from Africa to practice their pagan rites and insult the dead. So he hurried on, rather than stay an instant under such a baneful influence. He cannot have thought the idol would have tempted him had he stayed: he must have supposed that it had some spell that could overcome the just, some power hostile to salvation.

115

He left the poor African scientists with a haste not only of anger, but fear drove him too from the spot where a sudden curse seemed to be earned and overdue. You, reader, with your interests more scientific than superstitious, might perhaps thus hurry away from a group of men ignorantly shoving up a lightning-conductor into the sky on a stormy day, a day with clouds, low and intensely black, just overhead, and more coming up from far off, already muttering. You might be mistaken about the thunder, as Mickey was over the idol, but still there is little sense in fooling with a lightning-conductor.

Mickey went slow, for he had had one very long walk already; and it was not till night that he got back to his hills. It was still evening as he approached them, night only overtaking him on the slope, so that not till there did he see the number of fires that were burning round G.H.Q. There is a moment at which such lights flare forth and assert themselves, and at that moment the day is gone.

There was an irregularity in the lines of the fires that Mickey noticed at once. It was as though men had lit them to warm themselves, and not merely to show what a great army they were. Such men would be more confident in their strength than his own little force could be. He came very softly towards those threatening lights. Presently he heard voices. He crept a little nearer then, and lay down. For a long time he listened, and in all that time he heard no voice that he knew. He could not hear any words, or recognize Heffernan's voice or any other, but he did not like to come closer on account of the sentry, whose shape he could see pacing up and down before him along the edge of the wood. The sentry, like the voices, seemed unfamiliar, for this sentry carried his rifle over his right shoulder, whereas Mickey's own sentries usually held the rifle in both hands, with the bayonet pointing forwards, as being the most suitable position for the instant repulse of an enemy. He stayed there a while longer, then he went down the hill again, and there he gave a whistle, the long deep note growing louder and louder and the short shriller note that follows it, which is the call of the curlew. He waited, and heard no answer. Then Mickey went off to his left, and went into another part of the woods.

Mickey did not strike the woods until he was far enough from his old camp not to be heard by any men that might be there, when he stepped on twigs or rustled through dry leaves. The wood was full of sounds, the footsteps of the creatures that grow bolder by night, when the fear of man sets with the sun. At first the little noises startled Mickey, and then he reflected that it was he that had come to those woods to be their principal danger, and that it ill became anything to be terrible there but himself; and so he strode on, looking for his army. When he had gone some way from the strange force that was about his old camp, he gave the curlew-cry once more. This time it was answered.

Mickey moved t'wards the answering signal for some while, but perhaps, walking in the dark of the wood, he did not get so far as he thought. He did not whistle again, for suspicions would at once be wakened by the sound of an undue number of curlews traveling about the wood. It was just the time of year when one or two might go over at any hour, wandering far for their nesting, driven by spring. Presently he stood still and listened; and, after what seemed to him a long time, he heard a twig crack far off, and then the sound of steps coming through the wood. Then he whistled very low the call of the curlew, and it was answered low. The steps stopped as the answer was given, then they came on again. And presently Mickey heard his name being called. He answered, and it was Jimmy Mullins looking for him.

And Jimmy's first words were, "G.H.Q.'s lost, and the transport's lost; but we're still holding the wood."

"What happened, Jimmy?" said Mickey.

"Sure, Patsy came tumbling up the hill with his army, like a waterfall going the wrong way; and we could see he was that wicked that there'd be no stopping him; so we lit out of that and did as you said, and hid behind trees. And, wicked as he was, he couldn't find one of us."

"Was there heavy firing?" asked Mickey.

"There was not," said Jimmy. "Patsy was so wicked, lepping up the hill, that no shooting would ever have stopped him. We just lit out of it."

And suddenly Mickey thought of his provisions and ammunition; suddenly he remembered that he had given Jimmy no instructions about them. If they were left behind, his army was over; for a pursued or defeated army cannot forage with the assurance of an army that is a menace up in the hills. "The provisions, Jimmy. Where are they?" he asked.

"Sure, we brought everything," said Jimmy, "and the ammunition too. Only we left the canvas buried: it was too heavy."

"Well done, Jimmy," said Mickey. And there and then he promoted him to be General.

Thereafter, to mark the difference, Young Mickey was known as the Major General, while General Mullins was usually called the Lieutenant General. Mickey had not frivolously promoted him, but recognized that he could trust him with the command, and that he had saved the entire force. If Jim Brannehan was a little jealous he never showed his jealousy, unless by one remark that he made later: "Oughtn't there to be a colonel in an army, General?"

And Young Mickey had recognized the justice of the complaint, if complaint it were, and made Jim Brannehan colonel.

As the two Generals stood in the wood, talking in low voices, Mickey heard the dispositions of his own force, which were just such as he had ordered. They were far apart, in positions known to Jimmy, each man behind a tree with his three blankets. It might be possible for Patsy Heffernan's men to find one of them and to capture him, but to take the entire force would be an undertaking so difficult that Mickey felt he might safely defy any army in Europe. His principal anxiety was water: there was no water in those hills except the thin stream that was now behind Patsy's lines; all the other water seemed to follow the course that Satan took, when he cheated the archangel Michael of the vengeance so justly due. The holes here and there above that stream, on the eastern side, before it came to the hills and was only six feet from the surface, must henceforth be Mickey's water supply. "Have you the bottles and the string?" Mickey asked.

"We have," said Jimmy.

"You'll be a great general," said Mickey. "You think of everything."

What trivial conversation that appears! Yet the fortune of armies depends upon just such things.

"I'll inspect the outposts," said Mickey.

And Jimmy took him through the wood and showed him the position of each of the seven men. It was a perfectly good outpost-line. What was lacking was any army behind it. But I don't see why Mickey, merely on that account, should not have referred to his men as outposts. By the time the two Generals found them they were all asleep, and Mickey did not disturb them, knowing that they had had a hard day in the wood. He also had had a hard day, and he and Jimmy were soon as fast asleep as the rest.

A clear note called through the wood in the silence of night, followed by silence. It was the first blackbird. Then reveille woke the army. Not reveille from bugles or from any human instrument, nor did the music follow the rules of any human melody; for certain things are beyond us. The whole chorus of all the blackbirds in the woods was singing. Something short of our understanding, or beyond it, was greeting the dawn with a symphony such as man is uninspired to write. Nothing in the approach of dawn, nothing in the colors that crept into the sky when the last of the stars was gone, nor anything in the woods and fields, as they gradually received light, conflicted or disharmonized in any way with one note of the blackbirds' melody. And if any of us could make a work of art of which that could be said, we might then be nearing that point on the way to unity with creation, at which we might hope some day to catch up with the blackbird and thrush. What a meeting it would be. "I never knew you," we should say in astonishment.

"Didn't expect to see you coming our way," the blackbird or thrush would answer.

And then we would talk and talk, getting on well together as artists always do; if we were such an artist as that.

The first thing that Mickey did was to leave the wood and go down the eastern slope, before Patsy's army was likely to be about, and carefully to fix in his memory the line of the underground river, where the holes at which water could be obtained by letting down a bottle could be discovered here and there, wherever there were rocks. At one of these he filled a bottle, and returned unobserved to the wood. The bottle of water was for his army's tea, but first they needed a fire at which to boil it. The outpost line was mostly over the top of the hill, in the woods on the eastern side. Mickey gathered them all together on that side, and then sent four of them with bundles of sticks and bracken over on to the other side, the side of his old G.H.Q., that was now Patsy's headquarters, with orders to go to the edge of the wood there, and build a big fire, and light it and return as quickly as possible. This they did, and as soon as the four came back Mickey lit a small fire, over which they boiled the water and fried bacon. They had a leisurely breakfast; and the moment it was over Mickey marched his army a mile away, and ordered General Mullins and Colonel Brannehan to form an outpost-line. Thus Patsy by the time he found their fire, would discover no more troops than he found at the larger one. Nor did Patsy even look for it, merely remarking when one of his officers reported to him on the first fire: "Spry lad, Mickey."

Thus things were between the two armies after breakfast, and as the historian of this war I am at a loss to find a military parallel. What I look for is the commander of a greatly superior force enraged by an attempt upon the very source of his power; but the few instances that come to my memory, such as the Siege of Gibraltar, come only to be rejected; for, though Gibraltar is a fortress of first-rate importance, it was never so essential to the defense of England's possessions as that machine-gun was to the hold that Patsy had on the countryside. He determined to drive Mickey out of the woods; but for this he had first to find his force, and though he sent out scouts for this purpose, as soon as one of Mickey's men was found he changed his position, and Patsy was still no nearer to fighting a decisive engagement.

The time came, in the opinion of Mickey, when Patsy should advance with his whole force in line through the wood, spread out to a good many paces, for they were large woods, and beat for Mickey's army as for woodcock. He saw nothing else that Patsy could do; nor was there. And he was about right in his estimate of the time that Patsy would begin his drive, after his scouts had been unable to do anything useful. So Patsy with a hundred men in line came through the wood moving from the south along the top of the hill, while Mickey considered whether cover was thick enough for him to conceal his men so well that Patsy's force would pass over them. He decided that it was not. Should he then retreat? That would mean that eventually, though the woods covered the tops of the whole range of hills, he would be driven out of the woods. So he divided his force into two parts, and putting the eastern half under the command of General Mullins and the western part under the command of Colonel Brannehan he sent them out of the wood on opposite sides with orders to go round unseen and get into the wood again on the southern side, while he stayed in the wood himself to see what Patsy was doing. As Patsy began to do just what he expected, as he easily heard by the noise that a hundred men made in the wood, Mickey left his two subordinates to continue the movement on which he had started them off; and so by stone walls and hedges each of these two forces arrived unobserved at the southern end of the wood, behind Patsy's army, and advanced so far into it, as Patsy's force moved away, that they were soon at their old camp again. There Mickey joined them, slipping through Patsy's army by the help of a good thick evergreen. There was of course no machine-gun in the camp, but there were many of the useful trifles that make life out-of-doors more comfortable, such as saucepans, knives, glasses, blankets, tinned meat and pots of jam, which Mickey's men fell upon joyfully. But Mickey made them put them all down again, as any tampering with Patsy's camp would have given away his maneuver. He let them replenish the fire, and sit round it to warm themselves, but that was all. Patsy had taken every man, so as to make his line of beaters as thick as possible; so no one disturbed them there. Every hour of the daylight would be needed by Patsy, to drive those woods to the end; so Mickey had no anxieties for that day, and knew that Patsy would not be able to beat the woods for him on the way back, as it would be night by the time that he turned.

Mickey sat and watched his men sitting there in a wide circle, gathering that valuable if unconsidered thing that is one of the two for which civilization was principally originated, which are warmth and dryness; but he took no share in their comfort, for he was busy thinking, as he so often was in these days, what he should do next. And suddenly he smiled, and thought of a whimsical strategy.

CHAPTER XIX

Colonel Brannehan Arrives at the Fortifications

Before nightfall Mickey returned with his men to the exact spots that his force had occupied over night. Much of their provisions they carried, and the rest had been buried near where they now were, and was now uncovered. After supper they heard Patsy's army marching back, far off, through the wood, and then they wrapped themselves in their blankets and slept. And soon, as it seemed to them, in the night that wonderful bird was heard, the first blackbird waking the chorus that honors the dawn. And the chorus woke Mickey's army, that had heard that first blackbird too, but only as a call ringing over the fells of dreamland. Then Mickey gave his orders: the same men that lit the fire on the morning before should go and light it in the same place, on the very ashes of the old one, then they should return and light one where they now were and have breakfast, just as they had done on the day before.

"Won't Patsy be expecting us to do it again, and be waiting for us?" said one of the four men that were to go.

"Sure, it's the last thing in the wide world that he'll be expecting," said Mickey. "Didn't he beat the whole wood for us, and doesn't he think that he's driven us out of the hills? And when we're just where we were yesterday and doing the same thing, sure he'll think we're ghosts. Or maybe he'll think he's only a ghost himself and not able to push us out of his way. Begob, he may think he never advanced at all, only dreamt it."

And certainly Mickey had produced a situation that would be depressing to any commander: Patsy had advanced in line over the enemy's position, had taken it and pushed on for some miles, and returned to his camp; and there was the enemy next morning in exactly the same position.

Patsy was at breakfast, congratulating himself on his victory, believing that he had driven Mickey out of the wood, and contemplating a return to his business with the Dawn Insurance Company, and to the comfort of his house; when he suddenly saw the smoke going up from the fire, and later from the other one further off.

And right into the middle of his perplexities walked a flag of truce, coming from Mickey's army.

Mickey had felt sure enough, the day before, that from all they told him of Patsy, and the way he came up the hill, that day would not be the day to start poor parleys. Nor could he have hoped to have started them satisfactorily half an hour before he did, while Patsy was still flushed with the victory that he thought he had just obtained; but now, with that victory shown to be illusory, and an advance of his whole army unable to attain anything, now seemed a better opportunity than might occur again of adopting his grandfather's concept of the policy of Napoleon. So a flag of truce marched through the wood, and appeared before Patsy Heffernan.

The bearer of the flag of truce was Colonel Brannehan; and, having been blindfolded, which should always be done with flags of truce, to prevent them from seeing the defenses, he was now unblindfolded again, and stood by the fire by which Patsy and most of his army were having their breakfast. And thus Brannehan explained his mission.

"I'm Colonel Brannehan, and I'm sent by General Mickey Connor, to arrange what terms would be acceptable to both of yez, if you should care to have peace, in order to get on with your insurance business."

And Patsy replied: "I don't want any peace. And I'll fight to the last man."

To which Colonel Brannehan said: "Nor Mickey doesn't want any peace neither, and he'll fight to the last man and then get more. Only he'd like to know what terms of peace would suit you, if ever he did make peace; the way there won't be war in these hills for ever."

"I understand you, Colonel," said Patsy. "I'm not making peace nor Mickey isn't making peace; only I'll tell you my terms in case it ever came to it."

"Sure, that's all I want," said Brannehan. "This isn't peace; it's only poor parleys."

"Then," said Patsy, "let you tell him my terms are these: firstly for Mickey to be leaving these hills, secondly for him to surrender all his arms and ammunition, but for me to return him his transport; and thirdly for him to pay an indemnity of a hundred thousand pounds."

"Oh, General," said Brannehan, "how is Mickey to lay his hands on a hundred thousand pounds. Sure, you wouldn't drive him to go and crack open a bank, a thing Irishmen never did."

"Them's my terms," said Patsy.

So Brannehan saluted and was marched off through the outpost line, and blindfolded again when he came to the fortifications. It is not so much to the point to inquire what fortifications, as to understand, if I may venture to correct my reader, that this war was being run upon proper lines, and wherever there ought to be fortifications, or any other military appurtenance, they were not merely alluded to in conversation and in dispatches, but were treated in all other ways as though they were there. This rule was observed by both sides, so that my reader may feel assured that in reading this history of the war that there was in the hills he will miss none of the splendors to which he has been accustomed, and rightly expects, when reading military histories.

"Oh, General," said Brannehan to Mickey, "it's bad terms I'm bringing you, and sorry's the day that I bring them."

"What are they?" said Mickey.

"He said he'd fight to the last man. And, I told him you'd do more; and then he said for you to be leaving the hills, and to surrender all our fine rifles and all the cartridges, and he to give you back the ass."

"Good old Ned," said Mickey.

"But wait, General; the worst's to come," said Brannehan. "You're to give him an indemnity of a hundred thousand pounds. That's driving us to crack open a bank, and the sin will be on our souls, not on Patsy's."

"Them's good enough terms," said Mickey. "You did fine, Jim."

"But where will we find the hundred thousand pounds?" asked Jim Brannehan. "Sure we might have to go all the way to Dublin to find a bank that had that much money in it."

"Ah, not at all," said Mickey. "Sure, these are only poor parleys. It'll be time to be looking for banks when we get down to the actual peace-terms. Do you think I'm an English statesman?"

"You are not."

"Then I'll not be fooled by Patsy."

"Good for you," said Brannehan. "But what will we do?"

"Let you go back to his outpost-line," said Mickey, "and tell one of them to go and tell Patsy that I'll send my answer tomorrow, and that he's not to disturb us till then, because I'm writing out my dispatch to him. And let you say that I agree to his terms in principle. That'll help to keep him quiet."

So Colonel Brannehan went back through the wood and found one of Patsy's men, and told him to run and tell Patsy that he'd have his answer tomorrow, and that he was not to disturb Mickey till then, because Mickey was busy writing out his dispatch, and he agreed to the terms in principle.

That gave Mickey one of the quiet days that he meant to have in the wood, till the heathen were gone from Cranogue and the wise women done cursing.

He lit a large fire in the wood, a long way away from his outpost-line, and watched to see if Patsy would come for it; and, when Patsy left it alone, he had a good fire lit for his men, and they all sat round it and fried bacon for dinner.

"What'll we do next, Major General?" said Jimmy Mullins, looking up from his bacon.

"Begob," said Mickey, "poor parleys have to be written out, by both sides; and all that takes time. You wouldn't have us doing our poor parleys by word of mouth. Sure, the English would laugh at us, and so would any other country. We'll have our poor parleys done properly, the way Napoleon would have done them. And it'll take weeks. And it's the grand time that we'll be having in the wood."

"Why are they called poor parleys?" asked Jimmy. "Why not parleys, just plain parleys?"

Mickey having only heard of such things yesterday for the first time, from his grandfather, was all the harder on Jimmy for his ignorance.

"If you don't know the most rudimentary military terms, sure you had no right to be a general," he said.

"I only asked," said Jimmy.

And the difficult question was still open.

"I'm not here to give you military information," said Mickey. "Only to give orders."

"Maybe the man that first called them that knew best," said Pat Kelly, trying to restore harmony.

"Begob," said Mickey, "Napoleon and Julius Caesar and Hannibal and the rest of them knew what they were talking about."

And everybody allowed that that was so.

As evening began to bless the plain for miles, and gradually to give a glory to the woods, and the birds began to answer, thoughts far from war arose in the mind of Mickey, intensified by the uncertainty of the days ahead of him. He thought of the quiet fields round the house where Alannah lived, and of the days that passed over the farm, so serene and orderly, that they seemed to him like dainty maidens walking out of the sunrise, very different from the days that marched through the wood in which there were now two armies: there the days seemed to come to ripen the apple-blossom, here to give light to a rifleman.

All was quiet in the wood.

"Boys," said Mickey, "I'm going out to scout."

"Where are you going, Major General?" asked Jimmy.

"Ah, just round about," said Mickey.

"May I come with you?" asked Jimmy.

"Ah, sure, you may," said Mickey.

Each guessed at once where the other was going, and each guessed right. Mickey was going to O'Dwyer's farm, where the orchard was, and where the haystack had been: Jimmy was going to Patsy Heffernan's house to see the maid with the blue eyes.

"Colonel," said Mickey to Brannehan, "get all the water you can from the Devil's river, while things are quiet."

Then he and Jimmy set out.

Neither had very far to go when they came to the plain, on which men's shadows were already longer than men. They parted and General Mullins came first to his journey's end, to General Heffernan's house. There is often a bitterness in war that makes it impossible for a general in one army to visit the house of the general commanding the other, but let my reader bring no such feelings of bitterness, or thoughts of impossibility, to the perusal of this history. Let him rather be gratified that, amongst all the wars that work such ruin and havoc, there should be one war such as I tell of. Soon Jimmy and the maid, whose name was Aileen Flynn, were saying to each other very much what the birds were saying in the hedges all about them; and a little later Mickey met Alannah, outside the house in a field beyond the orchard. The bloom of the elm was out, though not a leaf upon one of them. The red trees glowing in the late light he remembered all his life, though he had never noticed that the bloom of the elm was red before: one girl had opened his eyes to the beauty of all those trees, though she never mentioned them to him.

"Mickey," she said as he came towards her, "are you still at war with Patsy?"

"I am," said Mickey. "But I'm going to make a treaty with him one of these days."

"Do, Mickey," she said.

"He's not an easy lad to make a treaty with," replied Mickey. "The English were the boys for that, but they're gone."

"Aye, they're gone now," said Alannah. "Did you have another battle with Patsy the other day?"

"I did that," said Mickey.

"Aye," said Alannah, "I thought I heard it."

Mickey sighed slightly.

"Ah," said Alannah, "don't be minding who won the battle."

"I'm not," said Mickey, "but . . ."

"Ah, if you won every battle," she said, "there'd be no fun in war."

And they walked together over the beautiful earth, whose light, flung out into space, fell on the new moon; so that, above the silver bow reclining over the sunset, the rest of the circle gleamed like a disk of copper. Near to it hung a star in the luminous evening, and the shapes of trees darkened. Alannah and Mickey said little; the evening seemed to be saying everything. Sometimes with shadows it seemed to hint of terror, sometimes with lucid radiance in the vast of the western sky it seemed to tell of beauty so far beyond human thought that there was no need for it to be told in words, no man being able to comprehend them even should words be uttered. And what words could Mickey say in this splendor, whose hush seemed a language? Fewer and fewer were his lame sentences; then he let the evening speak. And he and Alannah walked in perfect silence. A late wanderer walking a lonely road saw them and left them to themselves; but a faint light from them seemed to shine on his loneliness, a light that was lovely and radiant, though far from him like a star.

CHAPTER XX

An Historic Document

*A*ll the stars were out when Mickey returned to the outpost-line, and when the army was all asleep Jimmy Mullins came through the wood. Again there came the call from beyond human boundaries, the song that does not make sense to us, the words that seem of no language, the blackbird's answer to dawn, the reveille of those whose ears are nearer than ours to simplicities that to us, when known at all, are known only as complications. Mickey woke and sent for his pen; and then began the penning of those preliminaries that were to bring peace to the hills. "I agree for to retire from these hills," Mickey wrote on a large sheet of paper, "their boundaries to be delimited by one officer to be appointed by General Patsy Heffernan, one officer to be appointed by General Mickey Connor, and one eminent jurisprudence, not residing within the British Empire, to be chosen by these two.

"ITEM 2. I agree for to surrender my arms and ammunition to a neutral country, to be held by them for General Patsy Heffernan until the time is ripe. And General Patsy Heffernan agrees for to hand over the transport of General Mickey Connor's army to an officer to be nominated by me.

"ITEM 3. I agree for to pay an indemnity of a hundred thousand pounds."

This he read out to his men rather with the air of a victor than as a man suing for terms. He had no illusion whatever as to the relative strength of the two armies; his victorious air came only from his sense of achievement at having drawn up so historic-sounding a document.

"But, General, where will you lay your hand on the hundred thousand pounds," cried Brannehan as Mickey finished his reading.

"Sure, England will pay it," said Mickey.

"England is it?" said Brannehan.

"Sure, there wouldn't be any war in the hills," said Mickey, "if England hadn't taken the army away. Then isn't it England's fault? And oughtn't she to pay?"

"She ought that," they all agreed.

"And, sure, doesn't England always pay?" said Mickey. "And isn't it right they should, having all the money?"

"But will they pay?" asked Brannehan.

"Ah, you'll see they will," said Mickey. "Sure, there's only two things England can do, govern and fight; and when she stops doing them and tries to talk, sure, she's as helpless as a child."

"She is that," said Brannehan.

"Begob, look at the Treaty," said Mickey.

"We'll have a great day when the transport comes back," said Jimmy Mullins. "We'll get a great bundle of hay for him."

"We will that," said Mickey, "and carrots. And I'll nominate you for to fetch him."

"Good for you, Major General," said Jimmy.

"What's a jurisprudence, Mickey?" said one of them.

"Sure, he's a lad," said Mickey, "that will come over and say 'What are these hills, and what county are they in, and where do they begin being hills and where do they stop, and who appointed them to be hills at all, and where's the charter appointing them?' And he'll want to see a map as big as a blanket, and when we have that we'll get it translated into Irish and then into French. And by the time we done that, sure, the wise women will be done cursing and we can go back to Cranogue."

"But, General, our lovely rifles," came like a wail from Pat Kelly.

"Ah," said Mickey, "what neutral country's going to bother about us? And doesn't it say 'when the time is ripe'?"

"Then we will keep them," said Pat Kelly, with hope lighting up his mind like a sudden dawn.

"As long as there's fighting in Ireland," said Mickey.

"How long will that be, General?" asked Pat Kelly, wanting to be quite sure.

"Ah, who's to stop us now?" replied Mickey. And Pat was happy again.

Then Mickey sent Brannehan off with his flag of truce to take the poor parley to Patsy; and, as soon as he was well on his way, Mickey lit a good fire and they got all ready for breakfast.

When General Patsy Heffernan received Colonel Brannehan and read the poor parley he realized that the first shot had been fired in negotiations that would demand his utmost thought, if they were to be worthy of their place in history. So he sent Jim Brannehan back, saying that the poor parley would receive his consideration. When the colonel returned, his piece of bacon was already fried for him.

Those were great days in the wood for Mickey and Mickey's army. The ways of men; what they think and how their thoughts will make them act; though they should be visible daily all round us, are so often hid from our sight. To Old Mickey, his grandfather, Young Mickey saw that these things were clear, and the poor parleys were bringing about exactly what he had promised. Perhaps those that follow Napoleon may fall into pitfalls over which Napoleon strode, or they may go further, to fall where Napoleon fell; but no such forebodings as these troubled Young Mickey.

That evening a Colonel Fogarty came through the wood, with a document addressed to General Mickey Connor. Colonel Fogarty was stopped by a sentry and not allowed any further, but he was offered a cup of tea in the outpost-line, and the document was carried to Mickey. When Mickey saw that Patsy's answer dealt with little more than one of his items, he for the first time saw the full promise of his grandfather's policy, a policy that seemed to offer him the tenure of his share of those woods for as long as he should want it, the promise of a holiday such as few countries are able to offer youth.

Patsy's answer read: "In regard to your item 3, the indemnity will be paid in gold, which not until that has been done your transport shall be delivered to you. Your further items are under the consideration of my Army Council, and you will be notified shortly. Patsy Heffernan, Major General."

To which Mickey replied: "Your communiqué of today is duly noted. I have appointed General Jimmy Mullins as the officer to receive the transport. Your further reply to mine of yesterday's date is awaited. Have you any objection to me shooting rabbits round here? Mickey Connor, Major General."

But this missive did not at once go back through the wood, for it had to be thought out, and properly written on paper; and above all it had to do the work of a poor parley, which is to gain time for those that need it. So Colonel Fogarty returned to his army, and on the following afternoon Mickey's answer went to Patsy by the hand of Colonel Brannehan.

The scene in the wood was idyllic. There two armies rested before each other, at peace; a model for the armies of the world; the uneasy world in which all neighboring armies watch each other, even in times of peace, with more suspicious distrust than did these two of Young Mickey and Patsy Heffernan, though they were then at war. Patsy had no reason for fighting Mickey, when he seemed about to gain so much from the treaty then being discussed, while Mickey only wanted to be left alone in the wood. And in the wood the buds were swelling and shining, and even opening at the tips and giving hints of the many gay shades of green with which they would soon build paradise. Already the woods at evening shone with a strange glow, as the buds drew in the rarest rays from the sunset to illumine their ruddy tints. Soon a scene more beautiful than anything ever known since a year ago would awake dull memories of last year in men, and to many a bird and badger and rabbit it would seem that suddenly earth had fulfilled their dreams.

CHAPTER XXI

Umbolulu Progresses Yet Further

While Mickey and his young army were living happily in the wood, a great joy was flooding the heart of Mrs. Patrick. The heathen Umbolulu, heathen no longer, was making progress that she was assured by all to whom she had written was unequaled in all their knowledge of missionary work. For instance, though knowing no more than a dozen words of English for his own use, he could repeat the whole of the catechism; and, if this wonder cannot be credited, he had certainly discarded his bones, never touched his drum any more, and attended church regularly. Also, to a certain extent, he sang hymns. Naturally this required coaching, and all the hymns in the service were chosen solely for Umbolulu; and it is right that they should have been, for no appropriateness to times or seasons could ever have been so edifying to a congregation as the spectacle of this heathen coming up from the dark of Africa into the light that glows from salvation. And in so short a time.

"It's almost a record, isn't it?" said the rector of a neighboring parish, who had come over to see. For the Church may have her records as well as the race-track.

Mr. Washington, Mr. Japhet and the rest of the party attended church too, and were kindly spoken to by Mrs. Patrick, who showed interest in their scientific discoveries; and there were

134

PAUL DRY BOOKS, INC.

1616 WALNUT STREET, SUITE 808

PHILADELPHIA, PA 19103

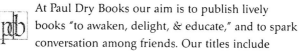

At Paul Dry Books our aim is to publish lively books "to awaken, delight, & educate," and to spark conversation among friends. Our titles include works of fiction and nonfiction—biography, memoirs, history, and essays. We also publish the Nautilus Series for Young Adults, great writing for avid readers of all ages.

To receive our catalog, return this card or e-mail us at pdb@pauldrybooks.com. You can see excerpts, reviews, news about our authors, and articles about us and our books at www.pauldrybooks.com. If you like our books, tell your friends about them.

Name

Address

City, State, Zip Code

Email (the best way for us to communicate with each other)

Book title

BOOKS TO AWAKEN, DELIGHT, & EDUCATE

accorded to them all the little courtesies that were their due as elders of the Church of Liberissima. Yet not in her heart could Mrs. Patrick feel for them as she felt for Umbolulu. Every truth of religion, every tenet, was new to him, and he welcomed each one with delight. Who, walking along the beach with the mayor of a maritime town, could feel the same joy at showing him a shell or a piece of sea-weed as at showing them to a child? Everything that Mrs. Patrick could teach Umbolulu, from dogma to table-manners, was equally new to him, and was received with the same smile of wistful delight. Sometimes at the end of one of her lessons in the drawing-room at the rectory Mrs. Patrick would ask Umbolulu about his earlier faith, but of this Umbolulu would not speak, turning back to these memories no more than Lot leaving Sodom; and all that Mrs. Patrick ever learned from him of this former religion was that it was "plenty bad." It is strange that in the same heart should have been both zeal and curiosity, yet so it was; and the two passions sought such contrary things, one to lead Umbolulu upwards towards the light, and the other to pry into darkness.

On various occasions, led by that less worthy passion, Mrs. Patrick inquired of other members of the party for what she could not obtain from Umbolulu; but they knew nothing at all of the faith of the forests of Africa. They would immediately tell her of all manner of sound practices; but of the faith of their fathers, nothing. Is my reader surprised at their ignorance? Let him or her ask a bishop what he did in his evenings at the Varsity, and he or she will receive the perfectly true answer, "I used to study." But let my reader persist, as Mrs. Patrick tried to persist, and say, "But did your lordship never dine out with your friends, other under-graduates? And what then?"

And a likely answer would be, "I do not recollect."

Not that there is any harm in any dinner of undergraduates; quite the contrary; but there is necessarily a limit to memory, or our brains would be stocked with more than they could hold. Mrs. Patrick never knew.

This chapter however is not written to tell of Mrs. Patrick's curiosity, and if it were there would be nothing to tell, for it accomplished nothing: its purpose is to record her zeal, and the fruits of it which were abundant. When I say that Umbolulu could repeat the whole catechism, I naturally mean when he had the cues: he knew all the answers with but little prompting. And though he did not as yet understand the words, more meanings were explained to him every day, and he received them as the flowers receive dew. Thus in Cranogue one was being rapidly led from tenets, whatever they were, of which nobody in Cranogue could possibly have approved, to a higher religious plane, to higher peaks of morality; and the whole main street of Cranogue looked on with a disapproval that almost verged on disgust. These things occur because parties are nearer to us than principles, and there are times that come to all of us when we find ourselves applauding the queerest things because the right side is doing them, things that would shrink and shrivel before our scorn if the wrong side should try its hand at them. The grab of the Protestant church for the soul of Umbolulu was not approved from the first: it was felt that it was not the right church to handle it. So might the cook feel if the gardener came in to cook a sausage: he would probably drop it into the fire. But when the soul of Umbolulu, far from going downwards, made this incredible progress, when the stolen rough African stone was cut by the thieves and showed the lights that flash from a diamond's facets, then had the good Catholics of Cranogue not felt jealousy, they would without death, without waiting two hundred and fifty years (as one of my own relations had to wait), without the usual formulae of canonization, have been saints already. They stood in their doors and watched him going to church; they watched him coming out; they recognized unerringly in his face a religious exaltation, a certain spiritual glow, as a thirsty man sees the warmth of alcohol shine from the face of one coming brightly out of a public-house, which his own principles or his lack of funds forbid himself to enter.

And Mrs. Patrick coming down the street upon one of these occasions while Umbolulu was still in sight passed Father Finnegan, the parish priest, standing outside his chapel, and made the great mistake that Lucifer made before he fell from Heaven; she let pride touch her spirit, and she boasted.

"He's coming on well, isn't he?" she said to the priest, with a glance towards Umbolulu.

"Bedad, he is," said he. "And do you know the little glass house I have, over beyond, at the end of my bit of a garden?"

"Yes, I do," she said.

"Bedad," he said, "I brought in a plant of strawberries to force them on."

"Did you?" said Mrs. Patrick.

"I did indeed," he said. "And I thought I'd be eating strawberries maybe in March, for all the heat that I gave them, or at any rate by the middle of April, before any one else had heard of a strawberry."

"Really?" said Mrs. Patrick.

"I did that," said Father Finnegan.

"And how did they get on?" asked Mrs. Patrick listlessly.

"Sure, they died," said Father Finnegan.

CHAPTER XXII

The Calm Before Storm

A white flag came through the wood, carried by Colonel Fogarty, with another letter for Mickey. Again he was stopped by the outposts and the letter carried on. "Will you have a sup of whiskey, Colonel?" said one of them.

"I will that," answered the colonel; "for it's the kind of day when it would do you good."

So the whiskey was brought and they all sat there talking, while Mickey read the letter.

"War's a fine thing," said Colonel Fogarty drinking the whiskey. "It puts heart into a man."

"Please God, now the English are gone, we'll have plenty," said Pat Kelly.

"What's to stop us?" said the colonel.

"Will Patsy Heffernan be having any more wars soon, after this one?" asked Christie Ryan.

"He will not," said Colonel Fogarty, "for he has his insurance business to do. But you never know. His firm might give him a holiday."

"Aren't they all slave-drivers, those English firms?" said Christie.

"They are," said Fogarty, "but they might give him that much holiday."

"Don't you find it hard to support your old mother, Colonel," said Christie Ryan, "when you're away up in the hills?"

For he knew the old woman, who lived in a small cottage with very thick white walls near Knocknavogue.

"Ah, sure, we all have pensions from the government," said the colonel.

"None of us have any pensions," said Christie Ryan, with just an echo of that note in his voice that you hear in the voice of a child that is going to cry.

"I never heard that much was done in Cranogue at the time of the troubles," said Colonel Fogarty.

"We burnt the Post Office," said Christie Ryan.

"It was not enough," said the colonel.

"We should have had our pensions like everybody else," said Christie.

But acrimony is a poor thing for any man's pen; and, as this discussion was growing acrimonious, I leave it; I neither dip my pen in gall, nor care for other men's bitternesses and grievances as material for my chronicle. Nor have I any need to look for such things, for it was a beautiful spring morning, and for any one grievance that these men had they had twenty jests: of these I shall make my story where this is possible. And the limits of this possibility stretch further in Ireland than in any other country that I know.

Soon Mickey came up to the outpost-line with the letter in his hand. The letter said, "You may shoot rabbits behind your own lines, and I to shoot pheasants up to a line to be demarcated by Colonel Fogarty, whom I have detailed for this purpose. All other points in your communiqué are still under the consideration of my Army Council. Patsy Heffernan, Major General."

"Begob," said Mickey, "you'll not get as fine a pheasant as ours. He was the finest bird ever. He was bright red all over, with gold on him like a lord mayor, and he had a voice on him you could hear roaring through the wood a mile away. He was the fine bird surely. And there was great eating on him."

"B'jabers there was," said Christie Ryan.

"We saw a bird finer nor that," said Colonel Fogarty; "and as big as a fox."

"Sure, ours was bigger," said Mickey.

"Will we mark out the line?" said Fogarty.

"Aye," said Mickey. "Go you with the colonel, Christie, and let you make out a line with him between the two armies."

"What officer is that?" asked Fogarty.

And Mickey realized that he had been about to detail a private soldier to do work of a diplomatic nature with a colonel. So he made him a captain.

"Captain Ryan," he said.

And away the captain and colonel went through the wood.

Now that the success of the poor parleys was so brilliantly evident, Mickey withdrew his outpost-line to a camp near a big spruce that would shelter the army from rain, and they collected sticks and made a fine fire at which they fried their bacon for dinner.

Over their cheery meal Mickey said: "We've more generals in Ireland than any other country; and better generals, many of them. But I'm thinking we've only one statesman."

"And who's that?" asked the army.

"My old granddad," said Mickey.

"Good Old Mickey," said the army.

"These poor parleys that he told me to have," said Mickey. "Aren't they great? He said they were what Napoleon would do. But he's wiser nor Napoleon."

"He is that," said they all.

"For I never heard," Mickey continued, "that Napoleon got peace for himself. Weren't all the nations biting at him like wolves, and England wanting to torture him. Sure he never got peace at all. And haven't we all we want up here in the wood?"

"Aye," said Colonel Brannehan, "except a little milk."

"We'll get it," said Mickey. "Now that Patsy's no longer feeling wicked, we'll walk out and get it."

That was the happiest day they spent in the wood. The weather had been growing milder every day, while they, growing daily more experienced in their contest with little discomforts, felt the equals of any weather. Glades of green grass shone in the wood, and there they went to shoot rabbits, taking the muzzle-loader in turns. Often through trunks of trees they saw the plain shining, like a huge stage set for spring, a stage up which she had just daintily entered, in a play made by enchantment. Nearly all the thorntrees now were green on one side; and even the latest of them, those huddled in shadow of trees and still remembering winter, had a greenish haze about them, like an elf that had draped herself in a piece of mist she had snatched from a stream at evening. Squirrels scampered over the ground in front of them, as though showing them the way through the wood, as though leading them on to some hidden court held in the hills by spring; and suddenly ran up trees and deserted them. Flowers peeped out where yesterday none had been seen, and primroses shone like a hoard of very pale fairy gold, not up to the standard of the world's currency. A larch shone gold here and there, barely yet green; and once they saw a green one in all its splendor, sudden and green in the wood like a meteor lighting the night. Sometimes a black-thorn flashed at them, the mass of white blossom amongst the solemn trunks looking like a fairy strayed from the gardens of elfland into some grim meeting of giants, some giants perhaps plotting war against the tops of the hills, being able to bring as allies the strong North wind and the thunder; but she had come from tending the buttercups guarding her borders, and giving to each its allowance of fairy gold. And all the while there was something haunting the wood, something that no man saw at once as he looked at the trees; twig for twig they stood every one as they had stood a month ago, yet they were not the trees of winter: look very close and you saw round them all a certain indistinctness, blurring the lines of the branches, hiding the ends of the twigs; it was the enchantment of Spring blessing the buds.

And, far off, other hills, where other bands of young men were perhaps enjoying themselves in the same way, looked at them from the rim of the earth, and slowly changed their colors as the hours went over them. And all this beauty of the wood, and beauty of the plain shining sleepily round it, and of the grave far hills, watching like aged giants leaning their chins on their knees, all seemed intensified strangely by a sense that haunted the wood, by a feeling that hovered like a strange bird in the air, that this was the last day of it.

CHAPTER XXIII

The End of the Poor Parleys

When dawn came through the wood, led on as it almost seemed by the chorus of blackbirds, and woke the army of Mickey, any forebodings that may have touched their spirits, only the evening before, were gone like the smoke of a camp-fire whose ashes are cold, were gone like mist out of air that is crisp and bright. Sometimes the lucent, almost invisible air is heavy, sometimes it is light, and though nothing changes before our eyes and though our ears hear nothing, our spirits are sometimes strangely oppressed by its weight, and in their oppression they may prophesy evil. In the bright morning all this oppression was gone, and if any of Mickey's men remembered it they put it down to strange fancies with which the evening had cheated them. A whole chestnut tree beside them had burst into leaf overnight, each leaf hanging limp and fresh like a moth with bright new wings. The men warmed themselves around a merry fire, and after breakfast went to the edge of the wood to look at the clear morning. There they saw a little field far up the hill, plowed and sown, but so far from the cottages that it almost had the air of having strayed; a stone wall was piled up round it, and in the middle of it there was a scarecrow. They all began shooting at the scarecrow, though they had not hit it by the time that Mickey stopped them, when he felt that they had wasted enough ammunition. Their provisions were running low, so they shot more rabbits with the muzzle-loader. Then they sat and watched the far hills changing their colors;

and the plain below continually changing, as wide areas of sunlight changed their places with shadows: white spires of churches arose to greet that wandering sunlight, and entirely disappeared as it passed to flash upon further fields and pursuing shadows of clouds hid the remoter distances. They sat there bathing their minds in the beauty of Ireland, while their thoughts running back down the ages pictured the men that had trodden those hills before them, spears-men that watched for the Danes, and kings in their collars of gold. With the glories of legend and the beauty of spring they were full of the past and the present: only of the future they had no thought whatever. By the time that evening came and they went back into the wood to build up the fire for their tea the whole scene below them had altered; the distance seemed to have shrunken, far hills to have disappeared, while nearer ridges took their places as boundaries: it was as though the stage that was prepared for spring had suddenly to be altered to something quite different and smaller, to suit some new and whimsical mood of her temperament.

They were all sitting round the fire drinking their tea, waiting for Colonel Fogarty to return with the next move in the poor parleys, and Mickey was wondering why the move was so long delayed; when suddenly there came the sound of firing from Patsy's end of the wood. Frequent shots broke out, and all at once they blended into that long rattling sound, rising and falling like waves, that is the sound of heavy firing. Yet still, for many seconds, no bullets came over them. The seconds passed and some bullets began to crack by, while a few ricochets whined over. Then the machine-gun lifted up its unmistakable voice. Very soon the sound of heavy fire ceased, and only separate shots were heard, and one long burst of fire that the machine-gun uttered. Then everything was still again. The birds that all this time had gone chirrupping to their branches, chirrupped still.

What was Patsy doing? So poor parleys ended like this. Mickey got his men into line and saw that they were all hidden, and that each man had in front of him a field of fire of at least twenty-five yards. And then he waited. But nothing happened. The birds ceased their chirrupping, and all was still in the wood.

"Shall we scout, Major General?" asked Jimmy.

"No," said Mickey. "There's nothing to find out. We know where Patsy is. When he comes for us we shall see him. But have a man out on your flank. He mustn't get round us."

That was the left flank, and Mickey put out a man to watch the right.

Still no one came through the wood.

When night came Mickey put out a sentry at the edge of the wood on each flank, and kept all his men awake and allowed no fire. And in the night they speculated; and the dead hush of the wood increased their speculations and doubts, faster than noises coming towards them would have done.

"Practicing, do you think?" said one of them.

But there had been a hurry in the roll of the fire, that had spoken clearly enough so that even their inexperience had understood; and something in the manner or voice of the machine-gun as it joined in, had told them that it was not practicing. They only shook their heads at the questioner, scarce troubling if it was too dark for him to see. But why this silence in the wood? What had Patsy begun, from which he had so suddenly ceased?

Patsy was only a year older than Mickey. But in experience he was as far beyond him as Old Mickey was. And both were puzzling him now: the poor parleys in which he had put so much trust had suddenly failed him; while Patsy, who only the day before had seemed so reasonable, had suddenly made this attack and seemed to have broken it off with a suddenness that was petulant. Was it the fault of something in the poor parleys, or of some queer streak in Patsy? But this book has no space for me to tell all the speculations that perplexed him and his men in the silent night, whose very silence seemed the most mysterious thing about it. He walked about and saw nothing, stood still and heard nothing. Then he went down the eastern slope to the edge of the wood and sat there waiting for dawn.

—————— ❧ ——————

CHAPTER XXIV

The Poor Old Woman's Gun

*B*efore the sun had risen, before any clear light had come to the fields at all, Mickey looked on the sleeping landscape and saw the outline of a stone wall away at the bottom of the hill begin to move slightly. He watched it and saw the outline wavering all the way along. Then he made out that it was troops crossing the wall, and coming up the hill in the dim light towards him. So many they were that they seemed to Mickey to be the whole of Patsy's force. He ran to his men and got them in line facing in that direction, then ran down the western slope to the other edge of the wood to see that no one threatened his rear; and there, coming out of the night that seemed just rolling away, he saw, about as far from the wood as the others, what seemed as many men as came over the stone wall. He ran back to his men, who were beginning to fire.

"Cease fire," he shouted to them. And to Jimmy he said, "Patsy's got lots more men. They're behind us. We must get away this way."

And he pointed north through the wood.

That way they went, catching glimpses now and then, through the trees, of the men that were climbing the eastern slope on their right. Suddenly Mickey heard the noise of a dry twig cracking. He halted his men and listened. There were more men coming that way through the wood. Brannehan too heard them, and pointed.

"Ah, what matter?" said Mickey. "We'll dodge them."

But at that moment Jimmy Mullins ran up to him from the right, with his mouth and eyes wide open.

"Oh, Mickey," he said, "it isn't Patsy! It's the lads from the Curragh!"

Mickey went to the edge of the wood. Sure enough it was true. Green uniforms coming up the hill. No way seemed open except to the south; but it was no use going there, for that was the direction these men had come from. With swift flashes of thought Mickey disposed of his entire force. He looked round him for hiding places and saw one thick spruce that could be climbed and could hide a man; and he saw an old tree covered in deep ivy, that should be able to hide two men. In the brief time that he had to look he saw other possible hiding places, but none that would not be searched immediately.

"Which of you lads can climb?" he said. Two came forward.

"Up that tree," he said. "And get into the ivy. And I want one more."

Another came up, Pat Kelly.

"Can you climb that spruce?" asked Mickey.

"I can sure," said Pat.

"Then up it," said Mickey.

And Pat went.

The way to the little field where the scarecrow stood was still open.

"Christie," said Mickey, to Christie Ryan, "let you run to the field where we shot at the scarecrow. Get into his coat and put his hat on you. And slip your hands inside the sleeves and let the sticks show at the ends of them, the way they do now. And let your knees hang sideways."

"And what'll I do with my rifle?" asked Christie.

"Ah," said Mickey very sadly, "maybe we'll not want it any more. Run."

And off went Christie.

Four remained.

"And now," said Mickey to Paddy Mulligan, "run you that way." And he pointed southwards to where G.H.Q. had been, and Patsy's camp, "and tell any one you meet in a green coat that I've been robbing your mother's farm and I'm just here, and ask them to come and arrest me to get back her blankets."

"But," said Mulligan.

"Run," said Mickey.

And now there remained Jimmy Mullins, Jim Brannehan and Young Hegarty.

"Jim," said Mickey to Brannehan, "hide your rifle as well as you can in that bracken, but let you keep your old muzzle-loader, Jimmy."

And Jim Brannehan did as he said.

"Young Hegarty," said Mickey, "you'll have to be a corpse. Stay dead as long as they're near you, and bide your time. Come here."

And he took out a knife and began to cut a small circle of skin from Young Hegarty's forehead up at the edge of the hair.

"Hell! That hurts," said Young Hegarty.

"Not so much as a real one," said Mickey.

"Begob, you're wrong," said Young Hegarty. "Because then you're dead, and you don't feel it at all."

"You'll be dead if you don't stay quiet, the way I can finish this job before those lads get you," said Mickey.

"It's not a job I like," said Young Hegarty.

"Ah, be quiet," said Mickey as he finished the job, "and behave yourself as a dead man should. Now lie there and keep still."

Then he walked Jimmy Mullins and Jim Brannehan away out of hearing of Hegarty. He knew he had kept the hardest thing for them.

"Jimmy," he said, "you two have got to arrest me, for stealing provisions out of the farms down there and taking the food from your mothers, and hand me over to those lads as a prisoner."

"B'the holy, we will not," said Jimmy.

"Begob, we won't," said Jim Brannehan.

"I order it," said Mickey. "And stand at attention when I give you your orders."

The troops were coming nearer. He stood between his two men, and dropped his rifle.

"Catch hold of my arms," he said. "Properly. Not like that."

And by the time that the first green uniform came into sight past a tree, the two reluctant men were just holding Mickey.

Reader, please judge Mickey by the care that he took of his men, rather than by his ignorance or his childishness (if you see any harm in childishness). May I ask you that favor?

Tree after tree seemed to disclose a green uniform, and soon there were a dozen there. Mickey dragged his captors towards the green army, with such appearance of being marched off by them as he could put up.

"Can't you look more threatening with your old gun?" whispered Mickey sharply to Jimmy.

"Sure, how can I, with one hand holding you?" complained Jimmy.

"Then run off and pick up my rifle, and give it to them," said Mickey.

"What's that you're saying?" said the nearest man in green.

"I'm saying," said Mickey, "they've no right to creep up on me the way they did with their gun and hold me up because I took a little food from their mothers when I was hungry. Sure, I was doing no harm. Let you tell them to leave me alone and give me back my rifle."

"Had you a rifle?" asked the green man.

"Sure, I had. Why not?" said Mickey. "That lad's got it."

"It's illegal," said the green man.

"Sure, I only had it to shoot a policeman," said Mickey.

And then an officer came up.

"Ah, what do *you* know about shooting at Black-and-tans?" he said.

And indeed Mickey knew nothing.

"Whose is that rifle?" the officer said to Jimmy.

"Sure, we took it off this lad," said Jimmy, "for robbing us of our food."

"And what's that gun in your other hand?" he asked.

"Sure, that's my old mother's," said Jimmy.

"An' what does she want a gun for?" asked the officer.

"Ah, sure, you wouldn't grudge it to a poor old woman," said Jimmy, "and she nearly eighty years old."

"And nothing but her old age pension in the wide world to support her," joined in Jim Brannehan. "And her rheumatics are terrible."

"And had ten children," said Jimmy.

"The poor old woman," said Brannehan.

And already this officer of a free army was beginning to feel a touch of that odium that he had thought only rested on England, for his own men were looking towards him with sympathies shown in their faces that were obviously for the poor old woman who had had ten children and who was now grudged her old gun.

"Ah, get along with you both," he said to Mullins and Brannehan, "but give me that rifle. And bring this man to the General."

So Mickey was marched off.

"The poor old woman," said Jimmy as he marched away with the muzzle-loader.

"Aye, the poor old soul," said Jim Brannehan.

And even though the officer had given up the gun he felt that a certain opprobrium still clung to him, and so did all his men.

Paddy Mulligan escaped in the same way as Mullins and Brannehan, and the green army found none of the hidden men for themselves. They found Christie Ryan, only because when some of them began shooting at the scarecrow just as Mickey's men had done, Christie Ryan ran away. They came after him and asked him what he was doing.

"Sure, I'm scaring the crows for my old mother," said Christie.

"Why doesn't she use a scarecrow?" they asked.

"Sure, she can't afford the clothes for it," Christie said.

"Couldn't you hang up that coat and hat that you're wearing," asked one of them.

For Christie was still wearing the scarecrow's coat, and a tall hat that had been made by one of the best London hatters when the Prince Consort was young, but had been later found in a hedge after a run with the Mountain and Valley.

"Sure, they'd be no good without a man in them," said Christie. "No good at all."

"Couldn't your mother find a better job for you than that?" asked another.

"Sure, she said I wasn't able for any other job," said Christie.

"She ought to know," said one of the green soldiers.

"Sure, she does," said Christie.

"Did you have anything to do with these lads in the woods?" asked one of them.

"I don't know any of them," said Christie. "Who do you mean?"

"We mean those lads that have been fighting up in the hills."

"Ah, I know nothing about fighting," said Christie.

"What do you do when you are not scaring crows?" they asked him.

"Sure, I watch my mother knit."

"Where does she knit?" one asked him.

"At home," replied Christie; and added, "By the fire."

"Ah, let him go," they said.

So Christie walked home to Cranogue.

The three men in the trees bided their time, and also got safe to Cranogue; safe but nearly in tears for Mickey; and they had reason, for he was in great peril.

CHAPTER XXV

Mickey Appeals
to Patsy Heffernan

General James Cassidy sat in a hay-barn among a few of his officers. He had been sent down there to investigate a rumor that there had been firing among the farms and up in the hills, the rumor in fact of the two battles between Patsy and Mickey, which he had been unable to get corroborated by anybody. But he had found Patsy's force in the wood and defeated it; and the following morning his men had taken Mickey, who was now led before him.

He was first asked his name, and told it.

Then, "Do you belong to Patsy Heffernan's force?" asked the General.

"I do not," said Mickey.

"Then what were you doing in the hills?" he was asked.

"I was operating against him," Mickey replied.

"How many men had you?" was the next question.

"I was quite alone," said Mickey.

"Where do you live?" asked General Cassidy.

"In the woods," said Mickey.

"How did you get your provisions?"

"I took them from the farms."

"Did they give you them willingly?"

"They did not. I had my rifle."

"How did you get a rifle?"

"Sure, you gave it me yourself."

This was not true; but General James Cassidy had distributed a good many rifles at the time of the troubles, and Mickey counted on his memory not tracing all of them. And it worked, so far as deceiving General Cassidy went, though not so far as exonerating Mickey.

"What were you doing when you were arrested?" was the General's next question.

"There were two lads that grudged me a little food," said Mickey. "I don't know their names. And they came after me, and they came up behind me, and one of them held me up with a shot-gun."

"You're for court-martial tomorrow," said General Cassidy. "March him away."

Mickey was marched away to another farm, between two men under command of a colonel. There he was brought to a hay-barn, and left on a bale of hay, with a wall of hay to lean against, and the two men remained with him. The colonel went out, and fastened the door with a padlock. Mickey began immediately to look round the barn, while one of the men pulled out a pack of cards and was soon at a game with his friend. Mickey noted that the walls were of thin boards, and that the door was unaccustomed to being shut, and was flimsy and had large gaps between it and the hasp of the lintel. Mickey looked then at the far end, where it was quite dark and mostly hay, but he could see where the walls ran, in spite of the dark. He looked next at the floor, which was of hardened mud. The men went on with their cards.

But Mickey had yet some things to learn. He made firstly the mistake of supposing that, as soon as these men began to play cards, complete oblivion of all else would come over them. And secondly, he supposed that, though they might have noticed him walking about the barn to inspect all its corners, they would not notice his eyes. However, one of the men saw him looking: they had both of them had similar experiences themselves. "Watch him, Mick, while I get a cord," said one of the men to the other.

Then he went to the door and shouted through the crack to some man outside for what he wanted. And presently the padlock was unfastened and a length of cord brought in by one of the others, who put on the padlock again as soon as he had gone out.

The man called Mick had put his cards carefully down on the floor, face downwards, and the other had put his in his pocket when he got up.

"Don't walk on the cards, Jack," he said, as the other came up with the cord.

"Get a hold of his hands," said Jack, "while I tie them."

And the man got Mickey's hands behind him.

"I say! That hurts," said Mickey, as the man with the cord bound his wrists tightly.

"That won't matter," said Jack. "You'll be dead in a few hours."

To that remark Mickey said nothing. He knew that the court-martial could only go one way. He would be charged with being illegally in possession of a rifle; and he had no defense. The sentence would be Death, as Jack knew already. And yet he had a good hope. He would tell them when they sentenced him that he was a friend of Patsy Heffernan's. He would tell them to ask Patsy himself, and he felt sure that Patsy would speak for him. To him Patsy Heffernan was such a national hero that he did not think they could shoot one of his friends. Buoyed up by this strong hope, Mickey did not feel the sinking of the heart that Jack's remark might have induced had he been hopeless.

The end of the rope that bound Mickey's wrists they tied to a post that there was in the barn. Then the game of cards was resumed.

I do not mention what food they gave Mickey, or who won the game of cards, for these things are trifles beside the rich material for many books that was now passing through the mind of Mickey. All the memories of his life went by in that procession of thought, some dim, some gorgeous; and among them, like guests uninvited slipping amongst the rest, were memories he did not even know that he had preserved. Into the future he looked too, the future that now seemed more radiant than he had ever dreamed it could be: clinging to his one hope of a good word from

Patsy Heffernan, he looked even into the future. He saw Alannah there, and the apple-blossom blooming about her, as it had been when first he had seen her. And fears sometimes pushed him away from his gaze at the radiant future, through the gates of the garden of Time. And then he would push away the fears and peer into the future again, for he did not really doubt that Patsy would speak for him. "What if Patsy won't speak for you?" the fear said. But Mickey felt sure he would. He was most of the night with these thoughts, and it was long before he slept, with his wrists still bound, on the hay.

At dawn Mickey was woken by one very ragged volley a little way off. For a few moments he hoped that some one might be attacking General Cassidy; but there came no more firing, and Mickey had to abandon this hope.

The morning passed quietly. And at about noon Mickey was marched before the court-martial. He was charged with "being illegally in possession of fire-arms, in that he, being a soldier of irregular forces, on April 6th 1922, in Drumlinvara hills, did have a rifle." Mickey had no defense that would not have led to questions that would have incriminated his men, some of whom General Cassidy might have been able to find; so he pleaded Guilty.

"Have you anything to say in mitigation of sentence?" Mickey was asked by the president of the court.

That was the moment on which his hopes had been focused all night, the hope that supported him still, and held him up unruffled before these men.

"I'm a friend of Patsy Heffernan," said Mickey.

It was all he had intended to say. But he saw no answering interest in the face of the president. And with the rapidity with which men in such circumstances see and feel, he observed that none of the men at the rough table before him appeared to have noticed what he had said. So he added, "You can ask him yourselves."

And then the president answered.

"Sure, we shot Patsy hours ago," he said.

That was the real sentence on Mickey; that was the blow over the heart from which he felt the approach of death. They had shot

Patsy Heffernan! All the room seemed dark to him. How could they have done it? They had shot Patsy.

"The court is closed for consideration of sentence," said the president.

Mickey was marched out. He saw from the way his escort looked at him what the sentence would be. They stood there rather curious and quite silent, and taking looks now and then at his face.

He was marched into the barn again; and there sentenced to death. It was no shock to him: the shock was over and he was still dazed by it, and unable to feel the weight of any more blows. They had shot Patsy Heffernan. And he must have heard the shots that killed him. That volley that woke him at dawn must have been the last of Patsy.

He was marched back to his barn again, and again tied to the post, with the same two men to watch him. Mickey was now quite hopeless. The men who had shown no mercy to Patsy Heffernan would never show any to him. They gave him something to eat, but he ate little.

"Are you good at digging?" asked one of the men.

But Mickey scarcely answered him.

His men were safe; the only good that there now seemed left in the darkness of this world.

Then more men came in, and untied the cord from the post, but left the other end round Mickey's wrists, and he was marched away towards the hills, which were quite close. He noticed that one of the men carried a spade. They did not go up the hills, but halted below them. And there Mickey's hands were untied. And again he was asked, this time by the officer in charge of his escort, "Do you know how to dig?"

"Sure, I do," said Mickey.

"Then dig your grave," said the officer.

One of them gave him a spade, and Mickey fumbled with it, for his hands were quite numb from the cord. He leaned the spade against him and rubbed one of his wrists, then he rubbed the other. Then he stuck the spade into the earth and left it standing, and rubbed his wrist again.

"Give me time," he said to the officer, "I can't use my hands yet." And he went on rubbing his wrists.

There is a certain awakening that comes to numbed fingers; but it was Mickey's mind that was awakening now. And while he stood there rubbing his wrists, it was not his hands that he was preparing for work, but his wits; for all of a sudden had come a gleam of hope.

CHAPTER XXVI

The Grave

"*I* wouldn't like to dig here," said Mickey.

"Do as you're told," said the officer in green. "And what does it matter to you where you dig?"

"Sure, I wouldn't like to offend those that live under the thorn," said Mickey, "with the last thing that I did."

"There's none of them here," said the green officer.

"Sure, there's plenty of them," said Mickey, and he pointed to a gnarled gray thorn a little way off, with its haze of green that was dimly shining all round it: by next morning it might flash out into full leaf. "And when they come out to dance round that thorn, and widen their circle a bit as more of them join in the dance, and maybe get as far as here, when they stumble over my grave they will be angry."

"Then let them be angry," said the officer, "and dig where you're told."

"It's not me that they'll curse," said Mickey, "for I'll be dead." And he looked at the green officer.

"Then where do you want to dig?" he asked Mickey.

"Oh, over there will do," Mickey answered and began to move slowly away.

"Ah, Timmy, let him dig his grave where he wants to," said one of the men to the officer.

"I'm not stopping him," replied Timmy.

Mickey went some distance, but walked as though he were continually about to stop, so that though his escort were often about to halt him they never did so until Mickey himself stopped; and so he went over eighty yards from where he had been told to dig. Even then he moved about, looking for a soft bit of soil to begin on.

"Sure, one would think you were choosing a nice coat for yourself," said the officer, "for all the fuss that you're making."

"Begob," said Mickey, "it will wear a long time."

And he began to cut a sod.

"It seems to take a lot of men to prevent me having a chance of escape," said Mickey. For there were thirty men surrounding him.

"Get on with your work," said Timmy.

Mickey dug. It is hard to say what forms of mental torture are worst. Perhaps waiting idly for death is as bad as any work that condemned men may be made to do. But there is no denying that this was a lonely task. Every stone sticking out of the clay left its vivid impression: it might be his eternal neighbor, or until the hills should shake themselves and stones and bones be all reassorted. It might be; but he clung to his hope, a hope of escape. Yet the hope was not strong enough to overcome the cold and the damp and the grimness of the walls of the grave. It needed religion now to remind him that this was not to be his eternal home, and yet earth was so very close as he dug, that with every spadeful it seemed to assert its claim to grip him for ever and ever.

"Can I have a priest?" he asked of Timmy, the officer.

"You can," said Timmy. "But you'll not want him till dawn. Now, get on with your work: we want to have everything ready."

The deeper he dug the more thoughts came to him from despair, and the fewer from hope. Among the myriad thoughts that came, were thoughts of Patsy Heffernan, the thought that he too had had this lonely task, and then the thought that never any more would he fight a battle with Patsy, one of those battles to which were brought no more hatred than boys bring to their games of football, into which the utmost of all their strength and endurance is put. With thirty men round him the circle of his guards was further away than they would have been had they been fewer. At first a few of them had stood near the grave; but the dust had pushed back those on the windward side, for Mickey was throwing the spadefuls high, while on the other three sides he was distributing stones. They were all well away from him now, except Timmy, who was walking up and down and continually peering in.

"Take a good look at it," said Mickey, "for it's where you'll be yourself some day."

And this had the effect of discouraging Timmy's interest.

Now no one was watching him, the cordon of men were round him standing at ease, with fixed bayonets, and his head was below the level of the earth as he stooped at his digging. And now he heard the sound of running water. Was it straight below him? Not quite, carefully though he had chosen the spot. He could see, as he chose it, two of the holes from which he used to get water, as well as the place where the river disappeared to go under the hill. He had aimed to dig on the line of Satan's flight from the Archangel. If the running water was not straight beneath him, it could not be far, because he heard it now and had not heard it before, so that his digging must have been going towards it, and must be near it now. It seemed down a bit to his right, and in that direction he dug.

"That's deep enough for you," said Timmy, coming by once more.

"Sure, it's I that have to lie in it," said Mickey. "Let me have a decent grave."

And he said it loud enough for the rest to hear, and in a voice the tone of which hinted a final ill-treatment of the man that had to die.

"Well, be quick then," said Timmy and went away again.

Mickey was quick. He dug with all his speed in the direction the water murmured as though some one were chuckling still at his escape from the lighting sword. He heard the steps of Timmy passing again. But Timmy passed on. The water was louder now.

"How much longer are you going to be?" shouted Timmy, but out of sight of the grave.

And at that moment some sandy earth, in the right-hand side of the grave, near one of the corners, began to run like quicksilver, and as it ran a hole began to widen, and the gray sand ran on. Mickey jabbed at it and the spade went in with the easiest thrust that he had made that day, and some of the earth came up with the spade and some went down the hole.

"Give me two minutes more," said Mickey.

He daren't ask for more. But would two be enough? He thrust hard again, and the hole widened. The right side of the grave was now joining in with the bottom of it in that cascade of running sand. Stones began to join in and all fell plopping into water quite close, though not close enough for any splash to come near Mickey, nor could he see it. Whether Mickey dug or not, the hole in the side of the grave was widening all the time, and he dug violently. He only just threw up enough earth for his captors to see that he was digging; so much fell down through the hole. With one thrust he thought he had nearly broken the spade, and an awful fear came on him lest thus at the last moment he should be left in these men's hands and have that dreadful task all over again, at some spot where there would be no hope.

The two minutes were up, and he heard the steps of Timmy coming his way; and at that instant a little avalanche fell and the hole seemed wide enough now for Mickey to squeeze through. But it was not the moment for the attempt, for if Timmy looked down as he was trying to wriggle away, there would be time to stop him. So he knelt, and prayed real prayers, though his kneeling figure covered the hole to the river. Timmy went on past, and Mickey gave three more swift thrusts with the spade. Now the avalanche was continuous, and the noise in the water began to be as loud as the noise of his spade which had hitherto concealed it.

"Have you done yet?" shouted Timmy from the other end of his beat.

"I have," said Mickey, and flung up one more spadeful of earth with his hands.

Then he crawled into the hole feet foremost. He could not feel the water with his feet. But what mattered how deep the drop? Better than waiting for the next dawn. Besides that, the little avalanche still ran, and he was slipping.

"Give me one more minute," he shouted.

"You've had time enough," shouted Timmy.

But Mickey was gone.

CHAPTER XXVII

An Old-fashioned Place

While Mickey was being taken to dig his grave, General Cassidy was having a drink in Sharkey's hotel in Cranogue. "One may be a general and at the same time want a drink," he sometimes said to his staff.

General Cassidy was well known in Cranogue, though he had first arrived there only four days ago. But he had made his influence felt from the moment of his arrival. He had come there in his Rolls-Royce on the day before his defeat of Patsy Heffernan, looking for information there, as well as on the other side of the woods, about the fighting that rumor had stated to Dublin had been going on in the hills. And the first thing he had noticed as he took a look at Cranogue was that there were no young men about. He saw Father Finnegan walking towards his chapel, and got out of his car and asked him about it.

"They were all at mass on Sunday," said the priest.

"Where are they now?" asked the General.

"Sure, I have my religious duties to attend to," said Father Finnegan, "and you have your military duties." And his face lighted up as though with the dawn of a delightful idea: "Shall we both attend to our own duties?" he asked eagerly.

"Begob, maybe we might," said the General.

"I think it would be a fine thing," said the priest.

"I think it might," said the General thoughtfully, and he went slowly away.

And he walked almost into the door of Old Mickey's house before he quite recovered the composure that a general should have, even after defeat. Old Mickey was in his doorway as usual. The General was walking across the street from the chapel, and suddenly drew himself up face to face with Old Mickey.

"It's a fine day," said the General.

"Bedad, it is," said Old Mickey.

"A fine soft day."

"It is, sure," said Old Mickey.

"Ye have a great view of the hills from here."

"We have that."

"I was wondering did any of you round here hear ever any firing up in the hills during the week?"

"We did not," said Mickey Ryan.

"Maybe some of the young lads may have heard it," said the General. "They often have good hearing while they are young."

"Maybe they did," said Old Mickey.

"Only I don't see any young men about," said Cassidy.

"Sure, there aren't any," said Old Mickey.

"And why's that?" said the general.

"Ah, it's a very old-fashioned place," said Old Mickey.

"Have you no children yourself?" Cassidy asked.

"I have not, only a daughter," Old Mickey answered.

"And has she no children?" asked Cassidy.

"She has not," said Old Mickey. "She lives there, and you can ask her."

And he pointed with his pipe.

"And the next house to you?" asked Cassidy. "Are there no young men there?"

"There are not."

"Why's that?"

"It's as God wills."

"And the next house to that?"

"There are none there either. I'm telling you: it's a very old-fashioned place."

"Then I think I'll be going on," said the General.

"God speed you," said Old Mickey.

And he came to the house of Young Mickey's mother, and knocked at the door. "I came to have a talk with your son," he said.

"Sure, I have no son," said Mickey's mother.

"Is that so?" said Cassidy.

"Sure, you can ask any one in the town," she said.

"I'll take your word for it," he replied.

"And what did you want with him?" she asked.

"Ah, nothing," he said.

And he went down the street inquiring for the young men of Cranogue, and asking if any one had heard any firing, and getting the same answers. It was a thankless task. Only a few months earlier, men had been making the same inquiries for him.

And it was a thirsty task. He went into Sharkey's hotel and asked for a drink. The waiter of Sharkey's brought it.

"Why are there no young men in the town?" he asked.

"Sure, they're all frightened out of it by the wise women cursing," replied the waiter. "And I'm frightened myself, for they have cause for it."

This was the first piece of direct information that he had had since he entered Cranogue.

"Will you have a drink yourself?" he asked.

"Sure, I will," said the waiter.

"Then get a large one," said Cassidy, "and bring it here."

The waiter brought the drink, by which I mean whiskey, and the two sat down at a table.

"Why are the wise women cursing?" asked Cassidy.

"Because there's black heathen from Africa disturbing Catholic bones," said the waiter.

"Do ye tell me?" said Cassidy. "Sure, why are they doing that?"

"They are digging up bones in the bog," said Sharkey's waiter.

"Begob," said Cassidy, "they've no right to be doing that."

"They're from Africa," said the waiter. "And they're staying in the hotel."

"Get them out of it," said Cassidy, who, having got to the root of the matter, made a quick decision. It was to keep the young men out of the hills that he had been sent to those parts.

"How can we do that?" asked the waiter.

"Give them no food," said the General.

"Sure, no one wants to give them any food," said the waiter. "But they do be getting bits of it."

"Find out who gives them any," said Cassidy, "and tell him to look to himself, or something may be happening to him that he wasn't counting upon. Tell him from me."

"I will," said the waiter.

"Where are the young men gone?" asked Cassidy.

"I don't know," said the waiter.

"What are their names?"

"I don't know," he replied.

"Have another drink," said the General.

"I will not," said the waiter. "For if I have two drinks I become talkative; and I'd be taking up your time."

"Ah, I've nothing to do," said the General.

"Haven't you a bit of an army to look after?" asked the waiter.

"I have," said Cassidy, "but I left another lad looking after it. Ah, have a drink."

"I will not," said the waiter.

And the General never found out who had gone to the hills.

He walked back up the street then till he came to his car, and motored back to the other side of the hills. In all that countryside, in all the land that looked on any part of those hills, there was only one man to give away Patsy Heffernan; and Cassidy found him. Others found him soon afterwards, and he is dead long ago. This man told Cassidy just where Patsy Heffernan was, and what he was doing; and Cassidy, making his plans at once, moved up the hill and surrounded Patsy at evening, and gave him some sort of court-martial next day, and shot him at dawn the day after.

Having ordered that Young Mickey should be court-martialed the day that Patsy was shot, and that he should be executed the day after, he was now back in Cranogue having another drink at Sharkey's, while Mickey was digging his grave. He had considerable facility of maneuver, as was shown by his defeat of Patsy, which was not solely due to superior force; and yet he was unable to instigate Sharkey's waiter to have a second large whiskey. That fugitives must enter Cranogue he knew, and he felt fairly sure that a second large whiskey would be the key to their whereabouts, but to maneuver that whiskey into the waiter had been beyond him. So he drank his own in silence. There was no one else to help him in Cranogue. He had met Father Finnegan again in the street, and had asked him if he had heard anything of any young men; and Father Finnegan had answered, "Sure, I know nothing." And he had felt the stupidity of his own question, as some old fool might feel it who had questioned a child of four about the lore of Sir James Jeans. He had also asked some such question of Old Mickey. But Old Mickey had only said, "Sure, if there were any young men in Cranogue they might be coming home again when things are quiet and you are gone back to Dublin. But, sure, we never had any."

In one thing the General had succeeded in Cranogue; he had tightened up the boycott of the Africans. Not that any advantage came to him from that; but he had felt it was the right thing to do. The boycott made it difficult for any of the Africans to get food, but for Umbolulu it was impossible, for somehow the boycott seemed to be directed mainly at him, and a certain tactlessness of Mrs. Patrick intensified it. She had tried to get food to him, but it was intercepted. Some consolation she had, when she learned of this, from the thought that hunger quickened his spiritual perceptions. But for Umbolulu there was no consolation; and I feel that when I have laid the whole of his story before my readers, no one should judge Umbolulu who has not himself been starving. He fared hard in Cranogue; and it seems to me to have been no small part of his hardships that it was his rapid and splendid spiritual development that made him the objective in the struggle of jealousies of which he knew nothing, till his poor frame, growing daily thinner, may almost be likened to some peasant's cottage around which Armageddon is raging. And then again, warm-hearted overtures would be made to him by some who were envious of Mrs. Patrick's triumph, that she derived from his still increasing sanctity; and next day all trace of friendliness would be gone, and Umbolulu never knew why. And all the while he was starving.

One thing Umbolulu did understand, and that was that it was General Cassidy who was preventing him from getting any food.

When he had despaired of getting any more whiskey into the waiter, or more information out of him, General Cassidy walked out of Sharkey's. He stood in the doorway, all dressed in green, with leggings of red leather, wearing Sam Browne belt and sword; and there Umbolulu saw him. "Umbolulu hungry," he said.

Cassidy had come to Cranogue wanting a good deal, and from nobody could he get anything, except the whiskey he paid for. He was annoyed with Cranogue; and here was a man who wanted something too. And a black heathen. Should such as he have what they wanted, when a good Catholic could not get the information he ought to have? "Dirty heathen," said Cassidy.

Whether Umbolulu's English ran as far as these two words is doubtful; but he saw he was not going to get food. Yet he followed the General as he walked away, lifting up every now and then that piteous plaint, "Umbolulu hungry," for his only chance of food seemed to be to placate Cassidy.

Cassidy by walking fast shook off the hungry man. He had sent his motor away and was walking back alone over the hills, knowing that he should see no trace of fugitives from the high road, and combining his walk with a bit of scouting. There were reasons, rather beyond the scope of this book, why a knowledge of the ins and outs of the Drumlinvara hills was valuable to a general. He did not know the way, but he came to a stream that ran singing towards Cranogue, laughing with sunshine. He did not know the importance of watersheds in the planning of a campaign, but he did know that streams ran from the hills, so he followed this one homewards. And behind him still came Umbolulu a long way off, still hoping against starvation.

CHAPTER XXVIII

The Sword of Michael

When Mickey slipped though the angle of the grave between the side and the bottom of it, and went down with the little avalanche of sand, he fell some way, as it seemed to him, then hit the water and went down to the deeps. Actually he had fallen no more than three feet, and the depth of the water was barely four; but the darkness, the fall, the cold and the great noise of the water, all multiplied his impressions. He came to the surface and got his breath, and soon collected his thoughts, and realized that the mystery of the blackness ahead of him was not the enemy, but the thirty men behind, and that the cold and rushing water, with its roaring that so hugely filled the darkness, was his friend. He leaned forward and swam, and the current carried him on over large stones rounded by centuries of running water and smoothed with slime or moss. In the darkness there was only what he could hear and feel and smell. He smelt the water, a curious smell like that of unfamiliar plants growing on mud in the damp, he heard its huge voice all round him, dominating the darkness, and he felt the softness of the rocks as his hands hit against them at the sides with nearly every stroke and pressed a little way into their moss as he shoved against them. And they helped him on, as much as free strokes in open water would have done. Though he bumped his knees on the rounded stones below him, he was still carried on, as though the stream were accustomed to carrying things easily over them for ages. Presently he saw the curves that the water made as it slipped over the curving rocks, for a silver light gleamed on the water, from a hole in the roof ahead of him that flashed like a green flame, where the daylight came down past a few leaves and grass. It was one of the holes from which he used to fill bottles for the water-supply of his army. He thought of his army now, safe through the best dispositions of it that he had ever made, back in Cranogue with all the fun of that war in the hills for a memory. On the other side of the patch of light he stood still, leaning back a little against the water, and with a hand touching a rock on either side to steady himself. He knew now how far he had come, and he had gone so fast that he had confidence that at any sound of pursuit he could dash on again and keep his lead. He stood still and listened. There was no sound but the roar of the water. Certainly no one had come to the hole in the rocks; and, though he could hear nothing behind him for the roar of the stream, he felt sure that the approach of any one following him through the water must make some louder sound which he would hear even above that roar. But there was no other sound. It seemed that, careful though Timmy had been to guard against the escape of his prisoner upward out of the grave, with his circle of thirty men, he had not thought of escape where none had been made before, and had not yet looked to see if Mickey had gone; or, if they had found out, they could not know anything of the course of the river, for still there was no sound at the hole in the rocks. Mickey could touch the roof, and found it crumbly with stalactites, and spiders' webs amongst them. It cheered him to discover even that much sign of life in this dark annexe of the grave.

It was time to go on again, for when they did discover that he was gone, whether they tried to follow him, or whether they tried to find the course of the stream and plodded over the hills, it would be best to be well ahead of them. He left that green glow and the light on the water regretfully, and plunged on. Sometimes the water seemed shallow, sometimes much deeper, but as the width was always about the same, as he could feel by his fingers hitting with every stroke against the rocks at the sides, the depth required for that volume of water probably varied little, except where the current pouring downward over a larger boulder scooped out a hole as it curved. These holes seemed abysses to Mickey, passing them in the dark. A swim down a stream four feet deep, with the current to help one, seems no great Odyssey; yet in that darkness Mickey forgot his knowledge that the little stream soon emerged from the hills and rippled on t'wards Cranogue; for there were darker things to remember than this knowledge, things appropriate to the blackness and the noise. Every one knew, and few bothered, how that stream had been made, and Mickey had given it no more thought than the rest. But now in the darkness he wondered where such a stream might go, whether such a stream might not go straight to Hell, carrying its discoverer home. He had never seen the place where it left the hills, though he knew it further on. But was it the same stream? Or what if that dark one who first caused it, should come down it again, pursued once more, and taking the old line as a fox will sometimes do? Would he carry Mickey with him? And, if he did not want to do that, another thought presented itself, and a practical one too: would there be room for the dark one to pass? These are not thoughts to be entertained by any reader in sunlight, or sitting by the fire: there they must seem trivial fancies. But they were thoughts well suited to the darkness and the legend of that place, and cold reason dominates thoughts only at its appropriate desks. The sound behind him seemed different to the sound in front; no doubt, as we can see in the daylight, where nothing hinders reason, because the echoes were more voluminous in the direction in which they were pent up than in the direction in which they were nearer an outlet, or merely because there was some fall in the river far behind. But to Mickey it sometimes seemed as though there might be heard behind him the snarls of one pursued by frightful vengeance. It had been so once: why not again? And the vengeance would not overtake him: things never varied in Heaven: so that the dark one would come by Mickey all unhurt and angry, and would take him upon his way.

A pool of silver shone once more before Mickey, with flashes of green in it and a little gold. He was coming to the big shaft in the midst of the hills, that was known as the Devil's Chimney. As he saw the light the thoughts that were troubling Mickey faded as white April frost disappears in the sun, if anything so dark as those thoughts can be likened to such a brightness. He stopped when he came to the shaft, and looked up and saw a patch of the sky again. Green ferns between him and the light shone like enamel. He took a rest there, climbing out of the water, and standing upon a rock and leaning against the side. He was exactly under the center of the hills. The air had been good so far, but he had the long bit before him, with no cracks in the rocks that he knew of. Perhaps the running water would bring the air along with it. Such thoughts as this came to him now, that little patch of light having bent them that way; so easily are the calculations of the mind of the soi-disant lord of Creation turned this way and that by things beneath his considering. And now there came to cheer Mickey the thought that pursuit was almost impossible. There was only one way to go down that stream with ease, and that was to go with it as he had done. The current that helped him along would hinder men trying to walk: with every step they would have to fight against the current as much as if walking upstream; for, let it push them one foot too far, and it would have them down. Or would they take off their green greatcoats, he wondered, and swim as he had done? He moved downstream a little, and stood on the far side of the patch of light, and turned round and waited. He reflected that swimmers must come without their rifles, and only one at a time. Standing there in the dark he could seize the head of any man swimming towards him. But no one came.

The men in green were all strangers there, and knew nothing of this stream, and Mickey had little fear that they would find out its course and follow it over the hills and down the other side, and slowly pursue him that way. Nevertheless he went on; and so he entered the longest and darkest part of his journey. The noise of the stream wrapped round by the roots of the hills roared again with a great voice, and again the reasonable thoughts that had come in the light left him, and instead of his accurate calculations of the difficulties of his real enemy he thought of that old enemy of all of us, wondering if on that day, of all the ages, he would come down the stream again. He uttered a supplication to Michael. But would it make things any better if the archangel did come after the enemy there? In such a narrow space, with two immortals fighting to the death, what chance would Mickey stand? He had seen the sword of Michael: it was a frightful thing. It had hung in the sky over the bog for three or four nights when he was a child, in 1908. A great silver light pointing towards the West, and flaring upwards and widening as it went. His elders had spoken of it in low voices, out of his hearing, and none told him what it was or what it threatened. But what could it have been but the sword of Michael? And if such a sword should come behind him now, there would be no room in that narrow cavern to be neutral. Not that he ought to be neutral in such a cause. But what chance would there be for him any way? And if the dark one were not pursued, if he escaped again as of old, once more there came the thought, what would he do to Mickey when he came up with him? He had heard it told, by one who had actually seen it, how a hunted fox had run through a flock of poultry without ever touching one. Yes, it might be like that. But would he have room to go by? And the only answer that came to his thoughts was the roar of the stream, telling of tumult and hurry under the hills.

It may be considered that it was enough for Mickey to have asked of himself such questions once, and to have settled them; but that is not the way with thoughts in the dark, and again and again the thought occurred, could there be room to go by? And the chances against that day out of all the ages being the very one diminished suddenly with another thought: what if it happened often; as sunset and star-shining and dawn, and other heavenly things, happen again and again? And the dark and the roar continued, and the thoughts appropriate to them.

And another thing that was dreadful about this journey was that the river was continually changing its voice; sometimes when big stones stood in its way it muttered, sometimes when narrowing walls squeezed it and thrust it upward its voice turned to a roar; so that sounds of the complaint or the anger of a powerful everlasting thing in the dark were continually about Mickey. Once he came to such a narrowing between two pillars of rock that he had no room to stretch out either arm; the river rose near to the roof and swooped again, and Mickey's head went under; when he came up he heard a roaring behind him, and tried to swim faster, to get away from the anger there seemed to be in the sound, but could not hurry much faster than the hurrying of the current. It was then that he said out loud what perhaps he should not have said: "I never said a word against the Devil." And when the roar behind him sounded full of menace as ever, he added, "I always minded my own affairs, and took no part in religion."

It was not true; but, in addition to the noises with which all the air round him echoed, there was one thing perplexing him which cannot trouble any one of my readers as they read these words and judge Mickey; and that was total darkness. Strange sounds in the daylight are analyzed often by reason, and in the darkness by terror.

There was no pursuit, no dark shape fled that way, no lightning sword overtook it: would that I could say it had; for, even though many would have been out of a job, the world would have been a happier place. But it is not for me to moralize on this theme.

A patch of gold and green appeared on the water, further on were patches of silver; and pieces of daylight ahead shone framed with ferns, that glittered like green glass. With the light ahead of him all his fears disappeared, and soon he was rejoicing in the brilliance of daylight and the luxuriance of growth that flared on the very edge of the darkness. Every curve of the stream dipping over the rocks was now outlined in silver, then every runnel and every ripple, till the water before him looked like copious silver, inlaid on copper that showed through more and more rarely, and then upon sheets of brass. And Mickey ceased his swimming and tumbling and found his feet, and walked slow to the stream's exit, little dreaming that General Cassidy with his fine new sword was walking to the same point from the other direction.

CHAPTER XXIX

Umbolulu Breaks His Fast

As Mickey came to the rift at the foot of the hills, through which the stream poured out and sang on its way to Cranogue, he suddenly saw he had scarcely room to get out. A column of rock rose up in the stream's center and went nearly as high as the roof. There was no room to get over the top of it. He tried to the right and found there was no room there, but to the left there was nearly room. He stripped some of the moss off, and got his head through. Then he drew back his head and steadied himself against the rock, so as not to be carried into the gap and wedged by the rush of the water, and looked at the rock and considered what he should do. The rock was not hard; it was limestone; and it was wearing a jacket of lime that was softer still, that through the centuries it had got from the water. He took off a buckle of his braces and began to cut the softer lime away, and found that he could cut nearly half an inch of it before the rock got too hard. By removing all the moss on the other side, and smoothing the surface of the rock on that side in the same way, he calculated that he would just have room to get his body through sideways. Only a great deal of the rock would have to be scraped, all the way down on both sides; and Mickey, calculating this by the little that he had done, decided that it would be a matter of over an hour. He scraped for another five minutes, then put out his head again, to see how he was getting on, and looked right into the face of General Cassidy.

And Cassidy recognized him. "What are you doing here?" he said.

"Ah, what ought I to be doing?" asked Mickey.

"You ought to be making your confession," said Cassidy. "I ordered you to be shot at dawn."

"Ah, General, what did you do that for?" said Mickey.

"To learn you," said Cassidy.

If he couldn't get out, the general couldn't get in: that was a certainty. Mickey was wondering what he could say that might be of any use, when the general pulled out his sword and came for him. Mickey drew in his head.

"Ah, General, what's the good of that?" he asked plaintively. And it was so obviously no good, as soon as Mickey was the length of an arm and a sword back up the river, that the question enraged the general instead of soothing him. But after a few blind thrusts into the dark of the cavern he stepped quickly back and hurried away up the hill. Mickey went on with his work, but with despair in his heart. When the general got to the top of the hill he knew he would blow a whistle. Timmy and the thirty men who had surrounded his grave would come up the far slope at the double. A sentry or two would stop him from getting out by the way he got in, even if going back up that stream were possible; and the rest would come to the opening at which he was and would shoot upstream. There was nothing to do but work on, though the work seemed useless.

And then Mickey heard a voice so plaintive that it seemed attuned to his own plight, coming towards him up-stream: "Umbolulu hungry," it said. "Umbolulu hungry."

He put his head out again. He had one walnut left in his pocket, a very compact form of food that he had been carrying while in the hills. Umbolulu was quite close. Mickey stretched out a hand and offered the walnut to him. Umbolulu almost snatched it, and began to eat it immediately. His strong white teeth cracked it at once and, as far as Mickey could see, ate nut and shell together. Then Mickey remembered that he had had bread and cheese in his pocket. The cheese should be still there, though hardly the bread. He felt, and found that a bit of the crust remained. He stretched out a hand again with the crust and a piece of cheese. Umbolulu took it and drew out a large knife and spread the cheese on the bread, in a way that went better with his black frock coat and his envied spiritual progress than the way he had eaten the nut.

"The knife," shouted Mickey, "the knife! Lend me the knife!"

For with a knife like that, he felt, he might scrape the rock in time.

But Umbolulu went on cutting the cheese and laying it on the bread. "Umbolulu hungry," he said again.

"Quick then, when you have done with the cheese," said Mickey.

But that was more than Umbolulu could understand.

"Knife, knife," called Mickey again. "Lend me the knife."

But Umbolulu put it back in his pocket and, lifting up eyes in which there was real suffering, said again in that plaintive voice, "Umbolulu hungry."

"Black Protestant," said Mickey in his disappointment at seeing this sudden hope thus snatched away, for Umbolulu's reputation as a star convert had traveled far and wide. But Umbolulu merely went on up the hill, muttering once again that plaintive cry. And Mickey with his last glimpse of him saw slung behind his shoulders what looked like his drum, which no one had seen him with since his triumphant conversion. Was Umbolulu leaving Cranogue, he wondered, and taking all his belongings away?

When Umbolulu had gone Mickey worked on listlessly, but waited for death. There was no possibility of getting through those rocks till he had had another hour's work on them. The big knife could have done it in time, but he had no knife. There was scarcely a possibility of marching up that stream, and none of finding an outlet beyond the hills unguarded. At about the time that Cassidy should have got to the top of the hill, he stopped his work and waited to hear the whistle. When he heard none he supposed that Cassidy had signed to the men with his hand, or, worse still, met them coming over the hill already. There was no chance at all that Cassidy would spare him. Against these very reasonable fears the ones that he had had in the deeps of the hill seemed childish. He wished that he could go back there now, but he had no food and he could not live in the water, with men at each end and at any other exits waiting for him to come out. His temptation was to despair and to wait for Cassidy, but he worked on scraping the stone, and the work took the edge off his fears.

And so an hour went by, and more than an hour, and the brightness passed from the water; and a dreaminess came upon it, and soft colors, as though the stream were brooding upon other worlds than ours. And still Cassidy did not come. The soft lime came off easily, but it had to be scraped off evenly over such a wide area, that with the two small implements Mickey had, the buckles of his braces, and the difficulty of standing there in the rush of the water leaping out of the hill, it took him all this time to gain the inch or so which he needed to slip through sideways. And at last he felt he could do it. But where was Cassidy?

Darkness behind him, and the fading evening in front; there was still plenty of light to see to shoot. What would greet him as he crept out of the cavern? He put his head out and saw nothing.

If Cassidy had not met his escort of thirty, he still had heaps of troops on the other side of the hills and had had time by now to bring a battalion of them; yet all was absolutely still, all round the mouth of the cavern. It seemed unnecessary to prepare a trap for him, yet that Cassidy should show him any mercy he somehow knew was impossible. Why did Cassidy not come? And when he saw that he should find no answer to that question he slid quietly between the two stones, and stood once more in the open light of what was left of the day, and there was no sign of an enemy.

Mickey hastily left that spot in case men should yet come to look for him. He turned away from Cranogue where they would seek him first, and walked back t'wards the hills. And as he went he heard a gentle drumming, like the throb of a wild pulse, filling the air with mystery.

Looking upward in the direction of the soft sound of the drum Mickey saw a thin column of smoke going up at the edge of the wood. For at a little fire in the hills Umbolulu was eating Cassidy.

CHAPTER XXX

When Malachi Was King

Nothing was ever proved about Umbolulu and Cassidy. There seem to me to have been ample proofs, but no one appears to have marshaled them. Mrs. Patrick still asseverates that the whole story is due to sectarian jealousies, which is certainly unjust to the differences that there must always be in religion. Jealousy there was, and Mrs. Patrick herself was greatly responsible for it, for she had boasted too much of her convert's phenomenal progress; and jealousy makes strange stories; but it could not make the marks of a fire on the ground, and bones and boots and brass buttons. Mrs. Patrick's arguments were more eagerly listened to by those in authority than any that she had ever used before, for it was felt that such a thing could never have happened in Ireland, and argument in support of this was avidly welcomed. But Mrs. Patrick never boasted again. There were very large head-lines in those days to be seen in the Irish papers, saying "Horrible Murder," in big black capital letters; but all the murders recorded were always in England.

What I think happened was that Umbolulu, hungrier and hungrier as he walked, came up with the General at the edge of the wood, still trying to beg a respite from the boycott that was starving him. I picture him uttering again that plaintive cry of his, then perhaps stretching out his hands to the General in a way that Umbolulu had, and appealing to him in the name of their common Christianity; which had merely insulted Cassidy. What Cassidy had said, we shall never know. But I imagine that just as he spoke, the teaching of Mrs. Patrick fell like a cloak from the African; and he stood there between the terrible alternatives of starvation borne with Christian fortitude, and the dreadful teachings of his old religion, bred in the dark of Africa, that taught him he was in the presence of good food. As I have said before, let those that have known starvation judge Umbolulu.

Mickey kept away from the fire in the hills, not wishing to meet with any one, and it was not till long after that he knew why Cassidy never came for him, to take him away and execute him at dawn.

I may say, before I leave this distasteful topic, that a sum of money had been collected to record on a brass plaque the conversion of Umbolulu, and to have it let into the wall of the church of Cranogue, on the outside where every one could see it: the plaque was being engraved in Dublin, and was never completed. The residue of the money collected was set aside instead as a fund for providing meals for poor children in the parish of Cranogue. As there were not enough Protestant children, the Roman Catholic children got some too. Perhaps the last word of the little conflict aroused in Cranogue, by Mrs. Patrick's boast, was said by Father Finnegan when he met Mrs. Patrick one day about the time that the children's food fund was started.

"And what do you feed them on, Mrs. Patrick?" he asked.

"Beef," she said; and then, noting or fancying something in his expression, she added, "Have you any objection?"

"Not at all," he said.

"And bread," she added.

"Excellent," said Father Finnegan.

"And cheese," she went on.

"Quite excellent," Father Finnegan said.

I don't know what prompted her to go rushing on. She had far better have stopped.

"And jam, of course," she said.

"Excellent, excellent," said Father Finnegan.

"And a little butter," she continued.

"Ah, excellent," said Father Finnegan. "Best of all."

"And all the usual things," she said.

"Ah yes, yes," said Father Finnegan. "Really an admirable diet. Quite excellent."

It was on the tip of her tongue to say more, but at last she stopped.

Umbolulu and his vacillating religious persuasions, and the conflict that they gave rise to, are topics from which I gladly turn away. Even his fellow-countrymen spoke of him little next day, where they still worked in the bog. Sometimes when no one was thought to be within earshot, grave voices might have been heard mentioning the word "backslider," and solemn shakes of the head showed they discussed Umbolulu.

Mickey reached the woods, and, knowing that they would be well patrolled, he slipped cautiously through them, never stepping on any twig, and helped by the dimness of evening. He was going in the direction in which he had fled, and into the enemy's country; country he knew, because it had been poor Patsy Heffernan's country, and he had fought two battles in it with Patsy. And now it belonged, as Mickey supposed still, to General Cassidy. He was going in that direction for two reasons; because it was not the direction in which they would expect him to go, and because he had need of a hiding place, and trusted Alannah to hide him if he could get as far as her home. A star or two was shining as he came out of the wood, but there was light enough yet for Mickey to see that they had a sentry over his grave, and another over each of the two holes in the rocks that ran down to the river before it entered the hill. It was a light that Mickey liked, light sufficient for him to detect the presence of troops by watching carefully, and not too bright to prevent his easy concealment. And when it grew darker he heard their loud clear voices, ringing across the hush with which earth prepares for sleep, and sometimes saw their fires. There were a lot of them there, and Mickey studied their lines as well as he could, before it was quite dark, creeping nearer and nearer to them as the last of the daylight went. They were all between him and O'Dwyer's farm, a long line of them with campfires here and there. As far as Mickey could see there was no way round them; but he noted a gap between two lots of them, though it was only a few yards wide. If he could get to that gap unheard he could get through in the dark, but there were beech-trees dotted about just in the wrong place for him, and he knew that he would not get by unheard over the dead beech-mast. There was a sentry going up and down the whole length of the front of each company, or whatever they were.

Mickey went back to the wood and got a long stick, which in the dark would look like a rifle when he held it over his shoulder. Then he came down the hill again, and black night came with him. He lay quite close to the troops for a while and watched one of the sentries. Then he followed the sentry, but walking wide of him, away from the gap through which he wanted to go. When the sentry got to the end of his beat, the further end from the gap, Mickey slanted right on to his beat and came along it about fifty yards ahead of him, with the stick over his shoulder all the way along the line of the troops, and not fifteen yards from them. When he came to the gap he walked through it, and on t'wards O'Dwyer's farm. When he got out of hearing he ran, for fear that any one might have noticed the extra sentry, when the real one came into sight.

These plans were very good; but the night is full of surprises, and the plans did not entirely work. For Mickey bumped into one or two things, foremost and loudest amongst which was a bucket. And presently he heard footsteps coming behind him. Mickey stopped, and the steps behind him stopped. Then he walked on unconcernedly. Soon he came to O'Dwyer's house, and knocked hurriedly on the door. Alannah opened it. "Quick," said Mickey. "I'm followed."

She let him in at once and shut the door.

"Can you hide me, Alannah?" he said.

"Are there many of them?" she asked him.

"A whole army," he said.

Alannah thought a few moments. "There's the big bed," she said.

"They'd look under it," said Mickey.

"Not if Dad and Mammy were to go to bed early," she said.

"They would," said Mickey. "It's Jim Cassidy's army."

"Sure even he wouldn't do that," said Alannah.

"They shot Patsy Heffernan," said Mickey.

"They shot Patsy Heffernan!" gasped Alannah.

"They did that," said Mickey.

"Oh, the black hearts there must beat in them," cried she.

"They shot him at dawn," said Mickey.

"It was a black shame," said Alannah.

"It was that," said Mickey. "Here they come."

For he heard the steps that had followed him; and many more.

"Come in here," said Alannah, and led him into the kitchen where O'Dwyer and her mother were sitting.

Mickey had never seen Mrs. O'Dwyer before, and did not know O'Dwyer well. His principal link with him, if one may use the phrase, being that he had burnt his haystack. But he had now a far stronger link, indeed the link that in Ireland is one of the strongest of all: he was a hunted man.

"Can we hide him?" said Alannah. "They're after him."

"We've no longer got the haystack," said O'Dwyer thoughtfully, without any trace of bitterness, indeed without any allusion being intended at all.

"There's the big bed," said Mrs. O'Dwyer.

"They're Jim Cassidy's men," said Alannah.

"We'll go to bed," said O'Dwyer, "and see if they dare disturb us."

"Ah they could not," said Mrs. O'Dwyer.

"They're Jim Cassidy's lot," Mickey said over again.

"It's the only chance," said Alannah. And she was right.

"Show me the bed," said Mickey, as they sat undecided, and as the sounds of steps going round the house increased.

Mr. and Mrs. O'Dwyer and Mickey went upstairs, and there he saw the big bed, over five feet wide.

"They'll look under it sure," said Mickey. And a knock came on the door downstairs.

"They want me for dawn tomorrow," said Mickey in a low voice. And something in his peril quickened his wits.

"The bolster," he said.

He heard Alannah speaking to men outside the door, delaying with talk, and then delaying with unlocking the door, and later delaying with talk when armed men came inside. He took the bolster and shoved it into a cupboard.

"They shot Patsy Heffernan," he said, to show what sort of men these were.

Mrs. O'Dwyer gasped, as Alannah had done. Mickey took a blanket off the bed and wrapped it round himself. "If you'd go to bed," he said.

They both put on long night shirts over their clothes as they stood. And now they heard the sounds of steps on the stairs, and Alannah's voice delaying. Mickey lay down lengthways where the bolster had been and pulled the end of the sheet over him. The O'Dwyers smoothed it, as soon as they understood.

"Quick," said Mickey, for the steps were up the stairs.

Mr. and Mrs. O'Dwyer jumped into bed, and three knocks sounded heavily on the door.

"Who's that?" shouted O'Dwyer.

"The army," came the answer.

"For the love of God what do you want here?" O'Dwyer asked.

"We are searching the house," said the voice.

"My wife and I have gone to bed," said O'Dwyer.

"You're in bed early," came the answer.

"Isn't an Irish woman safe in her bed at any hour?" asked O'Dwyer.

"Sure such things have never been known," shouted Alannah.

"All the blessed saints defend us," cried Mrs. O'Dwyer.

"We're coming in," said the voice.

And they came, four armed men.

"When Malachi was king," said O'Dwyer, "a maiden could walk alone, wearing a bracelet of gold, from one end of Ireland to the other."

"Maybe she might," said one of the men with rifles.

"And men with guns didn't be coming into her bedroom," said O'Dwyer.

"Good for you," whispered the bolster.

And the men began to search the room, and the leader looked under the bed.

Mr. and Mrs. O'Dwyer had a pillow each, which were where pillows usually are, on the bolster; and their heads were each on a pillow. Mickey began to remember that his clothes were all wet; and he felt more compunction about the O'Dwyers' bed than he had about their haystack, the burning of which he felt had added a splendor to war, but he couldn't feel that about damping their blanket.

Again the leader looked under the bed. Then they opened the cupboards. Presently one of them stared at the bolster that Mickey had thrown into a cupboard, where it was now lying bunched up. The man lifted it up. A cry broke from O'Dwyer: "Our spare bolster," he wailed. "We've only two in the world. Are you going to take that from us?"

"Sure, we don't want it," said the man.

"When Malachi was king of Ireland," began O'Dwyer.

"Sure, we're not going to take anything," said the man who had found the bolster in the cupboard.

"I wish Malachi were back," cried Mrs. O'Dwyer.

"Aye, he was the lad," said O'Dwyer.

And the topic was well away from bolsters.

"A collar of gold he had," shouted O'Dwyer. "And the likes of you wouldn't have been allowed."

He was still thinking of Malachi.

And even Alannah joined in. "I'm thinking there's no one left now to learn you manners," she said; "and the respect that is due to a woman's bedroom that there was in the days of Malachi."

"Ah, what's the world coming to?" asked Mrs. O'Dwyer.

"I'm thinking it's coming to ruin," said O'Dwyer.

It seemed to these men unfair that the odium properly due to England should be so heaped on themselves, and it somehow hindered their search.

"Wouldn't you like to search my mother's bed?" asked Alannah.

"Sure, we wouldn't do that," said the leader.

"Ah, I didn't know you'd stop at that," she said. "That's why I asked."

They went out of the room and searched the rest of the house.

"I'm thinking they'll be disappointed," said Mickey, "when the dawn comes and they've nothing to shoot at."

CHAPTER XXXI

Old Mickey Uses His Wits

Mickey realized that, had he made his plans with sober judgment, or had it not been for Alannah, he would not have come where he now was. He sat in front of the O'Dwyers' fire in their kitchen, drying his clothes as well as he could and hungrily eating supper that they brought him. He discussed the situation with Alannah and her father and mother, and debated whether the green men knew it was he they were after, or whether they only knew him for a fugitive and were collecting fugitives. Whatever it was, all were agreed that he must get away from there as soon as he could. They sat there long talking, and the moon rose while they talked. Mickey got some dryness into his clothes from the fire; and then he went out to look and see in the moonlight where the men that were after him were. Alannah first put out a lamp that would have shone through the open door; and the first thing that Mickey saw as he looked to the hills, with Alannah standing beside him, was that there was a line of campfires now all the way between him and the hills.

"They're taking a lot of trouble to catch one man," he said.

"Ah, they're like that," said Alannah.

"Sure haven't they all been on the run themselves?" said Mickey. "And can't they leave others alone?"

"They cannot," said Alannah.

"I can't get over the hills," said Mickey. "And I can't stay here, for they know that I'm not far off."

"Maybe you could go the other way," said Alannah.

"I don't know the country," said Mickey. "I'm thinking I'd like to ask my old grandfather what to do, for he has the great brain in him. Only I can't get to Cranogue, for they're all the way between me and it."

And then an idea came to him. "Could you lend me one of your father's coats and a cap?" he asked. "The way they mightn't recognize me, if I got among any men that had seen me before."

"I could sure," she said.

And O'Dwyer had to give up a jacket and cap, for a fugitive had a right to make such demands.

"I'll come back some day, Alannah," he said. And they kissed and parted.

Mickey went a long way in the moonlight along the foot of the hills, and found the way clear to where he wanted to go, for his enemies now seemed to be all along the upper slope, cutting him off from Cranogue. When he had found out what he wanted, he returned to O'Dwyer's farm and took a spade out of a shed. With this he set quietly off again, and the sky lightened as he went. He was going back to his own grave, with the new cap pulled down on his forehead in case the sentry should still be there and awake. He made the journey unchallenged and saw the sentry standing there, and trudged towards him with the spade over his shoulder. Thus Mickey came to his grave at dawn.

"Halt. Who goes there?" shouted the sentry, bringing his rifle very martially to the first position in bayonet-fighting.

"Sure, I don't know," said Mickey.

"Then what are you doing here?" asked the sentry.

"Sure the General told me to come and fill in a grave," said Mickey.

"Did he tell you for why?" asked the sentry.

"Sure, he said it wouldn't be wanted now," said Mickey.

"Is that so?" said the sentry in a disappointed voice. "And why is that?"

"Because the general said it was for a young lad called Mickey Connor," said Mickey.

"It is, sure," said the sentry.

"And they shot the young black guard," said Mickey, "on the other side of the hills and couldn't be taking the trouble to carry him all this way merely to give him a grave."

"So what did they do?" asked the sentry.

"Sure, they left him where he was."

"It was all he deserved," said the sentry.

And Mickey began to fill in the grave.

"Sure, there's a hole in it," said Mickey, "and all the earth I throw in is running away."

"There is so," said the sentry.

And Mickey got into the grave.

"Put that rifle down," he said, "and hand me a good big stone, the way I can stop up this hole."

The sentry put the rifle down.

"Will this one do?" he asked as he stooped over the stone.

"It will, sure," said Mickey; though he could not see it, for his head was now at the bottom of the grave, and the rest of him lower.

The sentry heaved up the stone and carried it to the edge of the grave.

"Well, that beats all," he said. And after some moments' thought he added, "It does indeed."

And, reflecting again, he said, "It beats anything."

But he had not done thinking yet, and much light dawned on him, and he said, "The sly lad."

And then he went and reported what had occurred, to Timmy, his officer, and gave it as his impression that it was Mickey Connor who had gone, and added, "I'm thinking we shall have some trouble in getting him into his grave."

"Ah, we'll get him in," said Timmy. "But it's a pity he's not here now; for it's dawn and a fine light for shooting."

"What'll we do, Timmy?" said the sentry.

"Run, two or three of you, and shoot down those holes in the rocks into the water, and go on shooting till you see if he comes that way."

And all that they did; but Mickey was far past the holes before they arrived there; and, not untroubled by the old fears of pursuit by the enemy of us all, he came at last to the patch of gleaming light, and this time squeezed through at once, and was out again on the other side of the hills. He made for Cranogue as fast as he could go, and reached his grandfather's house as the old man was boiling his eggs.

"You're wet, Mickey," said the old man.

"I am that," said Young Mickey.

"You should keep dry," said Old Mickey. "And yet perhaps nothing matters that you do when you're young. Only it's a good thing to keep dry, for all that."

"Grandfather," said Young Mickey, "there are queer things happening. And I've come to ask you what to do?"

"And what's been happening?" said Old Mickey.

"It's General Cassidy," said Young Mickey; "and he was very anxious to have me shot at dawn. Terrible anxious he was. And he found me caught in the water where I couldn't get out, where the river runs out of the lull, and there wasn't room for me between the rocks. And he went away to get his men, and he never came with them. And when I can't find out what he's doing I can't make any plans. So I've come to you, Grandfather."

"He didn't come back?" said his grandfather.

"He did not," said Young Mickey. "And I got out at last after more nor an hour, but he never came near me."

"Let me eat my breakfast," said Old Mickey, "and let you put in another egg for yourself and boil it. And then let me smoke my pipe, and I'll tell you."

So they had breakfast together, and afterwards Old Mickey lighted his pipe, and sat and smoked in silence. And after a while he said again: "Jim Cassidy never came back?"

"He did not," said Young Mickey.

And Old Mickey took his pipe out of his mouth and said: "I'm thinking something happened to Jim Cassidy."

"Begob," said Young Mickey, "it might. For that black heathen Umbolulu was near him."

"Was he that?" said Old Mickey. "They made a great Protestant of the man; and, being all new to it, it might have gone to his head, and, Jim Cassidy being a Catholic, if they got to arguing about religion you couldn't tell what would happen."

"Be Jabers, that's so," said his grandson.

In writing a book like this about the Ireland I know, one must be continually touching on matters that some one or other thinks are better not touched on, or stating things with which some one disagrees, and often being thought to entertain views that one does not hold at all. But at least let me state here that, whatever Old Mickey thought, the Church of Ireland has nothing to do with cannibalism, either in dogma or practice.

"It's so indeed," said Young Mickey.

"Aye," said Old Mickey; "something happened to Cassidy."

"And what shall I do now?" asked Young Mickey. "For the others are all after me."

And sure enough they were, for a lorry swung into the main street of Cranogue, and every one knew from the sound and the pace of it that it held troops, and every one went further back into the houses away from the door to the street and all busied themselves very hard with household duties; and a certain light went out of their faces, so that they seemed to observe nothing and not to understand very much.

"That's them," said Young Mickey.

"Sure it is," said Old Mickey.

"Can you hide me?" asked his grandson.

"Sure I've only that cupboard and my old wits," said Old Mickey. "Hop in."

And Young Mickey got into the cupboard.

"Hi! Hi!" shouted Old Mickey. "Hi, you lads with the guns on you!"

The lorry slowed down, and stopped near the shouting old man.

"What is it?" asked the officer.

"Sure, we have no peace," cried Old Mickey. "No peace at all. Never tail nor trace of it."

"What's the matter?" the officer asked.

"Sure it's that lad Mickey Connor," said Old Mickey. "Do you know him?"

"It's him we're after," said the officer.

And all the men brightened up and got both hands on to their rifles.

"Then why don't you find him?" shouted Old Mickey. "Sure, he gives us no peace."

"What is he doing?" asked the officer.

"Sure, didn't I tell you?" said Old Mickey. "Didn't I tell you he gives us no peace. And he never will while he's roaming about in these parts."

"Where is he?" the officer asked.

"Sure, he's only after running out of that house," he said pointing. "It's his mother's house and he's only after leaving it. And it's plaguing us all he is. And it's times I wish the English were back. I do surely."

"What way did he go?" asked the officer.

"That way," shouted Old Mickey, standing up and pointing with both his arms. "That way."

"You've got your two arms pointing different ways?" said the officer.

"And why not?" shouted Old Mickey.

"You should point them both the same way," argued the officer.

"The same way is it?" shouted Old Mickey. "What for did God give us two arms? If there was only one way to point, sure He'd have given us only one arm."

"Which way did he go?" insisted the officer.

"Bedad He would," said Old Mickey, sticking to his point.

"Go on," said the officer to the driver.

"Find him! Find him! Find him!" shouted Old Mickey. "Sure, Mickey Connor gives us no peace."

They searched many houses. They came back again down the street, and Old Mickey ran out shouting. Then the officer spoke to the driver, and the lorry left Cranogue.

"You got rid of them fine," said Young Mickey, stepping out of the cupboard.

"Ah, sure, they've got no sense," said Old Mickey.

"And what will I do now?" Young Mickey asked.

"I'll tell you what for to do," the old man said. "Let you walk north from here till you get to the border; and let you cross it by night. And stay away out of these parts till them lads have had time to forget you."

"How long will they take over that, Grandfather?" Young Mickey asked, thinking of Alannah.

"Ah, maybe a while," said the old man. "Aye, maybe a good while. But give them time and they'll forget it. Other things crop up, and in a year or two they'll not be wanting to shoot you."

It seemed a long time to Young Mickey.

"And don't be eating in any house on the way," Old Mickey said. "You'd never know where they'd have spies looking out for you. Take boiled eggs and cheese and bread; they all go in your pocket; and you can drink water at streams: it'll do for a drink when you cannot get anything else. And many's the time I saw the Old Lord drink it, when he might have had all the whiskey there was in Ireland. Aye, often he did that when he was alone, although he never insulted his friends with it."

"I could do it in four or five days," said Young Mickey.

"Aye," said Old Mickey. "And four days would be better nor five."

"There's a girl over by the hills I'd like to see again soon," said Young Mickey.

"Is there so?" said Old Mickey. "Then she'd sooner you were walking about alive on the other side of the border, than lying about dead in these parts. She would surely."

"I'll get to the border," said Young Mickey.

"And you'll be right to get to it," said Old Mickey. "Sure, what is the border for? And let you put six eggs into that saucepan and boil them hard. You can get the cheese and the bread from your mother."

"Did the other young lads that were with me get safe away?" said Young Mickey.

But a vague look came over Old Mickey's face. "I heard some talk of it," he said. For the movements of fugitives were not a topic to be discussed even between grandfather and grandson. "And now," said the old man, "let you be drying your clothes. Leave them here in front of the fire, and you can go into the next room and get into my bed. And if I hear a lorry coming back I'll throw the clothes into that cupboard; and let you get in after them."

So Young Mickey did as the old man said, and no lorry came back. And the old man in front of the fire was soon asleep, and Mickey was soon asleep, and slept till shadows lengthened, the old man leaving him to sleep while he had his dinner, either because he knew that the lad needed rest, or because he had forgotten about him. And when Mickey heard birds singing and saw the rays of the sun all low, the song or the level rays having come into the room and awoken him, he got his clothes and dressed, and the old man made tea for him and boiled two eggs. And over the tea they talked again.

"When it is dark would be the time," said Old Mickey, thinking of the North and the border.

But Young Mickey was thinking of the South and of Alannah.

"I was having a lovely great war," he said, "and they should have left me alone. It was a private war and was doing no harm to any one."

"They had to stop you," said Old Mickey, "for they are trying to get it like what it was when the English were here."

"And look what they did to poor Patsy," wailed Young Mickey.

"Aye, that was terrible," said Old Mickey. "But let you go away for a while, the way they won't do it to you. And then one day you'll come back, and there'll be plenty more wars in Ireland, and you can go back to the hills and have a war again."

"I will, then," said Young Mickey.

"And maybe the lads that killed Patsy will be all shot by then, in order to learn them," said Old Mickey.

"Begob," said Young Mickey, "it would take that to teach them sense."

"It would, some of them," said the old man.

When it grew dark Old Mickey went to shut up his door, and as he did so Young Mickey slipped out into the street and stood with his back flat against the dark of the door-post, and looked both ways, and when he saw no one he went softly away and came to his mother's house.

CHAPTER XXXII

The Liberissimans
Turn Home

*T*he day on which Mickey slipped from his grandfather's door and went to his mother's house to say good-by before setting out upon his northward journey, was the last day on which the Liberissimans worked in the bog. That evening they were all in Sharkey's hotel, busily and rather silently packing up. They had a fine store of treasures; brown bones carved in many shapes to make pins; innumerable bone knives; fish-hooks of bone; flint arrow-heads, spear-heads of bronze and bowls of clay pipes; for in a few feet of bog where they dug lay many pages of the history of Earth, and the spade had turned the centuries as the finger of a reader of a book turns over the years. In a foot of soil at the surface there may be a thousand years of history; or in an inch of it, a little lower down. From these pages they had gathered their treasures, and had laid them to soak in oil, to prevent them crumbling away when the dry air took from them the moisture that was holding them together in the earth. They handed to each other pins shaped like sea-horses, from bone, showing that the people that had dwelt in that island-village must once have known the sea; pieces of crude enamel, and the ruins of crucibles in which bronze had been melted, stained still with the streaks of copper; brooches of bone and of bronze, stone querns and the idol of wood. Yet every one of these triumphant finds was passed from hand to hand and quietly packed, with no more than a nod of the head as it was received, with no comment and no apparent interest, but in a hush that all seemed half-afraid to break, lest anything should be said that was worse than the hush. One word hung over them all like the word of a dreaded spell, and that word was "backsliding." Behind them like an abyss was the past dark story of Africa, old practices of their fathers, thought of no more, but nearer to them perhaps than their tall hats and frock-coats suggested: over this abyss Umbolulu had now tumbled. Picture a smart young party in a restaurant, all in correct evening dress, well-fitting and enhanced with button-holes; and one of the party long ago was a boot-black and advertised some rather nasty boot-blacking: suddenly he pulls blacking brushes out of his pocket and goes to other tables trying to black evening shoes, perhaps shouting, "Blacko makes you smart." Imagine the feelings of his party. Yet this is only a social lapse. How much profounder the shock when the lapse is a religious one. All the way from grace to cannibalism in a single sudden fall. There is only one word for it—backsliding.

So they packed their treasures away in a grave silence, and Umbolulu sat apart with much the air of a child that has stolen jam. And what is that air exactly? I do not explain, because I cannot. So swiftly there passed over Umbolulu's features the lights and shadows of two emotions, that I cannot seize on one and say which predominated: the two emotions were contrition and satisfaction.

As dark rumors rippled outwards they found all parties happily united in one thing, and that was to assert (though "prove" was the word always used) that nothing of the sort could have happened. The Protestants were unanimous that no convert of theirs could ever have done such a thing; and, after all, Umbolulu did become a member of the Church of Ireland, and a very ardent one; and all the facts proving the point were very happily marshaled by Mrs. Patrick. The other side brought all the proofs they could find, to buttress up the assertion, that became their creed, that such a thing could never have happened in Ireland.

There may have been things in the past, they said, that Cassidy might have done, on account of which he might wish to go to America. He would naturally therefore discard his distinctive buttons; as for his boots and his bones, there was no proof that either belonged to Cassidy. And then the Dublin Press came out with a good many articles of scientific interest about Stonehenge. For about a week, if you turn up the files, you will find them full of such articles, and a great deal about the sacrificial stone; and about other monuments in England similar to Stonehenge but smaller. By the end of that week the word cannibalism could safely be mentioned, and turned naturally and innocuously to the topic of the savage habits of Englishmen.

So the little party of Liberissimans packed their treasures silently, almost furtively, away, thinking of home, home where the sun shone bright and strong and satisfying, where a black skin was no curiosity, where an elder of the Church, so long as he led a good religious life, was no heretic; where women would smile at them again, with lips that to them seemed lovely; where from every moment of mirth, or any happy emotion, around them from far or near, would drift up the African song for which they were home-sick. They would come back with the records of a strange people, triumphant discoverers, and friends would come round them to see: it was all different here; here they themselves were the strange people. And Umbolulu there would no longer be an embarrassment; not that they approved of his tenets, but in Liberissima where Umbolulu was a national hero, much as poor Patsy had been here, his tenets if disapproved, would at least be understood. All the anxieties of recent days were to be dissipated at last by the magic there was in the spell of the one word Home.

While the Liberissimans were packing up, there was movement in the army that had been General Cassidy's. They had surrounded the district in which O'Dwyer's farm was situated, and they were watching Cranogue. Another party had come to O'Dwyer's house, and it was being searched again. It was a party of men that were especially concerned in finding the man they were looking for, for they were the thirty men under the officer that was called Timmy, whose job it had been to shoot Mickey at dawn. Alannah was watching them as they searched, and Timmy was watching Alannah, with an admiration that he enviously suspected was shared by Young Mickey, of whom he seemed to know too much for the odds to be quite fair.

"And what are you looking for?" Alannah asked.

"We're looking for Mickey Connor," was the answer.

"And what's he like?" she said.

"An ugly lout of a lad," said the officer.

"He is not," said Alannah.

"You know him, then," said Timmy.

"I do not," she answered.

"Then how do you know he's not ugly?" he asked.

"Sure, I only meant by comparison," said Alannah.

"With whom?" asked the officer.

"With yourself, for instance," she said.

"And how do you know he's not less good-looking than me, if you never saw him?" he asked, pulling out a notebook to take down her admission.

"Sure, nobody could be," said Alannah, giving him a pleasant smile in case he should want to shoot.

"I don't know about that," said Timmy with more emphasis than the words seem to imply.

"Ah, you wouldn't notice it," said Alannah.

"Don't interrupt us while we get on with our work," said Timmy very officially. "We have to find that lad and shoot him."

"When will you shoot him?" asked Alannah.

"At dawn," said Timmy.

"Of what day?" asked Alannah.

"Tomorrow or next day," he said.

"Sure, you do your work very quickly," she commented.

"If we don't find him here or in Cranogue, he'll make for the border," said Timmy. "And we've a line of men waiting for him on his way."

"Do ye tell me?" said she.

"And if he gets through that," said Timmy, "we'll have another line ten miles further on. We'll move them in lorries while he goes on foot. He won't dare use the roads. And the border itself is watched too."

"And what for," asked Alannah, "are you so keen to shoot one young lad with all those men?"

"Sure, we're putting a stop to these wars in the hills," said he.

"Ah, what harm do they do?" asked Alannah.

"Maybe none," said Timmy. "But they're against the law."

"Ah, you're getting like the English," she said.

And a sad look came over Timmy's face. Because the accusation was true? Because it never could be? I do not know which. Please do not accuse me of having stated either of these two opposites.

"Ah, what do you want to be thinking of Mickey for?" he said. "We've line after line of men between him and the border, and we're watching the ports too. He's been condemned to death already, and he'll be shot in two days. What use is a dead man to you?"

Alannah had no answer to this, but her blue eyes looked at Timmy so thoughtfully, that after a while he had the impression that she was comparing him with dead men.

"What are you thinking about so much?" he asked.

"I was only wondering," she said.

Elba! and Farewell to the Old Guard

"Mother," said Mickey as he softly entered her house, "Grandfather told me for to ask you for bread and cheese and a few hardboiled eggs, the way I could walk to the border."

"And what for do you want to be going to the border, Mickey?" asked his mother, suddenly anxious.

"Ah, sure, I'm thinking there is not so much shooting over there," said Mickey.

"Are they after you, Mickey?" she asked, though she knew it.

"They are, sure," said Mickey.

"Then let you not stop in Cranogue," she said. "For that's one place they will look for you."

"They're after looking for me this morning," said Mickey.

"They'll come again and again," she said.

So Mickey got the bread and the cheese and six raw eggs; but his mother would not wait to boil them.

"Be off with you, Mickey," she said, "for you wouldn't know the moment that they'd come. And with the help of God you'll have another sixty years to eat boiled eggs; and if you waited now, sure it might be the end of you."

And then she put the lamp out and opened the door, and went out and looked up at the sky and at the top of her door-posts, and then went slowly in again.

"Go now, Mickey," she said, "and God's blessing go with you. There's none of them there."

"I'll come back, Mother," he said, "when they've forgotten about their shooting."

Then he kissed her. And the door was ajar. He slipped out with his back against the door, dark as the door in the night. He slid along it sideways as far as the door-post, saw no one, and was off. For a few yards he kept to the road, then he left it; and, so well he knew all the fields that lay round his house, that he traveled as fast over them and their boundaries as he did down the high road. Rabbits ran from him in the dark; he disturbed a snipe; nothing else stirred for a while. And then he heard the sound of steps running after him. He stopped to listen. One man's steps. And they had an honest sound. Then he heard a voice calling softly, "General. General."

It was Young Hegarty.

"Hegarty, boy! And how are you?" shouted Mickey, but shouting low like a very hoarse man.

"Grand," said Young Hegarty. "And how's yourself, General?"

"Fine," said Mickey. "You were a dead corpse when I last saw you. How did you get on?"

"They dug a grave for me," said Young Hegarty.

"Begob," said Mickey, "when I want a grave I dig it for myself."

"I have them dug for me," said Hegarty.

"And what did you do?" asked Mickey.

"Sure, no one was watching me," said Young Hegarty, "and away I went."

"Begob, they watched me better," said Mickey, "but I got away from them."

"Good for you," said Young Hegarty.

And then Mickey told him the story of the underground river.

"Oh, General," said Young Hegarty, "weren't you terribly afraid himself would come after you roaring?"

"I was that," said Mickey.

"Begob," said Young Hegarty, "I'd sooner have had the grave nor gone down the river with that lad behind me."

"He wasn't there neither time," said Mickey.

"Begob," said Young Hegarty, "you've a chance from the grave, if you've paid your dues regular, but none if that lad catches you."

"There's another lad after me now, and I don't like him neither," said Mickey, "and I'm off for the border."

"May I come with you, General?" said Hegarty. "For they know my face, and mightn't like the way I went off when they had a grave all ready for me."

"They will not," said Mickey. "And they'll be wanting to fill it. Aye, come with me."

"General," said Hegarty, "there's a lot of lads round here will be wanting to say good-by to you."

"Go and get them," said Mickey. "Do you know the old willow the far side of the next field, the white one with the two arms on it?"

"I do," said Hegarty.

"It's hollow on the south side," said Mickey. "I'll be there."

So Mickey went on over the dark grass, to the ghost-like old tree and climbed in, and Young Hegarty went back to collect what I may call the Old Guard, the army that had fought under Mickey.

And soon in the hollow tree Mickey heard the old call again, the voices of curlews over the marshy field, and then the sound of feet coming over the grass. And they were all there; General Jimmy Mullins, Colonel Brannehan, Captain Christie Ryan, Pat Kelly, Paddy Mulligan, Young Hegarty and two more of them, all coming to wish god-speed to Mickey, and Young Hegarty to go with him. They were all there. Once more I become the historian of an army. There was a sprinkling of white on the field, hail shaken down by thunder, a trick of spring. It should have been snow; wolves should have prowled on their flanks, watching the weary steps and the war-worn tunics, waiting to pick off stragglers. Was it Mickey's fault that no wolves were there? And I must make the best of what materials I have, and refrain from envy of men who had the retreat from Moscow to chronicle.

Before the hail melted the army was all gone, but not before every man had taken farewell of his leader.

"I'll come back one day," said Mickey, "when they've forgotten about that grave they have ready for me, and we'll have wars again in the hills."

"Good for you, General," they all said.

"Bloody great wars," said Mickey.

"We will indeed," said they all.

"And now farewell, I am going a long way," says Tennyson, as he tells of King Arthur's good-by to his eldest knight. And there is something so akin to poetry in the Irish mind and speech that Mickey's simple words followed so closely along that line as to be nearer to it than many a misquotation. Nor was there anything inappropriate in his words, nor alien to the spirit of idylls. His wars were too small for his fancies. Looked at in the cold light of reason they may even appear ridiculous; and yet for miles round Cranogue they dwell to this day side by side in many a memory with the great battles of Patsy Heffernan.

They took leave of him one by one by the old willow, General Jimmy Mullins first.

"We've had a great war, Major General," said Jimmy. "And, please God, we'll have many more."

Then Colonel Brannehan came by and gripped his hand. "The hills won't be the same when they're all at peace," said the colonel, "but you'll come back to us, General, and we'll have wars again."

And then the captain came up and shook Mickey's hand, Captain Christie Ryan, who was a captain once more, but who for a little while had done the work of a scarecrow. And he said, "Come back soon, General, and we'll go back to the hills. And one day, please God, we'll teach that lad Jim Cassidy."

For he did not yet know who had taught him already.

And Pat Kelly, who had gone up the tree at the end of the war, said as he took farewell, "You saved us all, Mickey, and one of these days we will make you general of all Ireland."

"Aye," said Mick Geogehan, "and crown you king at Tara."

And Paddy Mulligan came up to the willow and gripped Mickey's hand. And, "Many's the general I learned about," he said, "when I was a gossoon, and many a great war. But you are the greatest of them all, Mickey, and you had the greatest war."

And so said they all. And if any one doubts it, and should ever come to Cranogue, let him keep his doubts to himself while he is there, or he will soon find out his opinion is not the opinion of Cranogue.

There remained one more to say good-by to Mickey, a man I have not yet named; and as the historian of the war that there was in the hills I must rectify this now, for he fought as fiercely as any of them; the lad was Murphy, the postman. And as he took Mickey's hand there were tears in his eyes as he said: "Ah, come back soon, General, and give us another war."

And to all of them Mickey gave the blessing of God, and promised to come back soon. And they went away over the crisp remnants of hail, all but Young Hegarty; and the old willow seemed very lonely. They went back to sleep in haystacks, and then, soon afterwards, in their own homes, as they began to know that no one was looking for them, with a certain sense that they had for such things. For Mickey and Young Hegarty alone any such return was, for the present, impossible.

"Come now, Hegarty," said Mickey, "we must get away northward, and go a long way before light comes."

And they went north with the north wind in their faces to guide them, the wind that brought the hail. They kept to the fields for so long as they knew them, but when they were well away from Cranogue they got on to a road. Once they were challenged before they came to the road. But somehow they knew by the tone of the challenge that they were not really suspected.

"Sure, he was only roaring to show that he was a sentry," said Mickey.

And he had answered, "Herd of Old Lennahan," though there was no such man. And he and Young Hegarty had stepped back into the night. If there was any circle of men surrounding Cranogue that was all they saw of it.

Hours later Mickey lifted a somewhat weary head and saw suddenly a trace of light in the sky. "Get off the road, Hegarty," he said. "There's dawn coming."

They slipped into the fields again, and continued their way northwards, past sleeping cattle, through hedges, past a surprised goat, and by little cottages where none was astir. After an hour or so they saw a wisp of smoke going up pale gray from a chimney that rose from an olden thatch, and knew that they were no longer the only men awake. Mickey hoped he was not far short of twenty miles from Cranogue. Dawn widened; the sun came up, and began to warm the two wanderers.

"Have you food on you?" asked Mickey anxiously.

"I have," said Hegarty.

"Then eat it," said Mickey.

And they sat down against a bank and had their breakfast, Mickey beginning on his raw eggs, as he was more anxious about their safety than that of the boiled ones. And as they ate they heard an unmistakable sound.

"A lorry, by the holy," said Hegarty.

They were concealed from the road, but only had to peer over a bank to see what was coming along it. Sure enough it was a lorry, and full of troops.

"They're looking for you," said Hegarty aghast.

"Begob," said Mickey, "they're taking a lot of trouble to catch one man. Sure, it's because they've got that grave all ready, and don't know what to do with it."

"B'Jabers," said Hegarty, expressing a certain political antagonism, "they should fill it with some of the right lads."

"They're going North," said Mickey, watching the lorry out of sight.

They finished their breakfast and went on with their journey, but slanting away to the left from the road along which the lorry had come. And after a while, again the noise of a lorry. This time it was to their left, for they were near another road. They hid and watched, and again it was going North.

"Oh, saints and angels, what will we do now?" said Hegarty.

"Sure, they've a simple enough strategy," said Mickey, "if they're after me. They're getting ahead of us and going to line up between us and the border."

"Heaven defend us, why are they taking all that trouble?" asked Hegarty.

"Sure, they've nothing else to do," said Mickey.

"Oh, General, what will we do now?" said Hegarty.

"Sure, we'll go West," said Mickey.

"But that won't take us to the border," said Hegarty.

"It will not," said Mickey. "And it will not take us into the arms of them lads neither. We'll go West a long way; and when we get near the coast we'll turn North again; and that won't bring us to the border neither; but we'll go up past it into Donegal; and then one day we'll turn East and cross the border that way into County Derry, while they're all along the borders of Cavan, thick as fleas in a doe-rabbit's ear, waiting for us to come in from the South."

"Begob," said Hegarty, "you're the great general. But I'm thinking it'll be a long walk."

"There'll be no more walking for us," said Mickey, "if we go the way they're expecting us."

So they turned westward over the fields, only crossing roads after lying by hedge or wall and seeing that they were empty. Along their right all the way stood hills, where they knew men would be watching for them, and miles and miles beyond them they knew that the border would be watched by the same men again, for the lorries gave that advantage to them over two tired men on foot. Yet somehow the sight of the hills gave hope to Mickey. Roads and neat fields stood for a certain orderliness and law that had left with the English, and that poor General Cassidy had been trying to restore; the hills stood for untameable things, things wild and no more to be checked by laws than the bright clouds that sparkled above them, and whose shadows all along the brows of the hills lay like a frown. Young Hegarty too looked wistfully up to the hills, going up right into cloudland, but for the present they had to keep to the level land and go westward as fast as they could. They came to a river and decided to rest; but first they crossed it, and as it was too deep to wade, they found a bridge, which of course meant also a road, and all roads were dangerous to them. Young Hegarty insisted on crossing the bridge first, and whistled to Mickey when all was clear; for Hegarty had not yet been condemned to death, and if captured might not be, whereas the capture of Mickey would mean shooting for certain. They heard no lorries and got across unmolested, and went up the bank of the river into the fields, and sat down and rested. It came by, dark water streaked with flashing silver, parts of it hurrying as though on some urgent quest of remotest isles to which sea-currents would carry them, and parts of it floating by so full of dreams and ease that it seemed, as you watched those lazy slabs of water, as if nothing were ever important except to sleep. And this is what both Mickey and Hegarty did.

When Mickey and Hegarty woke, the sun was quite low. They woke together, hearing the words, "And what are yez doing here?" And there was a man standing over them, who looked like a farmer. Mickey grunted and made incoherent noises in his throat and closed his eyes again. He would not have done as a model for the picture of a thinker in an advertisement, choosing some quack remedy. But he was thinking hard.

"Sure we're looking for a young lad named Mickey Connor," said Mickey, "who has escaped from the Free-State army."

"And what do you want him for?" asked the farmer.

"Sure, there'd likely be a reward," said Mickey.

"And would you take money so dirty as that?" said the farmer. "Then get off my farm, and the curse of God go with you. Would you take blood-money from them lads?"

"I would not," said Mickey, "and I'll tell you for why. Sure, I'm Mickey Connor."

"My fine lad, are you him?" said the farmer, with beaming eyes.

He did not know Mickey Connor, but it was enough that he was on the run.

"I am that," said Mickey, "and this is one of my soldiers."

"What war were you fighting in?" asked the farmer.

"It was a private war," said Mickey. "But there was a lad named General Cassidy that didn't like it, and they want to shoot me at dawn. Sure they have my grave all ready, and I'm thinking they're standing round it and dropping tears into it because I'm not there."

"Sure, they'd do that," said Hegarty.

"Come now," said the farmer, "and I'll give you a good meal, for you need it. And I'll give you beds to sleep in. And tomorrow you can go on. Where are you making for?"

"Cork harbor," said Mickey.

"Begob," said the farmer, "you seem to be out of your way."

"No matter," said Mickey, "it's not the direct way we're taking."

The meal that they got from that farmer, whose name was O'Brien, the security of his house, and the long night's rest, were to Mickey and Hegarty like the turning point of a campaign. They were well on their way, and next morning they were to start fresh, with new provisions, and without fatigue. O'Brien brought them in to his wife, introducing Mickey with the words, "This is Mickey Connor. The army is after him."

And from the moment of that introduction Mickey was entertained with all the sympathy due to one oppressed by so much force. And that evening by a good fire burning in the cavernous fire-place of the kitchen Mickey regaled Mr. and Mrs. O'Brien with tales of his war in the hills, better told than this pen tells them, because they were seasoned, as they ought to be seasoned, with all the splendid exaggeration proper to the ambitions that made those battles. As the sole historian of these wars I feel a certain solemn duty to curb my pen, but no such necessity spoiled the tales that Mickey told; indeed gratitude to his host and hostess impelled him all the other way. And sometimes Young Hegarty joined in with embellishments that made it all better still, as when adding to Mickey's story of the battle that was spoiled by the arrival of the Mountain and Valley Hunt, he described the red coats flashing into sight and the charge of the English cavalry. It was a grand evening in that hospitable house.

Next morning they were off again, O'Brien carefully pointing out the road to Cork. But Mickey and Hegarty went West into Galway, leaving large prosperous fields and coming to the loneliness of great bogs. Always they avoided roads. And then they turned northwards, through Roscommon and Sligo. And sometimes coming within breath of the sea, and sometimes even hearing the dirge of it on the other side of low ridges, they at last reached Donegal and saw great hills again, hills going up with frowns into the clouds and breaking there into smiles, hills like old giants left behind by a retreat of the creatures of fable, and brooding on ancient wars. And they saw the glow of the gorse;

more and more as they came to the hills; like heaps of pure raw gold untouched by any alloy. And all the while as they walked, often on their feet, spring seemed to be on her tiptoes. Every day she led new leaves to the court of the sun; every day she inspired some bird to give forth his most magical note. One day they would see an elm that had flashed into greenery, on another the tip of one branch of a single beech that had broken before its time into leaves that were bright pale-gold, or brass that was only slightly tarnished with green; and then one day the brilliant flash of a lilac that was suddenly all leaf. Now Mickey and Hegarty felt themselves safe from pursuit, and with the great danger only ahead of them, where the border of wire would be guarded. All that Mickey knew of the border was that it ran close to the ancient fortress called Greenan of Ailach, and that the fortress was in the Free State; for the story of it had traveled down to Cranogue, where it was told how a certain doctor was a great lad, and how he had had the old fortress rebuilt from a pile of tumbled stones that lay in a ring on the top of the hill, till the circle of hollow walls stood up once more; and how the doctor had fooled all the people that built it.

"A great lad, the doctor," they said. "He promised that, all who would work on it, he would doctor them and their families free for the rest of his life. And they built it up as he said. And, sure, next year he died on them."

They came now to the fortress, and from its walls they saw the border of wire. And the border was full of troops.

"Begob, are they taking all that trouble to catch me?" sighed Mickey.

"And what will we do now, General?" Young Hegarty said.

CHAPTER XXXIV

Quis Separabit

Some weeks later, in a barrack-room of the Irish Guards in London, there was talk among men under their dark-brown blankets, uneasy talk before the quiet of the soldier's night. It was the eve of a general inspection. What would the General find? A single cold word to the colonel, and he would speak incisively to officers commanding companies. These would speak witheringly to their sub-alterns, who would ask the sergeants why it was that the men were not fit to be looked at, who would speak to the men themselves with the air of an angry farmer dissatisfied with the appearance of one of his scarecrows, while the rooks ate all his corn. Apprehension seemed to be rising, more appropriate to Adam in the cool of the evening, than to men with good enough consciences who ought to have been asleep.

And suddenly the newest recruit, a young fellow called Guardsman Connor, said: "Ah, sure, a general's only a human being."

My reader may accuse me of the trite and the obvious. But no such accusation was directed at Guardsman Connor. Quite on the contrary, it was felt he had founded a heresy the originality and daring of which could not excuse its falsity.

"What do you know of generals?" asked a guardsman with as many years service as Guardsman Connor had weeks.

"Sure, I was one myself," said the recruit.

Last Post had sounded an hour ago and the men were just going to sleep, instead of which they heard Mickey Connor's story; and the tale I have tried to tell was first told there between the hours of eleven P.M. and two A.M. And at the end of it, talking the old talk again, which a life in barracks was fast knocking out of him, whereby many fine fancies are being lost to the world, he said: "I landed on the English coast, and advanced on London, and there I met Sergeant Morrissey with ribbons in his hair. And I said, 'All men that wear red coats are bloody tyrants, but I want to enlist'."

"You said that to Sergeant Morrissey?" said a guardsman enviously.

"I did that," said Mickey. "And he only said, 'I am glad to hear it'."

Then he sighed wistfully, and added, half to himself, "And I never said anything like that to a sergeant again."

Afterword

BY MICHAEL GRENKE

This is a very funny novel. The main action is a private war in the Irish hills between nine young men from the village of Cranogue and a larger force of men from the neighboring county. The main antagonist is a former freedom fighter turned insurance salesman. The main intellectual challenge is presented by a bicycle-riding chewing gum salesman who stumbles into one of the battlefields and engages in a brief philosophic dialogue in the midst of the fighting. The course of the war is narrated ironically with all the pageantry of a major historical event. If one believes that it is impossible for a novel to be very funny without being about serious matters, then one won't be surprised to find beneath all the humor and wit serious lessons in statesmanship and generalship and deep, even perhaps melancholic, ruminations about the compromises and choices that human beings face in the modern world and about the costs of those choices. It may be that Lord Dunsany means to put us into a laughing mood, not only for our enjoyment, but also to enable us to look steadily at some serious matters.

For this is a novel about war. The war itself is remarkable for its high spirits and its friendliness. The sporadic shooting at each other neither damages the relations between the combatants, who think of each other as "great" or "lovely" or "sly" lads, nor does it corrupt the characters of the combatants in themselves. This aspect of the private war may prompt the reader to wonder whether what is depicted here is really a war. The English chewing gum salesman, who has been to war (presumably World War I), claims of this private war that it is "no good" and that the combatants "don't know what war is." Mickey, the "Major General" of the Cranogue army claims in response that the English "don't understand war." The novel begs us to consider which, if either, of them is right or the degree of correctness to be found in what each has claimed. We might be provoked here to try to see the possibility, within war or within wars of a certain kind, of trying to kill men whom one knows and likes and appreciates—the possibility of fighting without an issue of dispute, without a difference of principles, and without hatred in your heart. It might be best to conceive of the private war of this novel as a flashing forth of something more primitive or natural from within human beings, something that likes to fight and that makes it hard at times for us to live together in civilized fashion and that may also make it hard for our hearts to embrace civilization. The title of the novel marks the realm to which this private war belongs—"the hills stood for untameable things, things wild and no more to be checked by laws than the bright clouds." It is because of the opposition to civilization represented by Mickey's private war that the forces of "orderliness and law," the Irish national army, intervene to end it.

For this is also a novel about civilization. Dunsany directs our attention from the important questions of the nature and the goodness of war to the even larger questions of the nature and the goodness of civilization. Civilization in its very conception is something that is done to or imposed upon something that was not previously civilized (or as civilized). As such, civilization is necessarily opposed to what precedes it. Civilization is a human attempt, generally by means of politics, to make a change. It seeks to bring about outcomes that otherwise would not occur if things were left to their own course.

In *Up in the Hills*, Dunsany shows us a number of human societies at various stages of civilization and prompts us to assess for ourselves the advantages and disadvantages of each. In the first beginning of the novel, we confront a primitive lake settlement in ancient Ireland. The inhabitants are explicitly in conflict with nature in the form of their ongoing battles with packs of wolves. Even at this early stage, civilization is portrayed as opposed to nature. With their palisades, the lake dwellers seek to erect barriers to separate themselves from the rest of the world. With their power of fire, the lake dwellers' vanity leads them to consider themselves superior to other terrestrial beings and tempts them to claim kinship to the other light-giving beings that inhabit the heavens.

In the second beginning of the novel, Dunsany introduces a newly formed African nation, Liberissima. This nation has only just achieved independence by revolting from Liberia, a nation formed of repatriated slaves from America. Liberissima is rushing toward modern civilization. In their enthusiasm for all things modern and Western these Africans seek to imitate everything they have seen Europeans doing, and so they come to Ireland to dig up old things, to dig up the remains of the primitive lake settlement. The slavishness of the African's imitation of European ways is seen in their refusal to remove their frock coats even while digging in the bog. Because they have acquired these clothes so rapidly and recently, they are apprehensive about any laxity in dress which might tempt them back to their old ways. Their religious beliefs, Christian and protestant, are also brand new, and so they brook no superstitious exceptions. Liberissima is attempting to jump straight into fully modern civilization while skipping many of the intermediary steps.

The Ireland to which these African archaeologists come is, or has been, further along on the path of civilization, and thus it is more lax both in its religious beliefs and in its modes of attire. Some of its people believe in leprechauns and witches, and perhaps these superstitions indicate the difficulty that civilization has in gripping and keeping a grip upon the human soul. Although this Ireland is more advanced than Liberissima, it is still principally the Ireland of the rural village. The year is 1922, just one year after the conclusion of the Irish Revolution and the achievement (for southern Ireland at least) of home rule. The Irish Free State and its citizens are now struggling to sort out what it means for them to rule themselves as a fully independent people on the modern stage.

In addition to these three images of human society, England lurks in the background as an image of an even more advanced, more modern, more grown-up society. In this novel, "becoming like the English" is both an insult to and a fear held by the Irish. We get a glimpse of the character of England in the ruthless and impersonal upholding of the law by General Cassidy and his Irish national army. We can also look for clues in the figure of the English chewing gum salesman who passes the judgment on Mickey's war that it is no good. Mickey turns the tables on the salesman in their brief exchange and asks him what the good of chewing gum is. It "brings in money," replies the salesman. Is that all there is to say about England? Is this enough to prefer England to its alternatives?

Proponents of modern England and modern, Western civilization (whose preeminent model today is probably the United States) certainly tout its material prosperity over its more natural or primitive alternatives, but they are even more likely to tout its greater freedom. And *Up in the Hills* is also manifestly about freedom. The names of the nations involved trumpet the fact that freedom is their promise and their goal. The self-ruling Ireland calls itself the Irish Free State. Liberia literally means "the free place," and Liberissima is a play upon Latin superlatives meaning "the most free place." All these nations seek freedom in seeking civilization. In accepting limitations and boundaries upon their behavior and decision making, in embracing lawfulness and orderliness, these people seek freedom from the wildness of primitive conditions and from the occasional savagery and harshness of nature. But human beings can and do seek freedom in the opposite direction, by moving away from civilization. This is surely part of what draws Mickey up into the hills, and at least at one point in the novel he feels that "No man can be free when there's a government over him." How are we to assess and measure against each other these various attempts at freedom?

Where is the most free place? Is it to be found in some region, like the wild hills, without artificially fixed laws and limitations? Is it to be found in the midst of many laws and limitations, in the severely compromised condition that so many modern people accept and even seem to endorse as being "grown up"? This novel offers vivid images of both of these conditions and of several others somewhere in between. It helps us feel how we are drawn toward nature in its wildness and beauty, and how we are driven away from nature toward conditions that may improve upon it. It helps us feel how we admire and approve of youth in its sportive violence and carefree lawbreaking and why we endorse the limitation, or even the suppression, of such things. It helps us discover what in us objects to any law or limitation and what in us creates and embraces laws. It helps us measure the goodness of the modern civilization so many people and nations have sought and continue to seek. Yes, this novel is a great deal of fun, *and* it can also help us to think about and assess the life we have and the life we want.